"I suppose you want som...

Varian's face tightened with anger... something. My people's freedom from Your sick pleasures."

"Your people's freedom. How noble, my lord. Why not be honest and say that it's your own freedom you want?"... The Dark One raised an amused eyebrow... "What bargin will you drive with Me, beast-man?"

"The only bargin I can make, it seems. My own life. My soul, if You demand it."

The face laughed mockingly... "There is something I want. My enemy, My sister, thinks to lay a trap for Me, a trap you will help Me circumvent. I want your bride."

"My *bride*?" Varian sputtered in astonishment. "What bride?"

"I want—" and the face twisted in the first expression of consternation that Varian had ever seen. "I want 'she who snatches a rose from the fire.'" He looked down and frowned, as if He were reading something... "This girl is dangerous to Me. If you would pay My price, you will find her, you will wed her, and you will bring her to Me virgin."

LEOPARD LORD

Alanna Morland

ACE BOOKS, NEW YORK

This book is an Ace original edition,
and has never been previously published.

LEOPARD LORD

An Ace Book / published by arrangement with
the author

PRINTING HISTORY
Ace edition / March 1999

All rights reserved.
Copyright © 1999 by Lucinda Welenc.
Cover art by Jeff Barson.
This book may not be reproduced in whole or in part,
by mimeograph or any other means, without permission.
For information address: The Berkley Publishing Group,
a member of Penguin Putnam Inc.,
375 Hudson Street, New York, New York 10014.

The Penguin Putnam Inc. World Wide Web site address is
http://www.penguinputnam.com

Check out the Ace Science Fiction & Fantasy newsletter
and much more at Club PPI!

ISBN: 0-441-00606-X

ACE®
Ace books are published by The Berkley Publishing Group,
a member of Penguin Putnam Inc.,
375 Hudson Street, New York, New York 10014.
ACE and the "A"design are trademarks
belonging to Charter Communications, Inc.

PRINTED IN THE UNITED STATES OF AMERICA

10 9 8 7 6 5 4 3 2 1

Dedicated to

*The Barony of Lochmere,
especially
Alvaro de Leon and Ines de Avila
Baron and Baroness
for the inspiration,*

*The Staff and Patrons of
The Red Dragon Tavern
for the cheers and support,*

and always and forever

*my husband and our family
for their love.*

LEOPARD LORD

Prologue

Kyala was afraid. She knew every skill of the midwife's trade, had employed many of them tonight, but the girl in the bed still had a painful labor ahead of her. The baby was not lying right and had not moved as Kyala had hoped. She went to the window and twitched back the hanging, anxious for a breath of fresh air; the fire was blazing far too hot, even for a cold winter night, and the room was stifling. She glanced uneasily at the man sitting impassively in the corner. He frowned slightly and jerked his head, indicating that she must return to her patient. *As if I wouldn't,* Kyala thought indignantly. *Does he expect me to jump out the window and run?* A tiny voice seemed to whisper in her mind, *"Have a care what you think, Kyala. They say he can read people's thoughts."*

"Lady Damarisa, I must examine you again," she said softly. She ran her hands gently across the girl's swollen belly, then sat back and chewed her lip as she thought. Her mother had always taught her that keeping her patients unworried was the best policy, and certainly it worked very well in a normal catch-the-baby-and-clean-up birth. She didn't think this would be such a birth. *This girl is too young to even be having children. She's no more than a child herself. Doesn't he care that she may die? Why is he here? Most men don't want to see the effect of their bed-pleasures, no matter how they feel about their wives. And if you can read my mind, you just chew on that, Lord Baird!*

Reaching into her pocket, Kyala pulled out a small amulet, a circle of satiny wood carved with a twining vine and sheaf of grain. "Here, my lady, hold this and pray to Byela. She will help you," Kyala began, only to jump with pain and surprise as the man reached out, quickly as a striking cat, and slapped the amulet from her hand.

"My wife needs none of your foolish mummeries!" he snarled.

"But Lord Baird, Byela is Goddess of Childbirth as well as Light. Your wife needs Her help now," Kyala protested.

"I will not have your ridiculous superstitions prattled about in this room, woman! Now, tend to your work and get my son delivered, or I will have your head."

Kyala risked glaring at his retreating back, and her muttered "As you will, m'lord," came very close to making the honorific sound like an insult.

Damarisa gasped as another contraction began to build, the squeezing of her belly muscles obvious as she began to scream weakly. It seemed like an hour, even to Kyala, before the pain ended. She was certain that the girl was getting weaker, and she turned away to speak softly to Lord Baird.

"Will you permit my assistant to come in now, lord? The babe is not lying right, and I will need her help to try to turn it."

"If you must," he grunted and went to the door to shout for a slave to bring the midwife's apprentice. In those few brief moments Kyala whispered, "I will pray for you to Byela."

"I'm going to die," Damarisa whimpered. "His baby will be a monster; I know it will."

"Hush now, my lady," Kyala soothed as her eyes tried to warn the girl of her husband's return. "My apprentice Camiola will be here in a moment, and we will try to give your baby a little help. You'll be holding him in your arms before you know it."

"Are you sure, Kyala?" Damarisa asked weakly.

"Of course I am," Kyala assured her, although she was far from certain. She seldom saw births this hard, and the child being mislaid was making it much worse. She put on a smile for the girl's comfort, and added, "Everybody is afraid like this, but they forget after the baby comes."

Damarisa tried to smile also, only to break off as another contraction hit her. She tried not to scream, arching her back and biting her lip, as beads of sweat broke out on her forehead and rolled down her face to further soak her hair.

Though Kyala's attention was on her patient, she heard her assistant and friend Camiola come in and gestured for her to go to the other side of the bed.

When the contraction was over, Kyala spoke quickly and quietly to the girl. "Lady Damarisa, your baby has turned a little crooked, so we are going to have to turn him back the right way. Camiola, I want your hands here and here. I've got his little head here, so he's going to go this way. Relax as much as you can, Damarisa. Pant like a dog if it is painful. Camiola, now."

Gently but firmly the two women worked on the belly of the third, easing the baby's body around as best they could toward the proper position. Twice it slipped back stubbornly to lie crosswise again; then, as another contraction started to build, Damarisa's uterine muscles came to their aid and forced the small, round head down into place.

"Hold your breath and push now, my lady. There now, that's it, keep pushing. I can see the top of his head. Push hard, now take a quick breath, push, push, relax. He'll be here soon, one or two more like that, and it will be all over," Kyala said encouragingly. Damarisa lay back with her eyes closed, nearly too weak to nod.

"Lady Damarisa, when you have the next contraction, Camiola will press on your stomach to help you push. It might be uncomfortable, but it will help your baby come sooner. Camiola, here it comes, push, my lady, push *hard*!"

As Kyala positioned her hands to ease and support the baby, Camiola put both hands on the top of the girl's belly and pressed firmly down toward her feet.

"Yes, here he comes, that's it, my dear, easy now, we're almost done."

The baby's head appeared; it was red-faced and squirming even as Kyala tried to clear out its mouth. Then, with a slithering rush, the body was born. "It's a boy, Damarisa, and he's beautiful and strong—listen to him!"

He howled lustily, voicing his outrage at the cold world in which he found himself. His arms flailed so jerkily that it was awkward for Kyala to wrap him in a soft towel and put him gently on his mother's belly.

She was crying too, tears indistinguishable from the sweat on her face. Camiola helped her sit up a little, so that she could reach for him and touch him.

"He isn't—he's all right?" Damarisa begged.

"He's perfect, a beautiful baby," said Kyala firmly. "Ah, here's the afterbirth—you can hold him in a moment, my lady. Camiola, if you will tend to the cord, please."

Damarisa began to whimper weakly as the final contraction hit her. "No, it hurts, it *hurts,* you said it was over, nooo, it's happening *again*!"

"The afterbirth has to come, my lady; it won't be as hard. Everything is all right."

But as the words left her mouth, Kyala knew she was wrong. Damarisa was bleeding much too heavily. "Camiola, put him down and get a tight bellyband on her! Quickly!"

As the midwives worked frantically on the girl, neither remembered or noticed the man in the room. No one saw him take the newborn infant and leave.

Nobody knew how old the castle was; many of its secrets had died with previous generations. Only the lord that hurried through the twisting passage knew of its existence. Narrow, dusty stone stairs meandered downward through the castle walls, occasionally breaking for small landings and spyholes. After a time, the passage ceased being of worked stone; now it was carved from the same volcanic rock that formed the castle's foundations.

At last Baird came to an open chamber, formed in a forgotten time by some bubble in the rock. He laid the baby on a large, flattened stone that uncomfortably resembled an altar and busied himself lighting the candles and piles of herbs that he had carefully placed there previously. The newborn's fretful whimpering quieted as he breathed in the acrid smoke.

The man ignored his son as he finished his preparations. He carefully spoke words that had the ring of ritual, words that were at once command and beseechment, words that seemed to twist themselves and fly off flapping through the darkness that lived in this secret place. A knife glowed nearly white-hot as he lifted it from a brazier. The semblance of a face began to form in the smoke, and Baird brandished the knife in ceremonial salute above his head.

"O Master, Lord of Darkness and Fear, whose Name is unknown and unknowable, this is my son, my firstborn. Obedient to Your command, I dedicate him to You." Carefully, with the tip of the knife, he severed one of the baby's tiny finger joints. The infant screamed as the new sensation of pain penetrated even through his drug-induced stupor. His father ignored him, placing the severed fingertip into a black stone bowl filled with a clear fluid. Instantly the fluid coalesced around it, trapping it in a tiny crystal globe.

The face looked back at the baron with eyes that were pits of shadow, and a sneer curled over the handsome features. "You called Me for *this*? What use do I have for a screaming infant?"

Lord Baird stared back, anger and astonishment clear in his manner. "We made a bargain, master! I would give You my son, and You would release me from your control."

The god merely smiled. Baird jerked as though he had been struck. The planes of his face began to shift and the bones to thicken as a broad muzzle formed, and the eyes that glared back at the god were now yellow and slit-pupiled.

"Shall I continue until the were-change is complete, beast-man? It might be amusing to watch an ice leopard play cat-and-mouse with a human infant."

Baird snarled in silent frustration. All his life he had hated the times when his ice leopard body was not under his own control. The uses the god put it to were enjoyable, yes—but that submission to his master was becoming unbearable.

"A baby," the god smiled. "How disgustingly sweet. Will you tell it bedtime stories as it grows up, beast-man? Aye, tell it how its grandfather came to be baron here over his older brothers, how his own father outlawed him at fifteen. Tell it how a hill bandit just happened to have a were-talent I found amusing.

"Or would you like to tell it of your own treachery, how you came to Me of your own free will when you found out what you are? You made a bargain with Me then, too. Or don't you recall how you wanted your own father dead so badly that you were willing to become My creature as well?

"Take this puling brat away now, but take good care of it. I will want it back in fifteen or sixteen years." The semblance of a face vanished.

The baron stared after it in rage and frustration a moment longer, then abruptly bundled the infant back in its blanket and left the cavern.

The three women left in the birthing room nearly fainted with relief when Baird stomped into the room and dumped the baby back in its cradle. Kyala and Camiola had stopped the bleeding, and they knew that the Lady Damarisa would live, with proper care. The discovery that the infant had vanished terrified both midwives. Surely the lord baron would hold them to blame for his son's disappearance. Torture would be a mild word for what he might do to them.

Kyala picked the baby up and patted him to soothe his cries before she put him in his mother's arms.

"Shhh, shhh, little one, it's all right now," she crooned. "What is his name, my lady?"

"My lord says it must be Varian." As all new mothers did, Damarisa's first action was to push away the swaddling blanket to see for herself that her son was all right. Her eyes went to Kyala's face, full of sickened shock. "His finger . . . what happened to his finger?"

Kyala had no answer. As one, the heads of all three women turned in the direction Lord Baird had gone, and then they looked at each other in dismay and disbelief.

Swordsman

Year 404 D.S.: Month of Tallgrass

Swords rang against shields as the two opponents fought, testing again and again for some hole, some weakness in the other's defense. The hours upon hours of training each had received at the hands of a master swordsman showed in the smooth flow of blow and counterblow, the attempts of each warrior to force his opponent into a fatal error. So equally matched were the two that defeat for one came entirely unexpectedly. His opponent feinted, beginning a strike toward the leg, then suddenly snapped his wrist and elbow to send his blade skipping over the defender's shield for a flat blow to his head. At the same time, the defender's heel caught on some unseen obstruction; the combination sent him over backward as he fought unsuccessfully to catch his balance. Instantly his opponent was on him, sword at his throat.

"Do you yield?"

No answer came from the downed warrior. Instead, gusty breathless laughter rang hollowly from his helm.

"You are a dead man, Varian," said the one still on

his feet. "Is that a new style of defense, falling flat on your ass?"

"No, it's offense, Corven. Once I've perfected it, I'll be in position to cut your feet off at the ankle."

Corven laughed also and grabbed his friend's hand, hauling him to his feet. "Likarion, that was a good workout, Varian. It's been too long." He reached up and pulled off his helm, revealing a young man in his mid-teens, with a stubble of brown hair above a plain, honest face. "I'm slipping when I can only kill you once in an afternoon."

Varian squirmed out of his own helm. His shaggy, dark hair fell in his eyes, escaping the sweatband of cloth that had confined it. A small gold ring glinted in his left ear. "I can't see any way we can manage more than this. Getting both of us away unseen isn't easy. Lord Duer may be my uncle, but he won't wink at your arms practice the way Master Evan did at home."

"No, he won't," said a quiet voice from across the room. Both youths whipped around, startled. A younger boy was watching them with a troubled look on his face.

"How long have you been here, Niko?" Varian asked in dismay.

"Long enough. I saw that last bout. Corven's *good,* Varian. Too good. He's been fighting a long time, as long as you have, I think."

Varian didn't answer the half-question. He looked at his friend's face, white under its tan even though Corven had his expression under tight control. "Are you going to report us, Niko?"

"I have to. I like Corven, but he's a *slave,* Varian. You know the law. It's illegal for a slave even to touch a sword, even to clean it for someone else. And teaching him to fight . . ." His voice trailed off unhappily.

"We know."

"Why did you start, then? What made you do it?" demanded Niko.

Varian shrugged slightly, the gesture half-hidden by the armor he still wore. "I was about seven when I started arms training, Niko. Corven was my friend even then—and there was nobody else my size to practice with.

"Niko, please, you've got to understand, the king's laws don't—aren't always obeyed in the Northern mountains. We're so far away, and sometimes conditions aren't the same there. My father's slaves won't conduct an armed uprising because one of them is my sword-partner."

Niko was still troubled. He looked away from Varian's insistent, almost pleading green eyes to Corven, who had stripped off his armored gauntlets and was staring at his right hand, flexing and turning it as if to memorize the intricateness of it.

Varian followed the direction of Niko's gaze and desperately grasped at the straw that might let both of them survive. "Do you know what will happen to Corven, Niko, if you tell? *If* they let him live, he'll lose his sword hand. And the law says that *I* would have to be the one who cuts it off—or the one who executes him, because I am the one who is responsible. *Please,* Niko, forget you saw us, and we won't risk it again."

Corven lifted his head and broke his silence, forcing out the words almost voicelessly, "No, Varian, don't. Don't beg for me. I am responsible for my own actions, and I fight because *I* want to."

Varian ignored him, bringing his hand down on Corven's shoulder in the only gesture of reassurance he could make.

"Please, Niko," he repeated. "He's my friend, my swordbrother, not just my body-servant. Two years ago, he saved my life on the field. I can't let him die. If you keep quiet, I will do anything for you, anything in my powers to keep Corven alive and unmaimed."

The younger boy studied Varian intently, the signs of the man he would become already making themselves known on his young face, as he carefully calculated what advantage he could make of this. Slowly, he nodded his head, looking suddenly older than his years. "I won't tell. But there is a price on my silence. Loyalty like yours is not to be wasted. I want your pledge of fealty to me.''

''Fealty . . . ?'' Varian repeated, almost blankly. ''My lands are freehold, not a fiefdom. My bloodline has never sworn fealty to anyone, not even the king.''

''I know. My father says it makes you very dangerous men. I meant your personal fealty, to me alone. Remember, as your overlord, I would also be bound to serve and protect you . . . both of you.''

For a moment, Varian hesitated; then he stripped off the blunted practice-guards on his sword and went down on one knee before Niko, balancing the naked blade flat on both palms. In a low voice, he repeated the words of the formal vow that would bind him as follower and vassal.

''From this moment I am thy man; from this moment I pledge life and limb to thy service, as long as I have breath in my body. This I vow on the blade I hold and the blood I shed; if I dishonor or break faith with thee, may it twist in my hand to slay me as I stand.''

For the space of three heartbeats, Niko stood absolutely still, looking down at him as if to judge the integrity of his oath; then he covered Varian's hands with his own, so that the sword was clasped between them. ''From this moment I am thy lord; thou art mine to command or release, mine to protect with my power as thou defend me with thy body. This I vow on the sword between us; if I break faith with thee, may the gods above deal with me as I deserve. In sign and token of this I give to thee . . .'' Niko broke off, becoming only a slightly flustered twelve-year-old boy again. ''Damn, I don't have a ring or anything to give you.''

Varian looked up at him, a ghost of a smile on his lips. ''You have already promised me a gift . . . my lord.''

''Oh. In sign and token of this I give thee . . . this man's life. May it forever be a reminder unto thee.''

Niko looked down and fiddled with his belt knife as

Varian rose to his feet. "I'll keep all this secret, even the fealty, for now," he promised. "It might—it *would* cause a lot of questions. You know, I wouldn't have told, anyway. I like you, Varian. You don't treat us younger boys like we're dirt under your feet."

"Niko, who are you? Who is your father? I know you tyros are anonymous to be on an equal footing, but I'd like to know who I've just given my oath to."

Niko shook his head. "I can't tell you, even though I'd like to. My father . . . is a very powerful Southern lord. You won't regret it." He grinned at Varian impishly, all boy again. "For all you know, I could be somebody's bastard or the crown prince."

"Oh, yeah. As if they'd let one of their pampered princelings even this far north, where the bogharts might get him."

"You've seen real bogharts? In battle?" Niko asked with excitement.

"Seen them and fought them and been scared shitless the whole time," Varian answered dryly. "That was when Corven saved my life. You know, someone else will come looking for us if we don't leave soon. Corven?"

The two began stripping off armor. Corven unfastened the awkwardly placed buckles that secured Varian's chest armor, overlapping metal plates riveted to a heavy leather jerkin. His own mail hauberk came off more easily; he simply bent over and allowed it to slither off over his head.

Niko watched with interest. "How do you get Corven's armor back and forth without being seen?"

"We've been hiding it here. Who is going to look in a deserted storage room for a guardsman's armor that nobody has reported missing? I guess we'll have to sneak it out the way we brought it in."

"Abandon it, Varian," Corven put in bitterly. "I'll never get to use it again."

Niko turned his attention to him with interest. Now that he was stripped of mail armor and protective padded gambeson, the narrow black iron band of a slave collar was clearly visible around his neck.

"You haven't said much, Corven."

"I'm a slave, Master Niko. We learn early to speak when spoken to and keep our mouths shut the rest of the time." He added awkwardly, "I am grateful for my life, master."

"You know, you were lucky that it was me that caught you, instead of Paolon or one of the other sneaks."

"If we were lucky, nobody would have caught us," Varian observed soberly. "What we were is stupid, to think we could get away with it forever."

Faintly and far away, a bell rang.

"That's the warning bell for dinner. I've got to run— I'm serving high table," Niko said hurriedly. "Will you play shakarr with me after, Varian?"

"Of course, my lord."

Niko grinned at them as he hurried away.

Corven looked after him somberly. "He's right, you know, Varian. It's lucky we were caught by a kid who has a bad case of hero worship for you."

"Hero worship? Me? Let's hide this stuff anyway. Maybe we can think of some way to salvage it later."

"Hero worship," Corven repeated firmly. "We slaves see a lot, even if we don't say anything. That age needs someone to look up to. You're the best swordsman of the lot, and you've behaved decently toward him. You never served as a tyro like him. Watch how the other Swords treat them; as he says, like dirt."

"It's supposed to toughen the boys up, make warriors out of them. They can't be pampered in the women's quarters forever."

Corven shrugged as he hefted the heavy canvas bag that held Varian's armor. "I can't say. Nobody ever pampers slaves."

"Will you stop going on about being a slave?" Varian demanded angrily. "I'd free you if I could. You know that."

"I was stupid enough to try to forget I'm a slave these last years. Maybe if you rubbed my nose in it regularly, it wouldn't hurt like this," Corven shot back savagely. "You don't know—you *can't* know—how it feels to stand there, helpless, while two other people decide whether you live or die. It was like—no, it was *worse* than standing on the block again, waiting to be sold." The pain of that sale, now ten years in the past, was reflected in his eyes.

Varian's spark of anger died as quickly as it had flared, as he, too, remembered the sale that had put Corven in his life, remembered watching a six-year-old slave trying hard not to cry as his mother was taken away by her new master. "I'm sorry, Corven. You're right; I don't know. Come on, I'll be late for dinner, and I don't want to risk any attention from Lord Duer."

Corven stopped him with a hand on his arm. "Varian, I don't want you to think I'm not grateful. I know swearing fealty isn't something to take lightly . . ." He paused awkwardly, unsure what to say next.

"Niko's a good kid. It'll work out all right."

"Will it?" Corven asked bitterly. "Maybe I should just run before they come for me, try to make it to the mountains and disappear."

"Maybe you could, if we were home, Corven. But how far do you think you would make it here? It's all flat, open fields and little villages, remember? No forest, no cover at all for more than a day's ride. If you run, Niko will tell, and you won't have a chance. Even if I give you Rowan and delay them as much possible, they would still hunt you down. You'll be a dangerous renegade, not just a runaway. We have to trust him. There's no other way."

Corven looked frustrated. "I suppose you're right. I probably couldn't even make it out the gates with a collar locked on my neck and my head shaved so it screams 'slave' as far as anybody can see me.

"I couldn't leave you, anyway, Varian. You're in just as much trouble, and I know you can't run."

"Trouble is what I'll get if I'm late for dinner," Varian said grimly. "Let's go!"

In spite of his hurry, Varian knew he was late when he charged into the bathing room and found only a bath-slave in the middle of cleaning up. He hesitated only a moment before he stripped off his clothes and plunged into the lukewarm pool. It was better to be late by a few more minutes than to appear at dinner dusty and sweating.

He gave himself a hasty soaping and rinsing, then rubbed his hand over his jaw and decided that he could skip shaving. The bath-slave (who was hiding her annoyance at having her work interrupted) scrubbed his back dry as she handed him another towel to finish himself.

Corven hurried in with clean, dry clothes and watched with visible amusement while Varian attempted to pull tight breeches on over his still-damp legs, softly cursing at whoever had decided that tight clothes were fashionable and at his aunt who had decreed that the young men of her husband's Swordguard should follow that fashion.

He trotted through the empty halls, hurriedly combing back his wet hair with his fingers, then silently eased open the door to the great hall. He was out of luck. The dining steward said loudly and sarcastically, "How kind of you to join us, young sir. Pray be seated."

So much for trying to slip into his place unobserved. He could feel all eyes on him as he took his seat. The young woman on the other side of the table scowled at him. "Where were you?" she demanded. "I had to walk in *unescorted*. Everybody was *looking* at me. How could you *embarrass* me like this?"

Varian opened his mouth to apologize and bit his tongue as his neighbor elbowed him hard in the ribs.

"She had better be pretty enough to make up for it, Varian, because you are in deep trouble. Lord Duer is beckoning to you."

His stomach growled hungrily as he approached the high table and went down on one knee before his lord. "Command me, my lord," he said formally.

The Lord Duer, Earl of Sundare, stared coldly back at him, pinning him with a steely gray glare. "You have guard duty, boy. Take Aerdan's place." He motioned slightly with his head at the young man who stood ceremonial guard behind him.

Varian bowed his head. "You do me honor, sir," he said respectfully, although he and everyone within earshot knew he was being disciplined. Guards did not eat while on duty; the Swordguard scheduled would have eaten earlier.

Aerdan turned over his helm and sword and hurried off to take Varian's abandoned place at the table. Varian dropped into the guardsman's stance he would maintain for the rest of the dinner. Niko swept past him carrying a pitcher of wine and made a series of faces at him that he took to mean the boy was sorry but couldn't do anything to help him. Thank goodness Niko was quick though, and rapidly composed his face when Varian barely shook his head; just then, the visiting lord called for more wine.

Of all the duties of a Swordguard in the service of a lord earl, Varian hated ceremonial guard duty the most. It might be excellent training in self-discipline, but standing at attention, unable to move or even show emotion, was deathly boring. It was Varian's misfortune to have missed only a few minutes of this dinner. As there were guests, it was quite long and formal with numerous courses, all accompanied by pompous service and appropriate entertainment. He knew it was only about two hours that he stood there, but subjectively it seemed like half the night.

Even the end of the dinner did not release him to go and scrounge in the kitchens for something to eat. He was released from guard duty but was then expected to attend on his lord with the other Swordguard in the informality

of the little hall. It was not considered duty, as they were
free to talk or game quietly among themselves, but their
attendance was required.

Varian joined a group of friends at the far end of the
room where he hoped to be less conspicuous; he suspected that he was still in disgrace. Though most of the
young men there had been in trouble themselves at some
time, the odds were about even whether they would
commiserate with him or harass him.

Harassing won. Whistles and catcalls greeted him,
along with rather coarse speculation as to what had kept
him so long as to make him late for dinner. "Come on,
Varian, who was she?" "Yeah, Varian, that pretty little
blonde chambermaid?" "Oh ho, I tumbled her last
week. Is that why your armor was missing, Varian? She
scratches!"

Varian looked hunted. "Keep it quiet, gentlemen.
You'll get me in deeper than ever. I went off alone to
work out some fighting moves."

There was knowing laughter from the group. "Yeah,
we know what kind of moves, Varian." "You're not
supposed to fight them, Varian, you're supposed to . . ."
"Maybe that's the only sword he knows how to use!"

"Enough of that," warned Aerdan. "The ladies are
coming in, and we'll all be pulling guard duty if we
offend their delicate ears."

Lady Gavriveda swept in with her guest and both ladies' trains of Maidens. Just as the Swordguard were
young men of noble birth serving the lord in return for
training, so these girls were learning the duties and priv-
ileges of highborn ladies. Privately, Varian thought that
they were learning to be royal nuisances, good only to
chatter and giggle and gossip.

The young woman who had begun to scold him at
dinner broke away from the bevy and came toward him.
For a moment, Varian felt his belly roil, expecting her
to continue the scene, but she only fixed him with a cold
stare of scorn and distaste. "I wish my token of favor
returned, sirrah. I will not have my honor soiled by any

further contact with a churl such as yourself."

Varian bowed slightly as he pulled the square of embroidered linen from his belt. Though he heartily disliked both the playacting and the girl (who had been arbitrarily assigned to him as his "lady"), he knew how to play the courtesy game as well as any of them. "I deeply regret that I have displeased you, my lady Latetia."

She froze him with another cold frown, snatched the favor from his hand, then turned away with a swirl of skirts, sniffing indignantly as she retreated.

"Ouch. Is my broken heart bleeding, Aerdan?" asked Varian cheerfully. "Do you think I can hope she's off my neck permanently?"

Aerdan laughed sardonically. "I think you had the best of it this evening, Varian, even standing guard. I would have traded places back with you in a heartbeat. That girl has a tongue like a boot dagger, a little jab here, a little jab there."

"Don't run too fast, Aerdan. You aren't the only unattached Sword, but if you attract her attention, she'll be on you like ticks on a dog," said Niko's voice at their elbows.

"Where did you come from, cub? You belong in bed with the other babes in the nursery."

"Let up on him, Aerdan. He's too close to being a Sword himself to be packed off with the babes," Varian remarked with lazy good humor. "You wanted to ask me something about shakarr strategy, didn't you?"

Niko nodded. "I have the board all set up, Varian. Do you want black or gold?"

Aerdan snorted at the boy's insistent presumption. "Well, if you'd rather play board games with a babe than dice with the men, Varian, be my guest."

"Hey, let up on me now, Aerdan. Till my father shakes loose some more money, my pockets are flat as a beggar's." Varian pulled himself into a hunchbacked posture, thrusting a crooked hand under Aerdan's nose. " 'Alms for the poor, m'lord? Alms for the poor, kind sir?' '' he begged in a cracked, quavering voice.

Aerdan swatted at his hand. "Away with you, foul peasant."

Varian grinned and hobbled away to the shakarr table, begging alms from the rest of his friends as he went.

They were well into their game, with Niko mounting a strategic campaign that was decimating Varian's pieces, when Varian thought he heard his name called. He had raised his head and was looking for the source when he heard the visiting lord say loudly, "Now really, Duer, don't insult me with such nursery stories! Bogharts indeed! Next you'll be telling me dragons still live in your hills!"

Lord Duer caught Varian's eye and beckoned him over. With a soft word of apology to Niko, he jumped up and obeyed the summons, bowing his head respectfully to the guest.

"You called me, sir?"

"Varian, I would have you make the acquaintance of Lord Govert, Duke of Riaza. Govert, this is my nephew Varian, my sister Damarisa's son."

Lord Govert was a tall man with a warrior's muscular build now running to fat. Thinning red hair did not go with the piercing black eyes that stared out over his hawk's nose, and the wide gold rings of his rank seemed too heavy for his ears.

"I see you wear an heir's earring, boy," he said harshly. "Your father is . . . ?"

Varian's head went up proudly. "I have the honor to be son and heir to Baird, Baron of Leopard's Gard." His hardened stare seemed to dare the older and higher-ranking lord to find fault with his bloodline.

Govert broke the eye contact first. "I see Leopard's Gard raises fierce young cubs, Duer," he said grudgingly. "And yet I can see Damarisa in him, too."

Lord Duer grinned at both nephew and guest, clearly amused by their silent battle of will. "Govert disbelieves our tales of boghart hunting, lad. I'd like your help in convincing him."

" 'Tis naught to me, Uncle, whether a Southron lord believes me or no," Varian said with chilling quietness, his Northern mountain accent deliberately more pronounced. "But if I must prove it to ye on my body, m'lord, so be it."

He unhooked the embroidered cuff of his shirt and pushed the loose sleeve up to his shoulder, then displayed his left arm to the skeptical duke. A wide red scar ran from his forearm to just above the elbow, paralleled by three smaller scars, only now starting to fade to thin white lines.

"Likarion, man! What sort of a weapon leaves scars like that? I'm surprised you can still use that arm," exclaimed Govert, impressed in spite of himself.

" 'Nursery stories', m'lord. Those are boghart tusk marks. I was leadin' a hawkin' party that turned into a pitched battle." Varian stared challengingly at the duke, then turned away to look into the heart of the fire. "And before ye ask, Uncle, aye, I was a cocky young fool who underestimated them.

"We'd gone over the pass into the waste, hawkin' for grouse, myself, four other boys, a couple of guardsmen, and two slaves, one to handle the dogs and one for a beater. No shields, only three swords, one of them mine. It was new, and I was proud as a dog with two tails and didn't want to leave it behind. We'd had reports of a boghart pack in the area, but I'd disregarded them because they were tellin' some outlandish story of the creatures being armed. Bogharts are cunnin' brutes, aye, but just beasts.

"They ambushed us before we'd gone two miles, and they *were* armed. Just clubs and sharpened sticks for spears, but dangerous enough. They got up under my horse's belly and took her down. I got one as she fell and took off his hand, club and all, but that left him inside my guard, and he slashed my arm. I think he would have gone on to my throat, but a slave grabbed one of their stick-spears and got him in the back. I didn't even feel it, was yellin' like a gut-stabbed leopard and tryin' to form my men into some sort of battle formation when they broke and ran. I still don't know why.

"They won that one. Two of the men with me died to one of theirs, and another was crippled for life."

His voice had become quieter and harsher as he told his story. Niko had oozed into the firelight to hear better and saw the bright, hard glisten of Varian's eyes. Varian paid careful attention to refastening his cuff before he spoke again, fighting down the anger that had surfaced so unexpectedly—the old anger at himself, for causing the unnecessary death and mutilation of those under his command, and anger at the duke for scoffing at something that had caused him so much pain. "I lost two friends that day to yer nursery stories, m'lord. I hear ye Southron lords like huntin'. An' ye visit *my* lands, I'll show ye the hunt of yer life!"

The duke stared soberly back at him. "I apologize, Lord Varian. Duer, have your slave get this man a chair. He shouldn't have been made to stand like a peasant making a crop report to the steward.

"I was not doubting your word, lad, but your uncle and I are old comrades. He has been known to, hmm, twist truth's tail, shall we say? I'd like to learn more about these bogharts, if you'd not mind teaching an old warhorse new tricks.

"And what are you doing here, Niko?"

The boy grinned mischievously. "Learning, too, sir. If I may stay, please?"

Duer reached out a hand and ruffled Niko's hair affectionately. "This one has his nose in every stewpot in the castle, Govert. Don't you know that old saying, lad, about what curiosity did to the cat?"

"I was taught that curiosity is the father of wisdom, sir."

"Ah, well then," Govert said expansively. "Drag up a stool, lad. My lord Varian?"

"What do ye want to know, sir?" asked Varian, still wary of this Southern lord's unexpected affability.

"What sort of beastie are they? I had always thought

them vague monsters intended to frighten naughty children into obedience.''

"Quite real, sir. They look—mmm—rather like wild boars tryin' to be human. Short, spiky hair all over, tusks comin' out of their lower jaw like this,'' and he mimed jagged teeth sprouting from the corners of an elongated jaw. "They have stubby hands with a small hoof on the end of each finger instead of nails. I've heard that in my grandsire's time they ran on all fours, but the ones I've seen walk on their hind legs, sort of hunchbacked. They run in packs like wolves, and they'll attack for the sheer love of killin'.''

Govert was nodding at each detail, as if making a mental list. "How do you usually hunt them, then?''

"One or two alone can be treated like boar, with a cross-barred spear so they don't run up the shaft and slash you to bits before they die. A pack is a lot harder. We usually go after them with trackin' hounds and archers, with spearmen or swordsmen to take out the ones that don't die immediately. The few armed ones I've had reports of since that first pack are just as likely to revert to slashin' as they are to use handweapons.''

"You use dogs only for tracking them? And archers don't seem exactly sporting.''

"They'll rip their way through a pack of boarhounds in a heartbeat. We don't hunt them for *entertainment,* m'lord,'' and Varian's voice was harsh again. "We want to wipe all of them out right down to the cubs. They are gone from our southern valleys, but we still get some in the high slopes. Sometimes we go over the pass to take out marauders like that pack.''

Lord Duer sat quietly and watched his friend and his young kinsman. He had heard Varian's story before, and while he felt the weight of the young man's still raw grief, knew that no boy comes to manhood without trial. They were all so young, these boys under his care, tyros and Swordguard both, even though they considered themselves men. Perhaps of all of them, Varian was closest to understanding the deep responsibility of his

rank, rather than seeing only the outer seeming of privilege. Duer smiled a little sadly under his mustache as
he ran his eyes over the young men in the room, coming
back to rest on Niko, who was clearly bursting with
questions but too well trained to interrupt his elders. This
was not the first time he had noticed Niko's liking for
Varian; that would be a good friendship to encourage.

Varian was still explaining, his hands moving over the
table as he laid out imaginary terrain maps to illustrate
his points in the fine art of boghart hunting. Duer waited
for him to take a breath before he interrupted. "I think
Niko has some questions, Govert. Shall we let him ask
before he explodes?"

Govert chuckled. "Well, if you must spoil the lad,
Duer. And here I was thinking you kept them under
tight, old-fashioned discipline."

"Just the way we were under old Bardavin when we
were boys, my friend. Niko, ask your questions before
we pack everybody off to bed."

"Thank you, sir. Varian, that hunting trip when you
were hurt, what would you have done differently? Was
there something you did that you shouldn't, or something you should have done and didn't?"

Varian blinked in surprise. Questions on tactics were
the last thing he would have expected from a twelve-
year-old. "Other than not being a damn fool? I should
have listened to my horse. She tried to tell me there was
something around that she didn't like, and I ignored her.

"Since I did have reports of bogharts, I should have
taken a couple of guard dogs. The bird dogs we had
with us probably smelled the bogharts and ignored them.
You know how they're trained to disregard anything but
birds.

"What I should not have done was take command on
myself when I wasn't ready for it. I was fourteen and
thought I was a man. I found out I wasn't. That's why
I'm here, to get the training that I know I need."

Lord Govert chuckled again. "I hear he works you
lads hard, not only arms training but command training

like strategy and tactics. That's what we got as Swords, analyzing old battles and court intrigue and suchlike. Does he make you do stewards' work, too, so you know if the job is being done right?''

Varian grinned companionably at the older lord. "Aye, m'lord. And harvesting and milking cows on occasion, too.''

"And while we're on training and discipline, young man, why were you late to dinner?" asked Duer severely.

Varian felt his ears burn as he scrambled frantically for an explanation. He couldn't tell the truth, and he didn't want Niko to hear him in the dishonor of a lie. "I, uh, I was with a companion, my lord. We—we wanted to be alone and lost track of the time.''

To his surprise, Duer and Govert grinned at each other, although his uncle persisted, "And who was your companion, lad?''

They're thinking like the Swords, he realized and gratefully plunged into the opening. "It would be dishonorable of me, my lord, to reveal my companion's name. If any punishment is due for our actions, it is mine alone," he parried.

He was relieved to hear Govert laugh. "Let the man alone, Duer. As I recall, you didn't want to tumble your first girl in public either.''

Duer pretended to ignore him. "The punishment is certainly yours, since you choose to protect her. Report to the officer of the guard. Tell him you are to mount guard all shifts tonight, his choice of position. You are dismissed.''

Varian rose to his feet and gave a formal salute to his lord. "You do me honor, lord," he said, and made his escape.

Javis, the captain of the guard and the officer on duty, looked at Varian with mixed amusement and exasperation. "You again? What did you do this time?''

"Came late to dinner. I'm to take all shifts tonight.''

His stomach chose that moment to growl loudly as if in affirmation.

"Is that your belly or a bear?" Javis didn't wait for Varian's answer. "Take the first shift up on the ramparts with Leor. Fetch your own sword first. You've got a few minutes before shift change, and I won't ask you to use one of these issue meatchoppers when you've a decent sword of your own.

"And stop by the guardsmen's mess on your way back and grab some bread and cheese. I'll not have bears on my battlements all night."

Leor touched Varian's arm to halt him as they emerged from the guardtower. Two dark figures already occupied the ramparts they were to patrol. The voices that came to their ears were those of Lord Duer and his guest, no doubt come out for a last breath of fresh air and a little privacy before retiring for the night.

"And even seeing him doesn't change your mind, Govert?" Varian heard his uncle ask. "Does being Damarisa's son count for nothing?"

"I'll watch him carefully for the rest of my visit, Duer, but I don't think so. Yes, yes, he seems to be a fine, spirited young man, and if you had had the raising of him, I might agree to a betrothal.

"But I was there, remember, when your father told Damarisa she had to marry that hill-bandit who fathered him, and I've never seen terror like that since. She came to me in tears and begged me to help her. I can still see her face . . . and I couldn't do anything.

"No, Duer, I won't do the same thing to my Lariah, much as I may like the boy."

Varian was glad of the shadows that hid his burning face. So his uncle was matchmaking for him and not having any luck because of his father's bloodline? He didn't know whether to be angry or relieved; Likarion knew he didn't want any of those chattering females tied around his neck!

Summons

Varian stifled a yawn the next morning as he sat cleaning his sword. The sun was warm and he was sweating a little under his armor. Before him in the exercise yard other young warriors fought their own practice bouts, some under the sharp eye of the armsmaster, others on their own. The number of young men in training was uneven, so Varian was waiting for a partner to work with him.

But a warrior's training is not all swordwork. Ears trained to catch the slightest unusual noise heard a soft scuffling behind him. Varian suppressed a smile as a young boy's voice hissed, "You said he's *your* friend, Niko, *you* ask him, and don't blame us if he bites your head off."

"My teeth aren't that sharp, Niko," he said with amusement. "What is it?" He turned to see half-a-dozen boys, from Niko's age of twelve years down to about seven, grouped behind him.

"We wanted to ask you," Niko began and bit his words off as a somewhat younger boy elbowed him in the ribs. He glared at the other boy and continued aggressively, "*We* wanted to ask you if there are any training tricks that the armsmaster here hasn't taught us. Is there some Northern secret you don't let us Southerners know?"

"If there was, I couldn't tell you, now, could I?" Varian asked, both amused at the way the question was phrased and flattered to have been asked. "My only secret is a lot of practice. There isn't much else to do when you're snowed in five months of the year."

Niko's eager face fell a little at his words, and one of the younger boys whispered to a friend, "See? I told you he wouldn't."

"I'll tell you what," Varian relented. "If you have permission from Master Treon, I'll be happy to work with you boys. Since Kieran left home, I'm without a partner and have some extra time, but I can't usurp your swordmaster's training."

"We already asked him, and he said it's all right."

"All right, then, let me think . . . there's something my armsmaster at home had me do a lot that I don't see you boys doing much. Slow practice."

Niko made a face. "It's boring enough for warmup, why should we do it any other time?"

"Maybe not the way I was taught." Varian stood up and hefted his sword, then looked at it with a frown and sheathed it. "You boys are still working with the training swords, right? Good. We don't want you to lop each others' heads off in practice. Somebody, Niko, give me yours. It should be close to the right weight for me."

He caught the leather-wrapped wooden sword that Niko tossed to him and took up a stance, an imaginary shield held just so and sword cocked and ready behind his head. "Now, pretend, instead of swordwork, that you're serving high table at the great hall. This is Yearsend Great Feast and the king and queen are there and a whole boatload of nobles. Got that?"

The boys nodded but looked puzzled. Varian continued, "You're at the very head of a whole line of cooks and slaves and underservers, passing the food dramatically over your heads from hand to hand to hand. Someone puts a big heavy bowl of . . . of spiced peacocks' tongues in your hand and *you* have to put it down just so in front of the queen. You swing it down slowly and carefully, your hand rotating to keep it balanced so it doesn't spill, past your ear and under your nose,'' he demonstrated the movements as he spoke, ''but just as you start to set it on the table, the queen says, 'Eeeuw, spiced peacock tongues! How dis*gust*ing!' ''

The boys giggled, for Varian had pitched his voice into a high falsetto to mimic a nauseated queen.

''So just as slowly and carefully, you bring it back up over your head and pass it to the server behind you so he can pass it back down the line. And no doubt some poor slave will have to eat the stuff.''

He swung slowly through the movements again and added, ''Now, this is obviously either a very picky queen or the cooks are making some really outlandish stuff, because everything you serve you have to take away again.

''Try it that way for a while.''

The boys went to work with a will, some still giggling as they served their imaginary queens with the most bizarre things they could think of. Varian watched and corrected as needed. Once he had a boy drop his sword and work with a cupped handful of sand instead.

After a time he called a halt. ''I think your armsmaster probably covered this, but it doesn't hurt to go over it again. A good sword blow is a combination of strength, speed, and precision. Which of those three is the most important?''

''Strength,'' somebody guessed.

Varian shook his head. ''Anybody else? Niko?''

''Precision.''

''Why?'' Varian challenged.

''Well, I've seen you fight with the lord earl, and he's a lot stronger than you, but you beat him.''

''Only sometimes. But you're right, a man can have the strength of a giant, but if he can't put those blows precisely where he wants them, they don't do any good. That's the whole point of slow work, not only this par-

ticular type of blow but all of them, so that you learn to
move not just your sword arm but your whole body.

"If Swordmaster Treon agrees, I'll work up some
more exercises for you boys that don't interfere with his
teaching but don't necessarily cover the same ground,
all right?"

"Yeah, thanks, Varian," Niko grinned.

"So then—" he broke off as he saw a familiar figure
in a dark green tunic approaching. "What is it, Corven?"

Corven was being the perfect slave this morning, sub-
missive and quiet almost to the point of invisibility. He
went to his knees, his eyes down as he said, "A message, Master Varian, from the lord earl. He bids you
attend him at once in his office."

"Did he say why? He knows I have arms practice
now. Can't it wait?"

The slave didn't quite shrug. "He said at once, master."

"Damn." Varian chewed his lower lip. If it was
something important enough for his uncle to call him
out of arms practice, and in those words, he ought to go
as he was. And yet he didn't want to go swaggering
through the halls in armor, as if he were a mercenary
guardsman trying to impress the girls. "Corven, run
back and tell him I'll be there as soon as I can get
stripped. Niko, will you help me?"

"Yeah, sure, Varian. What do you suppose it is?"

Lord Duer turned to look irritably at him as he entered
the office.

Varian gave him a formal salute. "You sent for me,
sir?"

"Yes. It seems your father wants you home immediately."

"Does he say why, sir? Is he ill?" Not that any illness
of his father concerned Varian. They lived in the same
household and shared the same bloodline, but that was
the end of the relationship. Varian would have said that

his father scarcely noticed whether his son was home or not, or at times even that Baird had a son.

"It seems it has come to Lord Baird's attention that you were not dedicated as an adult to any of the gods, as you should have been when you turned fourteen."

Varian frowned and shook his head in disbelief. "My lord father has never seen fit to do that, it's true. But I never expected to be dedicated by him. He says that the gods are foolish stories made up to keep fat priests and priestesses in idleness."

"I wish you had told me this, Varian. I would have held the ceremony for you if you had wanted it, but I thought surely you had been dedicated before you left home." Lord Duer looked troubled at the thought that he had failed in a duty to a kinsman.

The young man let a smile flash briefly across his face. "Thank you, Uncle. But I wonder sometimes whether I believe in gods or not, myself. Likarion is supposed to be the God of Warriors, but He doesn't fight for the warrior who is right, just the one who is more skilled. And who is to say then, whether He is there or not?"

"If you had been properly dedicated, you would know, son. When . . . well, I'm not allowed to say, that's only for the initiated to know." The older lord sighed and added, "Well, that's neither here nor there. You've been summoned home, and you must go, much as I'd like to keep you here. Since Kieran was fostered out, you've been a son to me in his place."

Varian's face was solemn, but his eyes brightened at the praise. It was unusual for his uncle to admit to any of the softer sentiments; he was a proud warrior, not a poet or bard. "And you have been the father I would choose, were such a thing possible. I would stay if I were permitted, Uncle. May I return after this dedication?"

"Of course, lad," Duer said gruffly. "I don't want to seem to be rushing you, but if you leave right after noon, you can get as far as Applegard tonight and Roskear

Keep tomorrow night. That would give you only two nights on the road and not too long a ride any one day.''

Varian shook his head. "I'll obey my father, sir, but I won't hop just because he says 'frog.' I have commitments here to end first. We can leave in the morning.''

"All right. How many men do you want as escort?''

"Escort, Uncle? Like a timid maiden being taken to her bridegroom?'' He laughed harshly. "Corven is all the company I'll need, and we'll have no more problems going than we had coming.''

It was Lord Duer's turn to shake his head. "The land's become more lawless in the last year or two, Varian. I don't want to have to face your father and tell him I let his only son ride out alone.''

"If it's that dangerous, sir, what will keep your guardsmen from being attacked after they've taken me home like a stray dog?'' *And why do old people always think that young ones will get into trouble if they're left alone?* he thought resentfully.

Duer considered for a moment, then smiled. "What would you say, then, to traveling with a Free Trader caravan? One is leaving the city early tomorrow, and the elder is a particular friend of mine, the one who gets me that summer wine that keeps so well. I'm sure they could use an extra guardsman.''

Varian grinned back. "Trying to hire my services out like a mercenary, sir?'' He knew perfectly well that his uncle wasn't trying to do any such thing and also that his uncle knew that he knew. But if humor would let them both save face, why not use it?

"Certainly, my boy. You have to earn your keep somehow, and you're not very good at milking cows.''

Both of them laughed out loud at that. Varian had tried as part of his stewardship training, and the wretched cow had stepped on his foot and swatted him in the face with a filthy tail. He was glad someone else had to deal with the clumsy animals.

• • •

Varian and Corven rode into a scene the next morning
that had all the chaos of battle. A full train of twenty or
more wagons stood with animals harnessed and almost
ready to roll as their passengers finished up last-minute
preparations. Dogs barked and small children screamed
and ran about getting in the way of people loading ham-
pers of food and other things. Women hugged friends
and kinfolk good-bye while their husbands bellowed impatiently for them to hurry, and the women said, "Yes,
yes, my dear, but first I have to . . ."

Corven, who was leading a baggage horse on a long
rein, crowded his Hazel up to Varian's side and said in
a low voice, "Who will be protecting who in this mob?"

"Damned if I know. It'll be hours before we get moving." Varian was not going to ride Rowan into that
crowd. His warhorse was already shifting uneasily from
foot to foot, and he did not want him to decide that this
was a battle to be dealt with appropriately. He finally
captured a young boy and sent him with a message to
the clan elder, then waited right where he was.

It was not, however, quite the chaos that Varian thought.
This was only the leave-taking that accompanied any
journey from the Traders' settled clan-village. Nor was
Varian as overlooked as he thought.

A small, dark-haired girl ran up to an older one and
said excitedly, "Auntie Cathlin, I've got something to
tell you!" She used the specific form that meant
"younger sister of my father's wife."

"What is it, Beka?" Cathlin could remember being
six, and seeing the little girl's excitement made her feel
much more elderly than her own age of almost thirteen.

"Do you see that boy over there? The one with the
black thing around his neck? Shonna told me that means
he's a slave!"

Cathlin knelt down and put her arm around the
smaller girl's waist. Although she understood the child's
excitement, she said seriously, "Sweetling, I know it
seems exciting to see a slave, since we don't own any.

But you have to remember that they're people, too, with feelings just like ours, and it would be cruel to do something that might hurt them. Don't go asking the poor boy any questions about being a slave. It might hurt his feelings and make him unhappy.''

Beka's eyes were still round with wonder. ''But he doesn't look unhappy. He was laughing with that other boy.''

''The other boy is probably his master. Maybe he's kind to the poor slave. He looks like a nice boy.'' *He* was the one Cathlin was dying to talk to. He was so good-looking, with hair as dark as one of their own and light eyes the color of . . . what? She didn't think they were brown like hers. And that sword at his hip added to his intriguing air of maturity. None of her male cousins were swordsmen. She wondered who he was. Her uncle had said something last night about a lordling joining them for the trip north, but this boy didn't look the way she thought a lord should. Weren't they all tall and fair-haired?

Eventually, the caravan sorted itself out, and someone (not Cathlin, to her sorrow) took Varian to the Clan Elder Adelgar. After courteous greetings, he found himself assigned to ride at the left flank of the train, partnered with a mercenary guardsman. Corven was not mentioned and was left to fend for himself; evidently none of them knew quite what to do with a slave, nor in these circumstances did Varian. After some thought, Corven took himself to the end of the train, asked permission to tie his baggage horse to the tail of the last wagon, and joined the boys who were driving the small herd of replacement horses.

In spite of their disorganized leave-taking, once started the Traders made good time on the road. The stop for nooning was a short one, no more than time to let the horses breathe and let everybody make use of the bushes. Women handed out chunks of bread and cheese for the light meal that was all anybody would eat just then.

Their destination that first day was Longlen, a middling large village that seemed to be very pleased to see them. Late in the afternoon the caravan stopped in a large, grassy field that was reserved for such purposes and swiftly set up camp, keeping a knowledgeable eye on the waiting villagers at all times. As soon as the wagons were parked to everyone's satisfaction, boards that had served as siding to the wagons were let down to become display shelves, merchandise was arranged seductively on them, and the villagers moved in to take advantage of this traveling market in the hour of daylight that was left.

After Varian and Corven had unloaded their baggage horse and cared for all their animals, they wandered around as well. The amount and kinds of merchandise boggled the mind; it seemed that an entire harvest-fair market must be on the move with these Traders. Everything one might want was represented: broad-brimmed hats rubbed shoulders with embroidered shirts and silky, brightly colored scarves and ribbons, and daggers with carved bone handles lay tangled with strings of amber beads and jeweled hat-pins. Furs and exotic feathers tempted the luxury-minded to feel their softness, and butter-soft leathers in bright colors demanded to be touched. Children from the wagon that was displaying simple musical instruments demonstrated how easy it was to make a pleasant tune with their wares. The woman who was selling herbs and spices had a pot of soup burbling gently over her fire so that all who were interested might sample a small portion of her stock, and the perfumer held out cloths scented with her fragrances. One young man was selling long-legged greyhound puppies, descended, he said, from the kennels of the king himself. Even so exotic a luxury as books was available, on display but carefully shielded from the grimy hands that might soil them. The scribe who was selling them usually contented himself with writing or reading letters for the illiterate and making fancifully decorated marriage certificates, much in demand as gifts for newlywed couples.

Corven stared wistfully at a dagger that had caught his eye, a slim leaf-bladed belt knife with a hilt of dark wood inlaid with bone in a zigzag design, and Varian was just as taken with a leather jerkin of dark green, inscribed with a pattern of gold leaves around the neck. But the pocket money Lord Duer had advanced them was not enough to buy either of these coveted goods and still leave them enough to buy meals, so Varian contented himself with buying a comb of scented sandalwood as a gift for a certain young woman.

A Trader caravan had never come as far north as Leopard's Gard in his memory, and he wondered why. Not only could they provide luxuries and goods unavailable at home, but no doubt they would appreciate the opportunity to buy or trade for things that his northlands home could provide. He had seen no liryal skins, for instance, in the tumble of furs, and when he asked the herbalist about kuta bark, she had only a tiny bit and that very expensive. Was the clan elder on this caravan? Varian resolved to find out and to talk to him or whoever was in charge. He could make no agreements himself, of course, but surely his father would be interested.

These Traders certainly seemed to be more organized in their selling than in their leave-taking that morning. As the sun set and the light dimmed, they brought out lanterns for the ease of their customers. At the same time, Varian and Corven could smell food cooking over communal fires and hoped that their coinage would be enough to buy sufficient food to satisfy their ravenous hunger.

"Lord Varian?" A voice spoke at his elbow. A young man of about his own age was standing there, staring at him; when he knew he had Varian's attention, he gave a slight bow. "My father would be pleased, sir, if you and your . . . servant would join us for supper."

Varian grinned at him. "I never turn down an invitation to supper. If you would be so kind, your father's name, and yours? I like to know my hosts."

The young man smiled uncertainly back, perhaps expecting more coolness from a lord. "My father is Eleran, of sept Brighthawk of Clan Leioness. I'm Tarver, sir."

To Tarver's surprise, the young lord winced exaggeratedly. "Please, don't call me sir. I keep wanting to look over my shoulder for my lord uncle. I'm Varian; he's Corven."

"Oh. All right. We're this way." He led the way to one of the communal fires and introduced Varian to his father. This Trader, in turn, introduced him to a bewildering series of wives, children, brothers, and the brothers' wives and children until one commanding middle-aged wife pushed plates into both their hands and a piece of bread into her husband's mouth.

"There," she said with satisfaction. "That ought to shut him up long enough for you to catch your breath, Lord Varian. Eleran, the poor lad doesn't need to know all the relationships, just names so he can be polite. He'll talk all night if we let him," she confided to Varian. "And most outsiders, *horen,* we say, can get so confused they never sort us out, and he'll let you starve to death when everything is ready to be served, just trying to get you unsnarled."

"Thank you, Mistress . . . Davora, is it?" Varian said uncertainly.

"No, Davora is my sister. I'm Barvara. Now, this is rabbit stew, that's mixed vegetables, biscuits are here with butter or honey; just help yourself. As our guest—guests, you get the place of honor and go first."

Corven flicked an eyebrow at Varian that said as clearly as words, *"Me, a guest of honor?"* but obediently took the plate handed him and stood behind Varian.

The food was good, and plentiful. More Traders came to all the fires now as they began to shut up their displays for the night. Small children ran from fire to fire, carrying messages for their elders or playing now that they were no longer confined to wagon or pony.

Varian watched them somewhat wistfully. These people treated their children with so much love. More than
one child sat on a parent's lap or cuddled near them,
and nobody pushed them away or told them not to be
childish. He had vague memories of his mother holding
him and singing to him, but that was all. She had died
when he was three, giving birth to a babe that also died.
Only once could he remember his father ever touching
him, to "teach him to be a man." He had gone crying
to his nurse over some childish hurt, and Baird over-
heard him. The baron had beaten his four-year-old son
with his belt and had forbidden him to cry.

But that was long ago and far away; he didn't cry
anymore, certainly not just because of some pensive
longing. Yet it didn't help his mood when the woman
from the music wagon brought out a kithara and began
to play the stringed instrument in an eerie minor key.
Everybody about the fire quieted. "'The Two Rav-
ens,'" she said softly, and began the ancient tale of a
nameless lord betrayed by all those who should have
been faithful.

Though he had heard the song before, the last lines
still made the hair prickle on the back of Varian's neck.

> *Many a one for him will mourn,*
> *But none shall know where he is gone;*
> *O'er his white bones, when they are bare-o,*
> *The wind shall blow forever more-o.*
> *Wind shall blow forever more.*

The caravanners gave her a tribute of a moment of
silence, and then soft applause. Other people brought out
their own instruments, and other songs flowed through
the night. Varian listened with keen interest. Most of
them were new to him, for these were the songs of the
commoners that he had little contact with. Beside him,
Corven listened intently, too, and occasionally joined in
on the choruses.

At the close of the fifth or sixth song, Eleran rose to

his feet and bowed slightly in Varian's direction. "Lord Varian, I believe it is time for you and your servant to pay for your suppers. No, not in coin," for he had seen Varian reach for his belt pouch, "but some song of yours. If you please."

Varian slowly rose to his feet and returned the bow. "Alas, good Trader, it breaks my heart that I must refuse. The Lord Duer has forbidden me to sing anywhere in his domains. He says my singing voice causes children to cry, ladies to faint, and strong warriors to tremble." He looked down at Corven, still sitting at his feet, and his friend returned his gaze with laughing affection. "Am I that bad, Corven?"

"I'm not permitted to lie, master. You sing . . . about as well as you milk cows."

Varian laughed and shook his head, spreading his hands out in a gesture of helplessness. "So you see, since my voice is being saved as a weapon to use against our enemies, I must ask my friend Corven here if he will pay the toll for both of us."

Corven grinned and bounced to his feet, only to throw himself to one knee at Varian's feet. "Command me, lord!"

"What about 'Home from the Tavern'? I can do the spoken parts of that, at least."

"Yes, that's a good one." Corven rose, turned to the people around the fire, and said, "Good gentles, while we know your family life is very different from that of the great lords and ladies, there are some things that must be much the same. Such as the problems of an old man with a young wife . . ."

He hummed a few notes of a bouncy tune, then began to sing the tale of a hapless old man who came staggering home from the tavern every night, and every night found things that shouldn't be there in his home: a horse, boots, a sword, a feathered hat, and a shirt. His wife said that they were a milk cow, a bucket, a broom, a cooking pot, and an apron. Even though they suspected what was coming, it was the final verse that sent people rocking with laughter. The poor old man found a young man in his own bed, and the young wife told him:

> *Bless your soul, my husband dear! Are you so*
> *   drunk you cannot see?*
> *'Tis but a milkmaid, a nice new milkmaid, my*
> *   mother sent to me.*

" 'A milkmaid?' quoth he. 'Aye, a milkmaid,' quoth she,'' Varian said.

> *Tipsy may I be, but drunker have I been,*
> *And a well-trimmed beard on a milkmaid's chin*
> *   never have I seen!*

Cathlin laughed as loudly as anybody, even though later she went to her bed yearning for the young lord. When he confessed that he couldn't sing, she had fallen in love that instant. She couldn't sing, either, and it was so brave of him to admit it!

Their departure the next day was considerably more organized. Varian had not bothered setting up the small tent the baggage horse carried, preferring to sleep by the fire, so he and Corven were as ready as any of them. He even had time to work out a little with the mercenary who was his assigned partner. Corven watched to keep small children and dogs out of their way, and was very mindful himself of the young women watching.

Cathlin was among them, sighing with her romantic dreams of the young warrior lord. She really wished he would come and talk to her, or that she had even another night on the road so that she could watch him. It soothed her self-esteem only a little that he paid no attention to any other girl, either. Oh, some of them tried to flirt with him, but he only made polite responses and didn't flirt back.

And this was her last day on the road for *years.* She wanted to go to the Sanctuary of Byela for learning, but it would be so much better if the Sanctuary could be put on wheels and come with them instead.

It was the best of days to be on the road. The sun was just hot enough that the light breeze felt good on one's face, and there were high, puffy white clouds that forecast good weather ahead for the next day or two. Long before they came in sight of the fields, Varian's nose told him that the peasantry were getting in the first cutting of hay.

The order of the day, however, was not the same as yesterday. The sun had an hour's climb yet before noon when they came in sight of a village dominated by a walled structure perched on what passed for a hill in these parts. *Not a castle, there's no keep and too many buildings,* Varian thought. *This must be the Sanctuary they said we would be stopping at.*

So it was. The wagons parked in a long string and repeated the setup of last night's market, while Clan Elder Adelgar requested audience with the Mother Priestess of the Sanctuary. This was only a formality, since the bringing of young girls to the Grove of the Lady for schooling was routine and the girls had all been tested and accepted beforehand. But proper form and respect must be maintained, and the bargaining for their fees must be done properly as well. One could not call it bargaining, perhaps, since the Mother Illyana refused to take payment for the teaching that was the Lady's gift to Her daughters—but she could be persuaded to accept gifts to the sanctuary in return.

Cathlin was not alone when she entered the gates later that day, as two cousins and a half-sister were with her, and she was looking forward to learning so many new things. Why then, did she feel that she was letting something very precious elude her?

Mally

Varian and Corven spent that night in his uncle's castle of Roskear Keep, rather than with the Free Traders. Before he left the train, Varian found time to query the Clan Elder Adelgar about trade with Leopard's Gard. It was not a satisfying discussion for either of them. Adelgar was reluctant to discuss his people's fear and distrust of the Lord Baron Baird with that lord's son, and Varian was not happy to hear the evasion in the Trader's words. His own dislike and distrust of his father had always been on a personal level; now he saw that Baird was harming the people he had been trained to think of as his responsibility.

When Adelgar's stumbling excuses came to an end, Varian nodded, his face serious. "I understand, sir. Believe me, I understand. I thank you for your hospitality and honesty. When I come into my lands, I hope I can persuade you to think better of us. I think we can do business that will be most profitable to all concerned."

The Trader looked troubled. "Profit is only one of my concerns, Lord Varian. I must think of the good of my people."

"As do I, sir, for mine. Again, thank you, and may the gods send you good weather and dry roads."

• • •

The River Sythyan marked the boundary between Sundare and Leopard's Gard. The ford that gave the town of Roskear Ford its name had long ago been superseded by a toll bridge. At each end, guards stood to supervise crossings and collect the tolls that helped keep it in repair. Varian briefly considered playing the lord and enforcing his right not to pay the tolls, but the memory of yesterday's discussion with the Trader caused him to think better of it. Perhaps this was how his father had started down his path, pulling rank and privilege at every opportunity.

Past the river, the mountains rose almost abruptly before them. The road ceased to run straight in the manner of the South and began curving through the valleys, always climbing higher as it went.

Varian stopped, as he always did, at one particular spot. Through a gap in the mountains one could see, so far away that it looked like a child's toy, the white stone castle that was Leopard's Keep. This was his first sight of home in two years, and the fierce rush of possessiveness was a new feeling for him. This was *his* land, his to care for and protect. King Tiorbran on his throne far to the south could not feel any of the special pride that was Varian's Northern heritage, the pride that came from mastering a harsh land and curbing it to one's will.

For harsh it was. No gentle soaking winter rains fell in these mountains. Instead, heavy snow closed the passes and caused folk to stay warm and snug in their homes. Crops that flourished in the South struggled here in the cold, stony soil, and taxes were collected not in grain and gold but in fleeces and furs and firewood.

Even the people were different: fiercely independent and stubborn. Baird had tried his best to squash them into the subdued mold of Southern peasantry, but they resisted him at every opportunity. There had been rebellions during the early days of his rule, cruelly suppressed. Fear ruled them now, fear of their lord and of the Dark God it was rumored he served.

Varian saw that fear on his ride home. Children ran and hid at the sound of riders, and those adults who could not take themselves away in time watched them pass with wary sullenness. They might not know it was their lord's son who passed, but an armed man on what was clearly a warhorse was one of *them*, and not to be trusted.

It was nearly noon before they rode into the gates of Leopard's Keep. The town that clustered at the foot of the outcropping on which the castle sat was not quite large enough to be called a city, but it maintained defensive walls and watchtowers, just the same. Varian, accustomed now to the spit and polish of the more regimented guardsmen to the south, looked with disfavor on the worn green and gold tabards that marked the Town Guard. Nor was he happy to see that they paid him no mind as he entered. Their job was to control entry to the town; as they were now, anybody could just walk in.

This was a time and place when it was appropriate to pull rank. Varian demanded and got the attention of the Guard Captain. A few pointed observations and questions made that captain realize that the young lord who delivered them knew what he was talking about. Nor did Varian accept any excuses. The Guard Captain promised "a thorough investigation, my lord, I assure you."

"Good," Varian answered smoothly. "Perhaps, then, the matter will not need to be reported to my lord father."

"Yes, sir. Thank you, sir," the captain muttered as he left.

Corven sidled his own horse up to Rowan's side as they rode on. "Bad doings there in the guard-quarters. The slaves were telling me that the whole unit is lackluster like that. They work out on an irregular basis, evidently only when they feel like it, and feel justified because the pay is poor and often late."

"Damn. What is my father thinking of?" Varian muttered. "Look at that, Corven. If that man there on duty is sober, I'm a little green lizard."

"Mm-hm," Corven agreed. "They told me duty shifts don't interfere with drinking and gambling. And that the ale comes regularly, even if the pay doesn't. You know how hard a drunk guardsman can come down on a slave. Those slaves there are *scared,* Varian, scared shitless. One of them showed me burn marks on his arm. Said they had a contest to see who could make him scream loudest."

"Gods! I wish I'd known that when I was talking to the captain. That will stop, Corven, I promise."

The street through which they rode now was the main road from the town gate to the castle drawbridge. It was deeply rutted, littered with discarded fruit rinds and other garbage, and the shops and houses lining it were grubby-looking. Had it always looked like this, so that seeing it with fresh eyes brought out what was always there, or had it deteriorated in the last two years?

The castle walls and gates, at least, were properly manned and maintained. The guards knew him, but even so, they detained him momentarily while Armsmaster Evan was called to confirm it. In the interval, stable slaves came and led the horses away, and word was passed for others to come and help Corven deal with their baggage.

The short, stocky armsmaster stumped into the room, his face lighting up when he saw that his young lord was here at last. "M'lord Varian! Welcome home! Everybody has been holdin' their breath, waitin' for ye."

"I wish I could say it's good to be home, Evan, but I just saw some things that I'd like to discuss with you later. It is good to see you again." Varian slapped his hand into Evan's outstretched one and the two clasped forearms hard.

"I think I know what ye mean, lad. But as ye say, later will be soon enough. Yer father wants ye brought to him as soon as ye've washed away the dust."

Washing away the dust was not the luxury it was in Sundare Keep. There was no large bathing room with good-sized pools here, only wooden tubs filled by buckets. As heir, Varian could have demanded a bath in his own room, but he chose to scrub up in the little room off the kitchen that served for most of the castle staff. The maidservant and the young slave who filled the tub smiled shyly at him before both scuttled out to leave him to bathe in solitary splendor.

In spite of his father's orders, Varian did not see him immediately. When he came out of the bathing room, a plump, somewhat elderly lady pounced on him and smothered him to her massive bosom.

"Oh, you're home, you're home at last, my boy. Oh, and it's a young man you've become, not my baby anymore. Have they fed you? I can see they've given you a bath. Why didn't you make these lazy girls pour you one in the comfort of your own room, my dear boy? You can't let them get away with a lazy, half-done job you know—"

"Maggie!" he managed to yell, somewhat muffled.

"Yes, Lord Varian?" Mistress Margretha said briefly as she remembered just who it was that she was hugging. Sometimes she forgot that the dear boy who felt like her own son was the heir, after all, her dear kinswoman Damarisa's boy, and not hers, not merely the son of the castle's chatelaine, but a young lord. Oh, my, what of it? She loved him as if he were her own, after all, having raised him from a tiny babe when poor Damarisa couldn't after such a hard birth, and then died, poor thing, with the poor little girl-babe that didn't live either.

"Maggie, I'm . . . overwhelmed to see you again, but I was told that my father wanted to see me as soon as I was done," Varian explained as he extricated himself. "Don't scold the servants. I told them I wanted to bathe here to be quicker about it."

"Oh, well, then, just as you say, Lord Varian, but isn't it a shame that nobody told you, you could have had plenty of time to bathe and eat in your own rooms, for, you see, since we didn't know when you would exactly arrive, and we've been expecting you for the last two days and all, His Lordship took some of the dogs and a few men and went hunting—deer, I think that's what they said they were going out after—so you've plenty of time to come to the kitchen, and we'll find you something to eat, some spicebread or something of the sort, you've always liked that, and a mug of milk . . .''

It was as impossible to resist Margretha in full spate as it was to resist a flash flood, so Varian suffered himself to be led off to the kitchen and stuffed with spicebread like a six-year-old. He was fond of the dear old lady who was his foster mother, but her love was rather like being smothered in a nice warm goose-down comforter—one about six feet thick.

Lord Baird returned late that afternoon, so late that Varian had only time for a brief greeting before his father left for his own rooms to bathe and change. They met again at dinner, served at the high table in the great hall. Leopard's Gard followed the old customs, and all the castle household dined with the lord, rather than sending the servants away to eat in their own hall. Only two orders of the castle staff did not eat with the lord: the slaves who served the meal, who would eat later in the kitchen, and the Lord Baird's bodyguard.

These men were not the ceremonial guard of the South, such as Earl Duer maintained, but true bodyguards. Baird was hated by his people, and he knew it. These men were his reluctant concession to the knowledge that even peasants could sometimes summon up enough courage to attempt to deal directly with a brutal overlord. One of them attended him at all times, even in his own stronghold, armed and alert even at his own table. When Baird rode out, all three of them were part of his entourage.

Varian noticed, as he had not as a child, the fear in the eyes and bodies of the slaves serving the meal when one of them was required to come within arm's reach

of either Lord Baird or the armed man who stood men-
acingly at his back. The serving slaves were wary, too,
of Varian himself, even those who had known him from
childhood. Who knew what sort of man he had grown
into?

The dark-haired young woman who knelt before him
with a platter of tiny meat pies caught Varian's eyes
especially, and it hurt him to see her flinch away when
he raised his hand. He remembered the skinny child she
had been, always begging to follow along after him and
Corven, and her spirited protests when they treated her
with the lordly condescension of boys for a girl a whole
year younger.

Now Mallena was not skinny, but clearly and disturb-
ingly female. The knee-length slave-tunic that was all
she wore did little to hide the curves of her body. The
dark brown hair that fell about her delicately beautiful
face was brushed and shining, and the lashes of her
downcast eyes formed soft crescents on her flushed
cheeks.

"Well, did you have good weather on your ride
home?" Baird asked his son, and laughed to himself as
he saw the direction of the young man's gaze.

"Yes, sir." Varian, interrupted in his thoughts, jerked
his attention back to his father. When Baird made no
other comment, he asked somewhat stiffly, "And has
the weather here been good?"

"About as usual. Here, you, more wine." Baird held
out his goblet (of expensive Riazan glass, Varian noted)
to the server who filled it in silence.

After that, the conversation lagged even more. Varian
could not talk of his experiences in his uncle's household, for he knew that his father disliked Earl Duer, and
his questions about happenings at home were answered
only superficially. The dinner seemed to go on for hours,
and he had trouble choking down even the most appe-
tizing foods.

After the meal's remains had been cleared away,
Baird challenged Varian to a game of shakarr, but nei-

ther had their attention on the game. Varian won, slashing through the terrain-board with his horsemen and besieging his father's keep until the older lord conceded defeat.

And at long last, it was bedtime.

Varian was relieved to have this uncomfortable evening over at last. Would his father expect him to eat with him every night? To try to talk into the strained silence?

There was no light in his room except the dying fire. No matter, nothing in it could have changed. He could see the dim bulk of the curtained bed well enough, and he always preferred to wash in the morning, anyway. He peeled off his clothes and dropped them in a heap on the chest. Flipping back the sheets and the silky liryalfur coverlet, he started to slide into the bed, then jerked back as his foot touched something warm and yielding; he heard a soft gasp as if whoever was in the bed had been frightened.

"Who's there?" he demanded fiercely. ·

"P-please, Master Varian, don't be angry with me. He m-made me come," a girl's voice quavered.

"Mally? Is that you?" Varian asked perplexedly. "Since when do you call me 'master'?"

"Since your father said everyone was to call you master." Her voice was still frightened.

"What do you mean, he made you come? Who? My father?" Varian could see a little better now; he caught the gleam of tear-wet eyes as she nodded her head. "Move over, Mally, these stone floors are too damn cold on bare feet." He sat down on the foot of the bed and flipped a corner of the fur up over his body, moving very slowly and carefully so as not to frighten her any further.

Her voice was so soft that he could hardly hear her. "Your father sent me here to be your bed-slave." She was shaking; he could feel the quivering of her body through the bed even from where he sat, although he could not tell whether it was from fear or shame as she continued, "Last year he told all the men in the castle that I was being saved for you, and that I had to remain v-virgin. This evening . . ." Her voice died as she began to cry.

Varian forced himself to stillness. His mind told him that this was Mally, his friend from childhood, almost as close as Corven, almost his little sister. But his body didn't want to listen; his body was reminding him that he was male and she was female . . . and that she was a slave, his for the taking, if he wanted her.

At last he said in a quiet voice that took all the control he could manage, "Mally, love, you don't think I would treat you that way, do you? I'm still your friend, not your master. Go on back to your own bed now, and he'll never know."

To his surprise, she cried harder. At last she gasped out, "No, *please,* Varian, you don't understand. If you don't, he'll . . ."

He couldn't stand it any longer; very slowly and carefully, he slid under the bedcovers and took her in his arms, pillowing her head on his shoulder. Her slim body was tense against him as she cried on his chest. He forced himself to do nothing but hold her and murmur soothing nonsense.

Finally, she quieted and put her arms around him in turn. Very gently, he said, "All right, love, what is it I don't understand?"

She went rigid again as she said in a strangled whisper, "Your father said it was my duty to . . . to make sure his son was a man. And he checked me today to see if I was still virgin . . . and he said if I still was tomorrow, he would beat me and give me to his body-guard."

Varian tensed in his turn as anger started to build in him. So that old bastard had doubts about his son, did he? He couldn't just ask if his son was virgin or not. No, he had to shove this poor frightened girl into Varian's bed, had to threaten her with his bodyguard. No wonder she was scared out of her wits. Varian had heard enough stories about them before he left home to know that the sinister trio were three of the most brutal men alive; all the servants and slaves were terrified of them, the girls who were assigned to serve them most of all.

He must have moved in some way that revealed his anger, for Mally drew away from him with a gasp of fear. Did the poor girl think he had become like them, that he was going to shove her down on the bed and rape her?

Now he was really angry, both at his father and, though he hated to admit it, at himself for frightening her, for reacting to her tempting nudity. He was forced into a corner; either he followed his father's wishes and used Mally's body for his own pleasure, or he refused her and left her to the merciless cruelty of others. *Not much choice, is there?* he thought bitterly. *I can't let him do that to Mally, and he knows it.*

Perhaps it was that anger that made his voice sound harsh as he said, "Come here, then. I won't hurt you any more than I have to."

She obeyed; he could feel her trembling against him as he kissed her. Somewhere in the back of his mind, he was ashamed to find that her fear was exciting him even more. He could understand now, a little, why some men enjoyed rape, enjoyed proving their power over someone who could not resist. *Poor girl, all she's ever learned to expect from a master is cruelty. Well, she won't get it from me.*

"Easy, love, easy," he soothed, although in the grip of his aroused senses, he didn't know if he spoke to her or to himself. "I'm not my father, and I'm sure not his bodyguard. Just relax and let it happen. I won't hurt you, I promise."

He took two deep breaths and deliberately banished his anger at his father; he would deal with that tomorrow. Now it was more important to care for Mally.

His hand brushed gently over her face as he kissed her again, more tenderly this time. "You're so beautiful, Mally," he murmured against her mouth. "When I saw you serving me at dinner tonight, I wanted you then. You were a skinny little girl when I left, and now I find a beautiful, desirable young woman. I didn't want you like this; if I had a choice, you would have come to me of your own free will, but I'm glad being mine has kept you safe, has kept you for me. Yes, Mally my love, that's it . . .''

Mally thought her heart would break. He had taken her as gently as he could, and cuddled her close afterward. Thank the little goddess that he had fallen asleep almost before she had settled herself comfortably; he wouldn't know that she fought back tears of relief and dismay.

She was safe from the threat Lord Baird had made, but what would Varian feel for her now? Would she now be nothing more to him than his bed-slave? They had all been so close as children, until he went away, even though she and Corven were slaves and he was the young master; she wanted things to be the same as they had been, and now it was impossible.

Varian awoke the next morning to the sound of the door opening. Corven entered, carrying a basin of hot water and whistling cheerfully, then stopped and stood staring at the bed before his face dropped into the emotionless mask of a well-trained slave.

"Forgive me, master," he said impassively and started to back out of the room.

"Corven, get your ass back in here," Varian said impatiently as he sat up. "I need to explain, and we need to talk, all three of us."

"What about, master? You don't owe your slaves any explanation for what you do." Corven's eyes were fixed firmly on the basin as he set it down carefully, not meeting Varian's eyes.

"Yes, dammit, I do. I know you spent last night in the great hall with the other servants. What did they tell you about Mallena?"

"That she was assigned as your bed-slave," Corven

said unhappily. Finally, he raised his head, and his eyes were full of hurt dismay. "But after last week, I thought I knew you better," he blurted. "That you wouldn't treat Mally like that."

"Did they also tell you what would happen to her if I refused her?"

Corven shook his head, then glanced at Mally, who was sitting up as well, tucking the sheet firmly under her arms to cover her breasts. "Mally?"

She blushed red and said in a low voice, "The master said that if I was still a virgin this morning, he'd give me to the Uglies. Please, Corven, don't be upset at Varian. This is the only safe place for me, and he did what he had to." Her eyes dropped briefly as she continued shyly, "And I liked it."

Corven looked from his master to the girl and back again, then sighed. "I suppose so then, Mally. But . . . did you get any greenflower tea?"

She nodded. "Mother made sure I've had it since the messenger was sent out for you to come home. We don't have to worry about that."

"Worry about what?" Varian asked, puzzled by their reference to an unfamiliar tea.

The two slaves looked at each other, then Corven shrugged. "Me and my big mouth. We might as well tell him now. I don't think he'll try to stop it."

"Tell me what?" Varian asked in exasperation.

Mallena grinned at Corven. "You know," she remarked conversationally, "if he was smart enough, he might be able to figure it out for himself."

"Yeah," Corven agreed, and grinned back, but his face sobered almost immediately.

"Insubordination," Varian muttered, and slid out of bed to pull on his breeches and boots. "A man asks a simple question, and all he gets is insubordination."

Mally giggled. "Oooo, big words. I'm sorry, Varian, but I had to see if I could still tease you."

"But it isn't funny, Mal," Corven said seriously. "Varian, Mally can't risk becoming pregnant by you.

Your father would sell her like he did Nadira.''

Varian looked up from his boots, his eyes full of shocked dismay. ''Mally, no! I never thought of that last night, I swear!''

''It's all right, Varian.'' She leaned forward and put a hand on his shoulder. ''That's what greenflower tea does. If a woman drinks it every day, she won't usually get pregnant. It's something we slaves like to keep secret; you can see why.''

''What about Nadira?'' he asked bluntly. He remembered his father's pretty bed-slave but didn't know that she had been sold because of pregnancy. Did he have a young brother or sister somewhere, being raised as a slave?

''Your father kept her locked in his rooms with him for a whole week last Yearsend. I guess she couldn't get any tea.''

Varian gave a sigh of relief, then looked from one of his friends to the other. ''I think I know how hard it is for both of you to trust me entirely. I'm one of *them,* one of the masters, and I can't be anything else. If it were up to me, you'd both have been freed a long time ago, but it isn't. You both belong to my father. But I promise you, the day he dies, you won't have those collars on another hour.''

He reached over and took Mally's hand in his. ''Mallylove, it's too dangerous for you, even now, to go back and sleep in the servant's hall at night. You'll have to stay here with me.'' He looked down at her hand resting trustfully in his, then into her eyes.

''Mally . . . I'm not the hero in the old tale, the one who slept with his sword between him and the beautiful maiden to ward off temptation. If you sleep in my bed every night, I won't be able to resist you.''

''I'm not sure I understand,'' she said slowly. ''Are you saying you don't want me in your bed?''

''No, I'm saying I do want you, but I won't order you into my bed. I won't expect you to submit to my demands. You have the right to refuse me, to say, 'Go away, Varian, and take a cold bath.' " He looked from Mally to Corven. "I'm saying if you want Corven instead of me, I'll step aside. Or if you don't want either of us, you have that right, too. But any way, it's *your* choice. I won't treat you like a slave."

"That's right, master," Corven said mournfully. "Just give me away to the first pretty face that comes along."

Varian reached over and cuffed him amiably. "You call me 'master' again when we're in private, and I will give you away."

Mally giggled again and gave a bounce. "Oh, goody! Can I have him? I've always wanted a slave of my very own." She stuck one small bare foot out of the bed and commanded haughtily, "Kiss my foot, slave."

Corven obediently dropped to his knees at the side of the bed. He rested her foot in the cradle of his hands and lingeringly kissed the instep. Then, with a look of wicked mischief, he grasped her foot tightly, kissed her ankle, and started to kiss his way up her leg. She shrieked and tried to pull away; that only succeeded in pulling Corven up onto the bed with her. He pounced on her and pinned her body down with his own.

Varian pretended to ignore them as he checked his face in the polished bronze mirror. He decided not to shave. If he had been summoned home for his adult dedication, shaving his beard would be part of the ceremony, so he needed something to shave. He ought to start growing his mustache, too.

The shrieks from the bed subsided to giggles and then contented murmurs as he washed in the now-cooled water, pulled on a clean shirt, and knotted his belt around his waist. When he glanced at the bed, Mally had her arms around Corven's neck, and he was kissing her expertly. Varian firmly stomped on the beginnings of jealousy; he *would* give Mallena her choice.

With a sigh, he reached over and hooked a finger in Corven's collar, pulling lightly. "I hate to interrupt this tender moment, swordbrother, but Mally will wind up

with the Uglies if my father thinks you did the job instead of me. I meant what I said, Mally. If you want
him, you've got him, but it will have to be later."

"What orders were you given for this morning?"

She blushed with embarrassment as Corven rolled
away from her and off the bed. In a low voice, she said,
"I was to wait here for your father and the midwife to
examine me."

"We'll go away then." Varian leaned down and
kissed Mally as she sat up to meet him. She hugged him
tightly and whispered, "Thank you."

"Thank me for what?"

"For still being you. I was so scared last night that
you might not be."

He didn't understand, but it seemed like a good idea
to kiss her again.

It was.

4

Betrayal

"Father!" Varian called as he entered the great hall that morning.

Baird turned away from the doorway. "Yes?" he said impatiently.

"I wish to talk to you, sir." Varian deliberately allowed some of his anger to creep into his voice. "Why did you take it upon yourself to assign me a bed-slave? And why Mallena?"

The baron looked patronizingly at his son, one black eyebrow raised almost to his hairline. "I've always found the company of a bed-slave . . . entertaining, shall we say, and thought that any *man* would, as well. And as for which girl was assigned to you, that one was kept virgin expressly for your benefit. Or do you prefer bedding a common guardsman's castoff?"

"No."

"A nice young boy then, perhaps? I understand some Southroners, Sargadans and the like, prefer them, but they squeal too much for my taste."

"*No!* Likarion, Father, what sort of man do you take me for?"

Baird shrugged imperturbably. "Then why all this fuss about the girl? If you want her, you may keep her.

If not, then there are plenty of others. Did you have anything else to complain about?''

''Not complain, no, sir. I did want to ask about your plans for my dedication. Isn't that why I was summoned home?''

''In my own good time, boy, in my own good time. There are certain preparations first. What is the phrase you youngsters use nowadays? Don't get your tail tied in a knot?'' With another condescending smile, Baird left the room.

Varian looked after him, fuming with futile anger. Nothing had changed here at home. What he said, what he did, affected his father no more than the barking of a puppy. And everything his father said or did made him feel like an ignorant, untried puppy, all legs and paws and eagerness. No, that wasn't right, either. A puppy was eager for attention and affection; he wanted neither from his father, just the respect one man ought to give another. And he would never get it from the cold, arrogant man who had sired him.

He skipped breakfast, ignoring the beginnings of a hurt protest from Margretha. There was one place here that he did get respect and even a kind of affection. Corven grabbed an apple and dunked a piece of bread in honey as he passed the table, following his young master. He saw no reason why he should remain hungry just because Varian was angry at the world.

The tiny room that served Armsmaster Evan as office was more home to Varian than any other place in the castle. He must have been about five years old when he first wandered into the larger guardroom, escaping for once the careful watch of his nurse. The guardsmen had called him ''Lord Varian'' for the first time and had been happy to show him their weapons. Master Evan had picked him up and set him safely out of the way so that he could see them at arms practice, and he explained what was happening as gravely as if he talked to an adult.

The armsmaster had become foster father to the lonely

little boy, and it was he who had instilled in him his deep sense of responsibility. It was Evan who had caught six-year-old Corven stealing spicebread under Varian's orders. He spanked Corven first while Varian watched, wincing in empathy with every smack. Evan then explained to Varian that privilege was not something to abuse, that it was paralleled by responsibility, and that it was his duty to care for the people under his command. It was Varian's fault that Corven now had a sore bottom, for he had ordered the slave to steal. The spanking Evan then gave Varian made more than his bottom hurt; guilt left him quiet for several hours before he apologized to Corven and gave him his own dessert in amends.

It was Evan who had given Varian his first wooden training sword, who had drafted Corven as his swordpartner, who had trained both of them into the young warriors that they now were. And it was Evan who Varian trusted now to tell him the truth about his home.

"Aye, lad," the armsmaster said. " 'Tis not yer imagination. The lord yer father seems only concerned about keepin' up strength here at the castle. He spends his own time drinkin' and wenchin'. There's not a lass in the barony that goes virgin to her bridegroom's bed, unless she's ugly as a mud fence. He claims the lord's right with them all."

"Randy old bastard," Varian muttered. "Will he interfere if I do inspections of the Town Guard?" He explained what he and Corven had seen and heard the day before.

Evan shook his head. "Sometimes I think that's the way he wants them. I know he has Roden see personally to the ale delivery."

Varian filed that away in his brain, intending to look into it later. He neither liked nor trusted the man who served as steward to his father for the local estates. He suspected that Roden was squeezing more taxes from the peasantry than he reported and pocketing the difference.

"And those shops that ye saw all ramshackle? No

doubt they're empty. Few merchants are prosperous here now, and the ones who can have left." Evan's voice grew grimmer as he went on.

"The only traveler's inn left is the Seven Stars, although the taverns still do a good business. Probably because those Town Guards themselves are more than half of them mercenaries, and ye know what hired swords are like. The castle has first call on any of our own people with enough trainin' to know how to swing a sword, and even they're gettin' scarcer. Yer father's not enforcin' the laws about arms trainin', even the archery ones. But here in the castle, I still hold daily arms practice; will ye be comin' today?"

"Yes. Both of us, if that won't cause any problem?"

"Both . . . ah, Corven, I didna see ye there. Ye've learned to be invisible down South, have ye?"

Corven grinned wryly. "Almost, sir. Not as invisible as I would have liked to be sometimes."

They talked for a long time after that. Evan had no personal knowledge of things outside of his own command, but he had heard rumors and knew who Varian should talk to. Besides the slack defenses and lax upkeep in the town, there was growing fear among the people of Leopard's Gard, especially the village peasantry. Attacks by bogharts and other wild beasts had become more numerous, and the baron did little to drive them away; some, indeed, he had forbidden the people to hunt. One peasant trapper had brought an ice leopard's pelt in to market; when the baron found out, he had had the man impaled in the public square and his family sold as slaves.

Varian listened, becoming quieter and more angry as the day went on. These were his people that were living under this brutal terror. Even the release of fighting practice did not quell his outrage at his father's treatment of the people he should be protecting. He knew, too, that he could not abandon them to return to his uncle's household; he had to stay here and try to help them, even though it might be more of a battle than he felt ready to take on.

That night at dinner, as the serving slave knelt in front of him with a platter of chicken breasts seasoned with a sauce of lemons (a Southern luxury he had not expected to find here), Varian wondered how to approach his father. Outright criticism wouldn't do anything but anger Baird, he thought.

They ate in silence for some time until Varian nerved himself enough to speak. "My lord Father, I have been noticing things here that are bothering me."

"Oh? And what are those, boy?"

"A number of things, sir. Riding through the town yesterday, there was no challenge to us at the gates, and the town itself looked dirty, as if nobody bothered to care for it."

Baird shrugged. "Peasants don't take much care of their property. And as for no challenge to you at the gate, there had better not have been. If the town guardsmen don't know my son and heir, they'd not be knowing anything much longer."

"Even so, sir, they didn't appear to notice that anybody was coming or going through the gates. That's laxness, nothing more. And the merchant's shops are hardly owned by peasants. The streets were littered with garbage, and the buildings themselves looked ramshackle. If there isn't plague and other diseases breeding there, I'll be surprised."

"Since when do dirty streets lead to plague, boy? You've picked up some odd notions down South. So long as the commons pay their taxes, they can live how they like."

Varian looked stubborn. "They'll be my people someday, sir. Yes, I've picked up some new ideas down South. One is that prosperous people can pay more taxes, and another is that contented people are easier to govern."

"Your people? Just you remember, boy, that as long

as I live, they're *my* people, governed and taxed as I see fit. It is not the place of a boy to tell me how to rule my lands." The baron glared at his son, and Varian glared back.

Suddenly, Baird began to laugh. "So, a gamecock you've always been, boy, and now you think you're an adult? But not one who enjoys adult pleasures, it seems. Why aren't you drinking your wine, for instance?"

"It doesn't taste right." Varian tried to keep his voice level and neutral—gods forbid he should sound to his father like a sulky child!

But Baird's voice was like the stab of a dagger in his ears. "So, I was correct. You're still a boy who can't appreciate mature pleasures like an unusual vintage—or a woman. Since you have no use for the little bed-slave, maybe I should have her myself. She looks like a tasty morsel."

Varian's eyes were hot with anger as he reached for his goblet. He finished the wine in two gulps. "Are you going back on your word then, sir? Did you or did you not tell the household that the girl was being saved for me? And she is mine. If I must, I will f-fight you for her."

Lord of Warriors, why am I stammering? The old bastard will think I'm scared of him!

But there was no anger in his father's eyes; he looked amused as a malicious smile spread slowly across his face. "Man enough, then, I hope," he murmured, almost to himself. "Have you anything else to say, boy?"

"Yes. I . . . she's m-mine . . ." The words were in his head; why wouldn't his tongue say them? He felt dizzy, and his stomach was suddenly protesting at the thought of any more food, though he had barely eaten a thing.

"Oh yes, boy, she's yours. But you, you are mine, my son," Baird said softly. Then his voice cracked like a whip. "Stand!"

Stand? Like a slave being put through his paces? I will not! But his body obeyed his father's orders, not his. His chair tipped over as he rose to stand, back straight and head up. In that moment, Varian understood why the wine did not taste right, why his father had goaded him into drinking it; it had been drugged. He fought to bring his body back under his control, to move even a fingertip of his own will. He fought, and he failed.

"Come with me," Baird said, not quite an order but not a request, either. Varian followed him obediently to the baron's bedchamber and stood motionless by the fireplace while Baird shot the bolt to lock the door and lit a tiny, screened lantern. "This is a secret, boy, known only to the lords and their heirs. Watch." Baird brushed his fingers over a particular spot in the carved paneling that flanked the fireplace. There was a soft click, and a narrow section of the paneling swung out to reveal a passageway. "In here."

Varian followed his father and watched again as he demonstrated the catch on the inside of the door, then followed him down the steep, narrow steps. The part of his brain that was still conscious fought back rising panic by carefully calculating where in the fortress that was Leopard's Keep they must be. Soon, however, they passed beyond his reckoning; they must be deep in the rocks under the castle. The way was endless—or was that the effect of the drug?

When they came to the open vastness of the cavern, Varian again did as he was told and moved to stand by the altar-stone, in the center of a complex pattern scribed on the floor. It was only dimly to be seen in the shadows flung by the lantern. Even the candles his father lit did not reveal anything more than echoing blackness around them. On the altar Baird set a bowl made of some dark substance, stone perhaps, and placed into it a tiny crystal globe.

The baron's eyes glinted in the feeble candlelight with an uncanny reddish reflection as he stared at his son. A brutal smile twisted his face into a horrible parody of pride and satisfaction. "My son. Out of my body, a life to take my place. This is your dedication, boy, and not to any weakling sword-god, no, to the One who in the end will claim all men.

"Strip. Throw your clothes over there, so they do not obscure the diagram."

As the drug took hold of him more fully, even panic began to dim for Varian. He did not fight the order to strip; somewhere in the back of his brain there was only a sullen resentment that his father should command him as if he were a helpless slave. Only a dull curiosity remained as his father spoke words that somehow left a foul remnant of themselves in his ears, as a medicine might leave a nasty taste on one's tongue. He wanted to forget them, but they burned their way into his memory, as did his first sight of the face that began to glow above the altar, a face that was both inhumanly beautiful and unbearably evil.

Varian took the black-handled dagger that his father handed him, staring dazedly at the flaked obsidian blade that somehow seemed more right than honest steel. At Baird's order, he sliced the blade across his own left little finger, across the old scar of amputation, and allowed the blood to drip into the bowl. The crystal dissolved into a clear liquid, revealing a severed human fingertip. He knew somehow that it was his own. And he knew, too, why Baird was also missing the end of one finger.

"Repeat after me, boy," Baird demanded." 'I, Varian of Leopard's Gard.' "

And his treacherous tongue followed orders as well as his body. "I, Varian of Leopard's Gard . . . do dedicate myself unto You, O Lord who rules the dark . . . that which hides in men's souls until You draw it unto Yourself . . . I am Yours, in place of the Lord Baird, as long as I have breath in my body."

The echo of the oath of fealty brought cold chills to his heart, and the panic that had been dulled rose in him again. He could not, he *would not* belong to this god who was evil personified!

And as if He could read Varian's mind, the god

laughed. "Oh, yes, boy, you are Mine. Shall I prove it to you?"

The god laughed, and so did Baird as he watched his only son grow wide-eyed with terror. Pain shot through Varian's body and face, a wrenching pain that twisted through his bones. He dropped to his knees, then to all fours as his arms and legs thickened and changed proportions. A lance of pain at the base of his spine grew into a long, heavy tail, and his skull imploded in agony as if his head was being crushed into amorphousness and molded into a new form. Even his senses changed; the cavern around them sprang from shadowed obscurity into sharp relief as slit-pupiled cat's eyes widened in his face, his ears caught the rustle of small, unseen things in the distance, and his nose was suddenly choked with the reek of his own human fear.

Where the young man had stood there now crouched an enormous ice leopard, more than half again as large as its normal kindred, but the scream that ripped from its throat still held some trace of the human that it had once been.

"So, Lord Baird, the gift of shape-shifting still runs in your line," the god purred. "And this one is an even better plaything; he fights Me.

"Oh, yes, I remember that silly bargain, but you are not released until I am fully satisfied with your substitute. You will wait here."

Silently, the leopard left the confines of the floor diagram and padded off, deeper into the passage, into the depths of the rock. And a terrified Varian rode in the leopard's brain and looked out through its eyes as a prisoner riding in a gaolers' wagon might look out helplessly through the tiny barred windows. This animal body was no more controlled by his will than his human one was.

But if the God of Darkness controlled it, He must have had much practice, for there was no stiffness or lack of skill in the movements of the leopard's body. All the silent grace of a consummate predator was there as it leaped fluidly from ledge to ledge, working its way up now and out through a natural maze of caverns into the open air. In the clear warmth of a summer night, only a thin fingernail sliver of moon showed, one day past new moon.

The leopard lifted its head to more fully catch the fitful breeze, but no scent of interesting prey caught its attention. The tangled brush of forest thinned out as it worked its way downhill toward more settled land, down to where a village gathered its houses into a tight cluster like chicks sheltering under a mother's wings.

Now here there was a richness of possible prey; farmlands meant farm animals. But the enticing scent of pigs and chickens and sheep held no allure for the mind-controlled beast tonight. The Being who ordered its movements had other prey in mind.

The two who cuddled in the shelter of a garden wall knew the dangers that sometimes stalked their land in the dark of the moon, but they were young and in love and, in their own minds, immortal. They did not know that thick-furred ears caught their soft gasps and giggles as their scent wafted downwind, an intriguing scent of male lust and female receptiveness.

Two would be delicious prey, the fear of each one feeding on the other's danger, and He who controlled the ice leopard was mightily tempted to begin His playtime right then. But this was a new body, one whose responses were as yet unknown, and He did not want it damaged; He had more plans for it than a single night of bloodlust. So He bided His time and crouched the leopard in the shadowed shelter of a roadside well, watching and listening.

It would be the girl; males, even peasant ones, were seldom unarmed, although their defense was usually only a blunt belt dagger. Girls were so soft, so tender, so fearful.

The two lovers, with sighs and much protestations of undying love, finally separated. The young man walked with his girl to the gate of her cottage home, and there

left her, mindful of his responsibility to protect her but
as yet unwilling to face the scrutiny of her family. She
lingered until he was out of sight, then sighed and
reached for the latch. Her hand never touched it. A
shadow flowed out of the night and snatched at her skirt,
pulling her backward off her feet. She fell heavily,
bloodying her hands and scraping her face as she hit the
stone wall, and looked about frantically to find the
source of her fall.

Varian, trapped in the leopard and forced to look out
through its eyes, could do nothing as she scrambled to
her feet and backed away, screaming in terror at the sight
of enormous yellow eyes shining out of the dark. For
one horrible instant as the dim moonlight shone on her
face, he thought she was Mally, though he knew that
she should be safe in the castle, in his own bed.

Shouts and dogs' barking cut short both the girl's terror and her life; as her father opened his cottage door
and rushed out, the ice leopard sprang and ripped out
her throat with a swift strike of gleaming, sharp claws,
then bounded away into the darkness.

When Varian stood before the altar once more in his
human body, there was one last shock for him. The Hidden Lord, back in His aspect of a face, ordered him to
stretch out his left arm along the altar-stone, palm down.
Helplessly he obeyed, his body still controlled by the
drug, and numbly he waited for whatever final torture
the god decreed.

Baird had not been idle in his absence. A brazier of
hot coals smoked on the altar, its heart so hot the coals
glowed not red or orange, but golden-white. A long,
slender metal wand, fitted with a wooden handle, rested
in that heart.

The baron drew it forth carefully, its tip glowing
bright cherry red. Plain to be seen even in the dimness
was its shaped end, not the sword that marked the dev-
otees of Likarion, or one of those that identified follow-
ers of the other gods, but one Varian had never seen

before. It was the shape of a clenched fist.

"Accept, O Master, this your new servant." Baird pressed the branding iron firmly into his son's upper arm, on the smooth muscle just below the shoulder, burning the mark deep into his flesh. Varian, unable to look away, unable to protest by even the flick of an eyelash, turned white and would have fainted if he could. It was done then, irrevocable, unless the god chose to release him. He belonged to a god he loathed, as much as any slave belonged to a master.

"So, beast-man, you have given Me your only legitimate son. This is a sacrifice most pleasing to Me. I release you from My control. Take out your crystal. Put it on the altar."

The baron pulled a small black velvet bag from its hiding place in his clothes. Out of it he spilled a tiny, smoky ball, no bigger than the yolk of an egg. Entombed in its heart was an animal's claw surrounded by red swirls. This he put on the altar as he had been bidden.

Blinding white light splashed from the altar as the crystal vanished. Baird screamed in agony and fell to his knees. The god's face twisted into a repulsive parody of a smile. "You are free to run the night as you will, beast-man, without control from Me. And you, boy, you have your own crystal now. Take it. Guard it well. Your soul is in there. Or at least such of it as I choose to leave with you."

Varian reached out a shaky hand and took the tiny globe that rested again in the bowl. Trapped in the center was a gray claw, surrounded by swirls of scarlet blood.

Corven and Mally were not initially alarmed by the absence of their young master. They waited in his room as they had been ordered to do, sitting on the shabby ancient bearskin that served as a hearthrug. Corven told Mallena of life in the great castles, much different from the simple life they lived here, and she in turn brought him up to date on the events of his home. Some of the things were homey ones—marriages, births, deaths—but some of them were the same things that Varian had noticed that day. When she spoke of the growing fear that hung almost visibly over the castle, she shivered.

On impulse, he moved closer to her and put an arm around her shoulders. She nestled gratefully into his comforting warmth and wondered how it was that two young men, similar in age and size, could be so different. Varian was all hard lean muscle; last night he had felt enormous in her arms. Corven was just as muscular, but he yielded, giving her the feeling of being wrapped snugly in a soft blanket. An itch of curiosity begged— no, *demanded* to be scratched; on impulse, she tipped her face up to his and pulled his head down. Yes, she had been right this morning. He kissed differently, too: less demanding. She loved Varian, and he tried hard, but he was still her master. Corven was her friend.

"Are you sure, Mally?" he asked when she guided his hand to her breast. "What if Varian walks in on us?" But even as he asked, he caressed her, and she felt like purring with pleasure.

"Then we'll find out if he meant what he said this morning. And I think he did."

Their lovemaking was sweet and satisfying, but without the fierce, overwhelming rush of possession that she had felt from Varian. Afterward, they cuddled again on the hearthrug, lying spoon fashion with Mally's back tucked snugly into the curve of Corven's body, so that he could continue to stroke her.

And Varian did walk in on them. They sat up, feeling guilty, for the expression on his face was one of deep shock, but he ignored them as if they didn't exist. Instead, he stumbled blindly toward the fire, seeking instinctively for light and warmth to banish the cold, dark chill on his soul. He fell to his knees on the rug and covered his face with his hands, rocking back and forth.

Mally knelt beside him and tugged in panic of her own at his rigid arm. "Varian, please, we didn't mean—"

"It's not us, Mally," Corven interrupted. "This is

battle-shock, or something like it.'' He hesitated only a moment, then took Varian's hands and pried them away from his face. The feel of those hands, cold and sweating and shaking, confirmed to him that his swordbrother had suffered a major shock. Varian's eyes were wide and unseeing, the pupils so constricted that they were mere pinpoints. His breath came in ragged gasps, like a dog panting. And as the two slaves watched, the shaking of his hands spread up his arms to his body.

"Grab that basin, Mally, he's going to be sick!"

She leaped up, snatched the washbasin from the top of the clothes chest, and dropped it in front of him. Corven held his head as he vomited, spasm after spasm, until he was drooling only long strings of mucus. Mally tenderly wiped them away and went on to strip off his sweat-soaked shirt. Neither of them could find an injury to his body, except for a slight cut on one finger and a small, dark, irregular spot that looked like a burn on his arm.

"We have to keep him warm. Help me get him onto the bed," Corven ordered. Mally stripped back the covers as he put Varian's arm over his shoulders and his own arm around his back. With Mally on his other side, they heaved him into the bed.

"These sheets are like ice. The best way to keep him warm is one of us on either side," and Mally put action to her words. Corven was warrior-trained and might know how to treat shock better, but she knew how to treat illness. She wrapped him in her arms and held him close. "Hug his back, Corven, the way you were hugging mine just now."

Sandwiched between the two of them, Varian gradually grew warmer, and the frightening rigidity of his body eased. His breathing steadied and became deeper, though racking moans still welled up occasionally from his diaphragm. They held him until his body relaxed completely and his head stirred, his hair tickling their faces. His arms tightened around Mally again, but this time of his own will.

"Mally?" Varian's voice was slurred and confused as he came back to consciousness. "Corven, where's Corven?"

"Right here, my brother," rumbled Corven's voice from behind him, and he became aware that it was Corven who was the comforting warmth at his back. "Varian, what happened? You looked like you've seen the Evil One himself."

"He—I did. My father—we're all his slaves. *All* of us. Me, too." And he would say nothing more.

5

Baron

Year 407 D.S.:
Twenty-sixth day of the month of Yellowgrain

Varian came out of his father's room, so tired that his
shoulders slumped, so tired that he could barely raise his
fist to study the emerald signet ring on his middle finger.
Thank the gods, any gods, it was over. Baird was dead.
The two days of fever-ridden, delirious screaming were
over, the days when Varian had allowed nobody in to
tend his father but himself. He could permit nobody, not
even Corven, to hear the foul confessions that had
spewed from Baird's mouth. Varian did not doubt that
his father had done the things he gloated about; in the
past three years, he had been forced to do some of those
things as well. What sickened him was that Baird had
enjoyed them.

Corven met his eyes from his place on the floor outside the door, a query clear on his face, a query he didn't
dare ask with the Lord Baird's bodyguard also standing
there.

Corlena, the pretty young slave seated next to him,
raised her face, too, dread and hope intermingled. The
priests might say it was wrong to hope her master was

dead, but she couldn't help it. Perhaps the master was no more cruel than any other man to his bed-slave, but she hated him anyway. She could have tolerated ordinary bed-sport, even pretended to like it, for she had been trained in the exotic bedroom skills of a courtesan, but the things he did to her were too painful and humiliating. He did them to make her hate him; he wanted her hate, because it made him feel more powerful when he forced her to pleasure him.

Varian continued to study the ring on his finger, then looked up at the bodyguard. His voice was not tired at all, but cold and hard. "Your services are no longer required. You and your two fellows have one hour to gather your belongings and leave this castle. By tomorrow noon, you will be off my lands, and if you harm any of my people in your going, you will be treated as the brigands you are."

The bodyguard's face twisted into a mask of hate and anger. "Your father is our employer, lordling. It is for him to dismiss us."

"The dead dismiss nobody. I am baron here now." His eyes were as hard and cold as his voice.

The man facing him did not quail, and his face remained twisted in anger. "Aye, we'll leave. And I warn you, lordling, the king's magistrates will be here asking questions about how the Lord Baird died."

Corven rose to stand at Varian's shoulder as they watched him stomp away. "Can he cause trouble, Varian? How did he die?"

"Blood poisoning from an infected wound. Nothing we have to worry about, once the leading citizens of the town have viewed the body." He scraped his hands distractedly through his hair. "Gods, that's something else I have to do.

"Corven, go tell Evan that I want those men escorted off my lands. Then find Roden and tell him I want messengers sent to the Town Council, summoning them here as soon as possible, the bell rung to assemble the house-

hold, and I want Roden's keys, all of them. I will meet
him in his office.

"Corlena, you run fetch me Mistress Margretha,
here." As the young slave girl started to obey, he
reached out and caught her arm. She froze, afraid of him
despite Mally's insistence that he was kind, at least to
her. His eyes, not cold now, smiled down at her. "You
don't have to pretend to mourn, little one. Nobody will
mourn for *him*. Not even his son."

And nobody mourned when Varian stood on the dais at
the head of the great hall, half an hour later. "The Lord
Baird, Baron of Leopard's Gard, is dead." Only a soft
murmur spread through the people, free and slave. They
might not mourn the death of their lord, but they were
not yet ready to cheer his passing, not in front of his
son.

The new Baron of Leopard's Gard continued to speak,
holding up his fist so that the great green signet ring
shone clear on his finger, and the two gold rings of his
rank gleamed in his ears. "I am his son and heir; does
any man here dispute my right to hold his lands, his
title, and his people after him?" The ritual words fell
into the silence like pebbles into a still pond. No one
spoke, yet he waited, his eyes moving over them all.

"I am, then, baron by blood, and if any shall come
forth to challenge me, I will be baron by right of arms.

"The slaves of this castle will assemble here before
me." This did cause a stir. Only Corven and Mally
moved forward willingly to kneel before him. The others
came reluctantly, for although the new baron had never
been known to harm a slave, wariness of free men had
been beaten into them for too long. And, too, the older
ones had particular reason to fear him and what he might
be about to do.

"In the old days, I am told, even as recently as my
grandfather's death, slaves accompanied their lord on his
last journey. None of you will do so for the lord my
father." Varian looked at their kneeling figures with un-

derstanding as many gasped in relief, some even covering their eyes to hide their sudden tears. "Instead, I choose to commemorate his death in another way. Corven, Mallena, come forward."

Only the two slaves who knelt at his feet saw his hands shake as he thrust the tiny key in the lock of Corven's collar. His voice was low, too, as he repeated the action with Mally's. "I free you both, my friends."

No slave, however, missed his next words, for his voice swelled to a shout of ringing triumph. "None of you are slaves any longer! All of you are free! Is it witnessed?"

The ritual words came back to him in an even louder roar. "It is witnessed!"

It was many hours later before Varian could collapse quietly in front of his own fire. The newly freed slaves had all been reassured that yes, they were truly free, and no, they were not being turned out to survive as best they could. If they wanted to stay and work, they might do so, free of the fear of lash and block, although wages might not be as high as he would like for a year or two. If they had somewhere they wished to go, they would be helped to go there.

After that, the Town Council arrived, as pompous and ceremonial a group as he had ever seen, dressed in their best to attend on the new lord. Their head praised Varian's wisdom in sending for them, for all agreed that the circumstances should be witnessed. "Especially as, er, the Lord Baird was not, ah, perhaps the most, er ... popular of lords, my lord Varian, you see," stammered the Council Head. He was even more cautiously circumspect when they were asked to examine Baird's injury, for following Varian's orders, the baron's body had not yet been prepared for burial.

The ugly gash on Baird's hip stank of gangrene, and the red streaks of infection leading away from it had not faded. If any of the councilmen had heard rumors of a peasant wounding a marauding ice leopard in a similar manner several days ago, none of them mentioned it. Margretha, who served as the castle's healer (for none of that guild would practice in Leopard's Keep) testified that she had cared for Lord Baird until he had become feverish and ordered her from his presence. The servants who had carried food in and chamber pots out were questioned; none saw any sign of the vomiting and purging that would have accompanied poison. Varian was relieved that those particular servants had been freed, for slaves were by law questioned under torture.

The councilors had also prudently brought along their own healer, who examined the dead man's body. Varian wondered how he could bear to inspect the stinking wound so closely; it turned his stomach.

"It is quite clear, my lord, that nothing more could have been done," the healer said firmly. "This wound shows clear evidence of having been cleaned and cared for as much as possible. There is no sign of any other cause of death on the Lord Baird's body. I will so testify in front of any magistrates' court in the land, should it come to that."

The formalities of declaring his father dead had been almost more than Varian had the strength to manage. Now he sat wearily at the fire in his own room, too tired even to eat the food on the table at his elbow. He didn't even hear the soft padding of feet and started when small hands came from behind and gripped his shoulders.

"Let me get that shirt off, then lean forward, and I'll rub your back," Mally said quietly. He obeyed, propping his elbows on his knees and allowing his head to drop forward. Her hands were strong and sure, kneading the tight knots of tension from his shoulders and the back of his neck.

"Oh gods, yes, right there," he groaned as her thumbs dug into the muscles between his shoulder blades, then worked down his back on either side of his spine. "Woman, you've got just one week to stop that, or else."

"Or else what?"

"Dunno. I'll think of somethin'."

"You've got enough to think about, don't you?" asked Corven's voice. "Come help me with this, Mally." He nudged the door shut with his hip, his hands full with a pitcher and three mugs.

She didn't stop the kneading motion of her hands. "You picked up that clutter, you can put it down."

"Hot mulled wine is hardly clutter," Corven said indignantly. He managed to set the pitcher down before untangling the mugs from his fingers.

"That's what I want to think about. Hot mulled wine. Corven, you'll have to hold Mally's mug for her. If she stops, I'll go to sleep."

"Our fiendish plan exactly. You're going to get some sleep if we have to hit you over the head to do it. That's the least of what we owe you, Varian." Corven's hand went to his bare neck. Even in the firelight, a band of pale skin showed where his collar had been.

"I owe all of my people so much more," Varian said tiredly. "There are so many things I want to do that *he* would never let me. This can be the most prosperous barony in the kingdom now that I have a free hand."

Mally hushed him by raising the mug of wine to his mouth. He drank slowly, letting the spicy flavor linger on his tongue. His eyes slid shut and his head drooped again when she took it away. She returned to his back, now making long, smooth strokes with her palms. "Get his boots off, Corven. Now, no objections from you, Varian. You will let us be your body-slaves one last time."

"Don't nnneed body-sslaves." He caught himself as his voice started to slur and shook his head. "Did you drug that pitcher 'f wine?"

"No," Corven said firmly but only half truthfully. The sleeping potion had been in the bottom of the mug instead. The man who had been his master shook his head again as his vision started to blur. "You're tired is all, and you have reason to be. Come on, we'll put you to bed.''

Varian didn't resist as they stripped off his breeches and stuffed him into bed. Just this once, it wouldn't make him soft to let himself be cosseted . . . just . . . this . . . once . . .

Mally brushed a kiss on his lips as she pulled the covers up and tucked him in. He was asleep before he had a chance to turn over.

Corven smiled and held out her mug of wine. She took it and smiled back, then clunked mugs with him as he held his up.

''To freedom!'' he said quietly. ''And freedom for him, too, I hope.''

Freedom was the last thing he felt in the coming weeks. Varian worked harder than he ever had in his life. There were so many things to be done, things that Baird had forbidden his son to meddle in, and it seemed that they all had to be done at once.

The ordering of the castle was first on the list. The steward Roden was dismissed, and his place was taken by his assistant, Migael. This was in repayment of a debt Varian felt he owed Migael, for the new steward had been crippled in the disastrous boghart attack. He still walked with a limp, but his voice was firm when he swore fealty to Varian.

Varian also dismissed many of the guardsmen who he knew to be brutal bullies, including their captain. Arms-master Evan took his place and hired a small band of mercenaries to reinforce the castle troops. The Town Guard, too, was cleansed and strengthened, and any guardsman caught drinking on duty soon found himself without a job.

Varian discovered, too, that the needless stinginess of his father, coupled with Lord Baird's selfish extrava-gance, had nearly brought them all to ruin. There was plenty of money in the castle coffers, but his father had preferred to spend it on luxuries for himself rather than the good of his people. What did it matter to him if the peasants' cottages were almost in ruins and most of his slaves were nearly in rags, so long as he had liryal-skin coverlets and the female slaves who served him were dressed in silk to tantalize him?

The new baron rode for many long hours to visit all parts of his lands. All his people deserved to know who he was, to know that he would care for them, not exploit them. He demanded and got full accounts from all the stewards who oversaw the outlying lands and spent much time going over them. Almost everywhere, he saw that the tax burden could be reduced and still provide him with enough income to fulfill his duties. He cut the taxes somewhat, but not as much as he could have, for he had plans formulated for the extra money.

Still more time went to holding judicial hearings, for Baird had left that to the stewards and local provosts. Varian uncovered many cases of injustice, for it was well known that many officials expected to be bought off; those "criminals" who had no money were of course much more harshly treated.

It hurt him that children still ran and hid when he passed, but as he made his way from village to village, hopeful rumors started to precede him. He emptied many prison cells along the way, for he reviewed all cases of imprisonment and pardoned most offenders. Only those few who had committed crimes that truly harmed another were punished, most of them executed as they should have been.

Rumors flew, too, about the oddities of the new baron. He took long walks at night outside the walls, for a number of guardsmen saw him and challenged him before they realized who he was. He did not punish them but commended them for their vigilance.

Also, he did not have the lecherous eye of his late, unlamented father. Several young peasant couples came before him asking permission to be wed, and he did not claim the lord's right with any of the maidens. One that had the courage to appear looking pretty instead of try-

ing to make herself ugly drew a smile from him; that
one he kissed soundly before swatting her lightly on the
rump and sending her back to her relieved bridegroom.

He enforced the king's laws and passed new ones of
his own. Slavers were banished, and while he could not
forbid the owning or private sale of slaves, people were
encouraged to free the ones that they did own. Further
spurs to that were the extra taxes imposed for each slave
owned. One of the most puzzling of the new laws,
though, was the one that imposed dusk-to-dawn curfew
during the dark of the moon and the two days on either
side of it.

Varian had thought for a long time over that one. The
Dark God did not always control him for those three
days, but often enough, he was ripped helplessly from
sleep and forced into the were-change, and always He
Who Had No Name preferred human prey. This law was
the only way he had to protect his people without giving
himself away.

The urge to change and run the night came on him at
other times, too, but his leopard body was under his own
control then. It was uncannily seductive to prowl the
moonlit mountainsides, to hunt for the beasts of the forest, and to taste the sweet, hot blood bursting into his
mouth as a creature died under his teeth and claws.

As the shape-shifting power had strengthened over the
last three years, keeping it from Corven and Mally had
grown more difficult. He slept alone now in the room
that had been his father's, only occasionally asking
Mally to come to his bed.

The geese were migrating overhead, and the leaves of
the trees were bright scarlet and gold by the time Varian
was ready for the next step in his plans to help his people. In his travels around his domain, he had marked the
names of promising young men and women; now he
began to call them into his presence.

Garek rose to his feet and watched warily as his new
lord entered the room where the steward had told them

to wait. He didn't know why the baron had summoned
him, nor did any of the other men in the room that he
had spoken to. They were all hunters or trappers, but
none of them had done anything to break the game laws.
At least he knew he hadn't; if any of the others had,
they certainly wouldn't admit it to strangers here in the
lord's own castle.

The lord smiled at all of them and said cheerfully,
"Please, sit down. First, I want to say none of you are
in trouble. I've called you here to ask for your help."

Our help? Garek thought in surprise. *How could we
possibly help him?* One of the other men echoed his
thoughts, hesitantly asking nearly the same question out
loud.

"You can give me knowledge that I don't have," the
baron answered easily. "The stewards in your villages,
and the tax rolls, say that most of you are hunters or
trappers. I have plans that need those special skills.

"You know what sort of prices you get now for furs.
I know what those skins could bring you if they were
marketed properly.

"But the knowledge I need from you is about the
animals themselves. Of all the fur-bearers, the meat-
eaters, which ones are the least vicious?"

The same older man that had asked how they could
help slowly held up his hand. "M'lord, I would think
. . . prob'ly liryals. They's not hunters, like, more scav-
engers. Ye don' have to be fierce when ye eat dead
things."

Baron Varian smiled, almost with relief. "I was hoping someone could confirm that for me. Would it be
possible, do you think, to raise them in captivity?"

There was a buzz of excitement, and as he explained,
Garek's suspicion turned slowly to wonderment that a
lord should think of something like this, for it seemed
he had it all planned out. How they could build cages
or pens, how they could feed the beasts on offal from
slaughtering or hunting . . . and here Garek himself
raised his hand. "They'll eat fruit and such, too, m'lord.

I saw one once that'd been eatin' windfall pears in m' father's orchard. It seemed drunk, like.''

The young lord (well, not so young, for he was about Garek's own age) laughed out loud at that and asked Garek's name. Then he said, ''I want you all to know that I'm not ordering anybody to try this. I'm asking for volunteers. If you need money or supplies to build cages and such, I will provide that. That's not a loan or charity, call it a return of your taxes. You don't have to give me an answer right now, either. Go home and think about it, see if you can see any problems that I maybe don't even know enough about this to imagine. Let me know in about a week.''

The commoners rightly enough took that as dismissal. Garek hesitated, and let the others file out ahead of him. Then he gathered his courage in both hands and turned back to the lord. ''M'lord, there was one thing I been thinkin' already about this. Ye c'n pen sheep an' such, an' make poultry cages out of willow rods and leather thongs, but how d'ye keep a toothy thing like a liryal from chewin' its way out? I . . . know they will chew on leather, I had one steal a glove once.''

Please, Vorndal, let him not be angry at me, questioning him!

The God of the Hunt must have heard his devotee's prayer, for the lord did not look angry, just thoughtful. ''That's the kind of thing I wanted to hear, Garek. Let's sit down again and think it through.'' He pulled a bell-cord, and when a small boy answered, ordered cakes and ale for two. By the time the food arrived, they had tentatively solved that problem (wire ties on the cages) and gone on to others. Garek looked up when a woman's soft voice said, ''My lord, your ale.'' In that one look, he was lost. She was *beautiful*. Her hair was so . . . and her eyes . . . and oh, dearest gods, her smile! He would give anything to have that smile turned on him.

The baron did not seem to notice that the most desirable woman in the world was standing there holding a tray. He gave her an absent smile and a pat on the hip, saying, "Thank you, Mally m'love. This is Garek, one of the trappers that I called in about the liryal project. Garek, this is Mallena."

Mallena. A name fit for a queen. And as gracefully as a queen, she set the tray down and took a seat. Took a seat next to *him*, dear gods!

"We've been throwing ideas around for the project," the lord continued, "and I think Garek's hooked."

Mally did smile at him then, and Garek all but fainted. The lord's voice became a faint buzz; only willpower kept him upright in his seat. He was saved from making a fool of himself only by the grace of the gods. A shout broke into the buzzing.

"Varian! That damnfool Rowan is trying to break down the whole stable!" a young man yelled from the doorway. The baron jumped to his feet with a groan and a soft curse. "On my way, Corven. Mally, you talk to Garek." He ran out of the room.

Garek looked at the young woman, still in his daze. "Who's Rowan?"

She laughed, a delightful ringing sound. "Lord Varian's warhorse. I expect there's a mare involved somewhere. Tell me, what do you think of his plans? He has a lot of them besides this liryal one, plans to raise or gather spices and dyestuffs, all sorts of luxury things that he thinks traders will be willing to pay good prices for."

"They're so beautiful . . ."

"*What?*" She stared at him in delighted astonishment.

"What did I say?" he asked in confusion. "Oh, yeah, th' plans. They sound good . . . but why does he care how we make our livin'?"

Mally's face was suddenly serious. "Because he cares about all his people. Because he'll never be the cruel master that his father was. He's worth serving and helping, Garek. You'll see."

For the second time that day, Garek grabbed for his courage. "Ye are all I see right now, Miss Mallena. I never dreamed there was anyone like ye."

"You don't know anything about me," she said abruptly and rose to her feet to begin collecting the dirty dishes. There was no need to tell this nice young man who and what she was. He was only making pretty speeches, perhaps thinking that flattering her would somehow get him in favor with the lord.

"I've opened m' mouth and put m' foot in it, ain't I?" he said mournfully. "I'm sorry, miss. Thick-headed and cack-handed, m' mother says I am. If'n I go home and have her whop me upside th' head, will that do?"

His sorrowful tone caused her to turn and look at him again. In looks he was much like any peasant of these parts, with ash blond hair and blue-gray eyes in a square, firm-jawed face. Now those eyes were as sad as any hunting hound's. *He means it. He wasn't just making up a pretty speech. You need to be whopped upside the head, Mally, hurting him like that,* she thought. "I'm the one who should apologize, Garek. I took what you said for something else entirely. I'm sorry."

"I ain't sure what I said, but if I do't again, ye jus' whop me yerself, yeah?"

His heart bounced again when her face crinkled into another smile. He smiled back and stood, and for the first time she could see how tall he was. Tall and sturdy, plain almost to the point of homeliness until he smiled— nothing like Varian or Corven at all, and yet somehow very attractive.

"Miss Mallena, I—th' lord says he wants us trappers' help on this job. So maybe I'll be back t' report every couple weeks. Do I need t' ask his permission t' see ye then?"

She shook her head and smiled her beautiful smile again. "You can see me any time. And when you do, I'd like you to call me Mally."

6

Bargain

Year 410 D.S.: Tenth day of the month of Springthaw

Garek approached the castle with eagerness, the load of furs heavy on his shoulders. Never before had he paid his taxes with such cheerfulness. But then, Mally had never sent him a message before, either. The guardsman at the gate grinned at him.

"I know a lass who'll be glad to see ye, m'lad. Yer lass is in th' kitchen, no doubt, but ye'll need to see Migael first."

The steward took his furs and recorded them in the big ledgers, turning them over and stroking the fine, soft pelts. "Beautiful lot this year. How many of these are wild caught, and how many are cage bred?"

"All th' liryal are cagers. Most of t'others are wild caught, sir."

"What's this? A white liryal?" Migael's eyebrow rose at the sight of the rare fur.

"Aye, sir. Four in one litter; I'm repeatin' th' breedin' and keepin' t'other three, hopin' to breed more. This one died, or I'd not've skinned it," Garek explained, half proud and half apologetic.

"Lord Varian will be pleased, I'm sure. I've no doubt

he will want to talk to you. Wait here.'' Migael limped out.

Garek, feeling abandoned, stood by the window, gazing out over the inner bailey. He started when small soft hands covered his eyes and a feminine voice cooed, "Guess who?"

"Allara? Opal? Meraud?"

One of the hands removed itself and became a fist in his ribs. He caught the fist, then the other hand still over his eyes, and wrapped the girl's arms around his waist. "Mally. Ye always greet me so lovin', m'sweet."

"More than you realize, my dear." She snuggled up next to his back and whispered in his ear.

"No! Mally, are ye sure?"

"How did I know you would say that?"

"Say what?" Varian asked as he entered the room.

Mally only smiled at him. Garek looked at her, then at his lord. "I—m'lord, I'd l-like to ask ye for audience wi' ye," he stammered.

"I'm already here, Garek. There's no need to ask for a formal audience to discuss liryals."

"Not liryals, m'lord." Garek straightened and his face became more solemn. "I'd like yer permission to wed with Mallena. She—she just told me she's carryin' my babe."

"Mally! Are you sure?"

Mally looked from one stunned man to the other and dissolved into helpless giggles. "Blessed Lady, are you all alike? Garek just said the same—hee, hee—the same thing!"

No wonder Garek looked stunned, Varian thought. He felt rather as if Mally had whacked him with his own sword. "Mally, Garek, sit down. I don't know what to say." *Except . . . is it mine?*

"Say 'yes'. And you don't need to count on your fingers, either of you. I'm sure I'm pregnant, and I'm sure it's Garek's babe."

Varian sat down and took Mally's hands in his. "Mally, years ago, I said I would step aside for any man that you wanted. I meant it then, and I mean it now. But does Garek know what . . . your position was in the castle before I became baron?''

To his surprise, Garek was the one to blush.

''M-m'lord, I don' think Mally's kept any secrets from me. I know she was a slave . . . yer slave, an' I know I wasn' the first man in her bed. I tol' her, an' I'm tellin' ye, it makes no difference. M'lord, when yer father was master here, not a maid in th' barony went virgin to her bridebed. Mally . . . well, Mally's jus' somethin' less virgin than that.''

Mally gave a muffled scream and pretended to hit him. Garek caught her hands and grinned at her. ''And aye, m'lord, I'll take her, temper an' all. I love her.''

''Then that's all you need to say, Garek.'' Lord Varian grinned suddenly, so that Garek thought he looked much younger. ''If I say 'no' she'll hit *me,* and we can't have that, can we?''

Varian gave the plans for Mally's wedding over to Mistress Margretha. He knew that Mally had always been one of the old lady's favorites, and that she would do her best to give her a suitable wedding. Indeed, the ''poor overworked'' chatelaine did so, grumbling happily the whole time (and secretly planning the wedding for her darling boy, when it came his turn).

Though it was not the wedding that would have been accorded the daughter of the house, nothing was omitted for Mally and her bridegroom. Varian's part in the ceremonies was short; as their lord, he joined their hands and kissed the bride, then discreetly vanished. Festivities and feasting by the castle staff and the populace of Garek's village went on until midnight, and the newlyweds were put to bed with all the traditional bawdy ceremonies.

''I'd always thought she might marry you,'' Varian said to Corven as the happy couple left the next morning. Though Mally had not shared his bed in months, already he missed her.

Corven shook his head. "No. We were—are—friends, but she never loved me, not like that. I'm glad Garek's parents seem to like her so much. I know she's missed her own mother since her death."

"Do they? They were so timid I thought Garek's mother might faint when I spoke to her. Why else do you think I made myself scarce?"

The immediate thought of *jealousy* was something Corven chose tactfully not to say. More than once Mally had cried on his shoulder, sobbing out her love for Varian and her awareness that she could never marry him, never be more than his concubine. Privately he thought also that perhaps Mally didn't love Garek but was settling for a man who loved her and could marry her. Instead he said, "They're happy, too, that she's pregnant. Garek's their only son, and they wanted a wife for him that would give them lots of grandchildren."

"Then I wish all of them luck," Varian murmured and turned away to his duties.

Year 410 D.S.:
Sixteenth day of the month of Sunheat

The heat of the day, even in the middle of the summer, rapidly eased with sunset, but in spite of the night chill, most folk saved their firewood for the winter. There was no smell of smoke, then, that dark of the moon, and no one was out and about in the night. No scent of human prey came to the ice leopard as He prowled the villages. Occasionally, a dog barked a warning, but He ignored them as if they did not exist. Perhaps for the Dark One, they did not.

Other scents came to the beast's nose; scent of pigs, scent of sheep, of chickens, of cows. All very dull and unappetizing, dull as the peasantry themselves, animals as staring and stupid as their owners. He was bored, deathly, utterly *bored;* this game was starting to pall.

A cool breeze flirted with the leaves of the trees, heavier gusts bringing down the occasional green apple or pear as the leopard padded through an orchard. And now on the fitful breeze there was a new scent, an intriguing one. Not dull grass-eaters, but the scent of other predators.

The Dark One probed deeper into the leopard's brain to bring out the identity of these predators: not a name, for the leopard did not think in words, but a picture. Small, long, slender; thick, dark fur; and a humping run. And a puzzlement to the beast, many all in one place, too many, for they should run alone.

He hid the leopard's body in the shelter of a fallen log, for now He must access the mind of the man who rode as unwilling passenger in the beast. And never did the man give in easily. This time, the battle was more furious than ever before, and the Evil One smiled at the challenge. Silent minutes went by, with twitches of the animal's body the only sign. An observer might have thought it slept and dreamed, were it not for the wide-open, yellow eyes.

Varian submitted, as he had known he must, his will stripped away and his mind naked to his master. But still he fought feebly to give Him only what he was forced to. Liryals. That much he gave up without a struggle. That these were caged animals, confined and nearly helpless, he tried desperately to keep to himself. It was no use, for the very fact of resistance told the Nameless One that there was something significant about these creatures. For a few minutes He toyed with the man's mind, then backed off.

He flowed the leopard to its feet and approached the farmstead cautiously. Here again, a dog barked. It could be safely ignored, for the foolish yelping thing was chained to its kennel. A quick, graceful bound took the leopard to the top of a small outbuilding for an intense, careful investigation, then down to the ground again. One claw emerged and delicately hooked into the latch-string of the door. It swung open of its own weight.

• • •

Garek heard the commotion of the dog, the racket snapping him out of his deep sleep. No doubt that marauding fox was after the chickens again. Mally stirred, too, and he shushed her with one finger to her lips, grumbling softly as he rapidly pulled on breeches and boots.

He snatched up his crossbow and hurried out the door, but the henyard was oddly silent. He bent and released Growler from his chain, expecting him to take out after the fox, but the dog whined and tried to hide behind his legs. "Go get him, boy," he urged.

Growler whined again and took two reluctant steps away from his master. There was a crash from the farmyard and a horrible soft noise of snarls and high-pitched cries, not from the direction of the chickens but the other way.

The liryals! Oh, please gods, no, not the liryals! Garek cursed, angry with himself now that he had not taken the time to light a lantern. And it would be the dark of the moon, no helpful light there. He ran for the liryal shed, nevertheless.

Mally cuddled drowsily back down in the blankets and waited for her husband to come back, all agrumble over plundering foxes and stupid dogs that couldn't be chained where they could protect the chickens. She heard a crash and smiled to herself; Growler was one of the clumsiest dogs she had ever seen, and she wondered what he had blundered into this time. All was silent after that.

Too silent. No sound of chickens, no sound of Growler baying after the fox—nothing. She propped herself up on her elbow, tension prickling along her back. For another dozen heartbeats she waited, then carefully heaved herself to her feet. She padded barefoot to the door and listened again, calling, "Garek? Garek, what's wrong?"

Her hands trembling, she lit the lantern. Outside, she froze in momentary shocked relief before she realized that the figure coming from the barn was not Garek but the hired boy, Remi, a neighbor's son. "Miss Mallena? I thought I heard a ruckus, but Garek didn' wake me."

"He went out—we thought a fox in the chickens . . ."

"No, I thought 'twas more like comin' from th' lir-yals." Even in the lantern light, he thought he saw her face pale. He tucked his own crossbow under his arm temporarily and handed her his dagger. Just like a woman, coming out unarmed with gods knew what out here!

But it was not Mally who yelped, startled, when a great cat leaped out of the liryal shed and raced past them into the night. Nor was it Mally who fired the crossbow so hastily that the shot flew far wide of the mark, the quarrel disappearing into the darkness.

"Garek? Please, answer me!" she begged, more frightened than she had ever been that he should be silent so long. *"Garek!"*

The light of the lantern lasted just long enough, before it fell from her nerveless fingers and went out, to show Mally her husband's bloody, ravaged body sprawled across a pile of broken liryal cages.

Somehow, Varian forced himself into the semblance of normality until Migael informed him that a messenger was at the gates, who told him of Garek's death. He expressed proper shock and sympathy to the young boy, who said he was one of those who discovered Garek's body. Corven volunteered to return with him to see if there was anything they could do to help and to bring Mally back home.

"I should do it myself, for Mally, but . . . somehow I feel responsible. It was my idea for raising the damned liryals . . ." Varian said gloomily, but inside, anger was starting to build. *Admit it, Varian, it was your fangs that closed on his throat, your claws that shredded his body. Your fault, Varian,* all *your fault that Mally's a widow and her child an orphan. And you came within inches of killing her, too.* "Tell his family that their taxes are remitted for the next two years."

"That will help them some," Corven said just as gloomily, and left.

He returned late in the day, alone. "Mally wouldn't see me, Varian," he reported. "Not me, not you, nobody. Her in-laws are caring for her in their own home."

Varian rubbed his hands down his face and distractedly through his hair. "Did you tell them that we would take care of her?"

"She won't leave them. They're her family now, all she has left. Don't force it. You've done all you could."

All I could. No, Corven, not all I could. I can fight Him for my freedom, for my people. I can and I will. This is the last one of my people He will kill!

In the six years that the Hidden One had owned him, Varian had never willingly approached His altar. This night, driven by rage and grief, he did so. Words that were engraved in his brain but that he had never before said crackled out of his mouth, seeming to take on a life of their own. They hovered over the altar, eddying the smoke of the burning herbs, twisting on the edge of vision.

The face of the god looked sleepy and bored. "I suppose you want something, beast-man. It's fortunate for you that I am wearied enough from our play last night to be indifferent to your petty demands. They might even be entertaining. I will not punish you this time, but know you that I am not to be summoned like your pretty little bed-slave."

Varian's face tightened with anger. "Yes, I want something. My people's freedom from Your sick pleasures."

"Your people's freedom. How noble, my lord. Why not be honest and say that it's your own freedom you want, that you don't care for being My toy?" The Dark One raised an amused eyebrow at Varian's stubborn silence in the face of His taunts. "Your father made Me a bargain for his freedom. What bargain will you drive with Me, beast-man?''

"The only bargain I can make, it seems. My own life. My soul, if You demand it.''

This time the face laughed mockingly. "Your soul is already forfeit to Me, and why should I take your life when I have it already? Do not think to escape Me by killing yourself, either. When the human in you dies, the beast will be free to roam among your people forever.

"But there is something I want. My enemy, My sister, thinks to lay a trap for Me, a trap you will help Me circumvent. I want your bride.''

"My *bride*?'' Varian sputtered in astonishment. "What bride?''

"I want—'' and the face twisted in the first expression of consternation that Varian had ever seen. "I want 'she who snatches a rose from the fire.' '' He looked down and frowned, as if He were reading something held in His unseen hands, something that He did not fully understand. "This girl is dangerous to Me. If you would pay My price, you will find her, you will wed her, and you will bring her to Me virgin.''

"As blood sacrifice on your altar?'' the man asked bitterly.

The god gave the impression of a negligent shrug. "What is one more? But as it happens, no. I want her alive and well and virgin. It will be doubly delightful that My enemy's tool will be My toy.''

His belly roiling with shock and disgust, Varian bent his head. Give an innocent girl to this monster?

"One innocent girl," a nasty voice whispered in his head. *"What is one wench, more or less? How many have we played with, beast-man? Remember how entertainingly they scream? How delicious their bodies are under our claws, how sweet their blood is on our tongue?"*

"All right!'' Varian cried desperately. "I'll do it, You bastard. This one girl for my freedom, and Your promise to leave my people alone!''

"Bind it properly, beast-man. Triple oath, unbreakable."

For a long minute he stood utterly still, his head bowed. Then his hand came up to brush over the Evil One's brand on his arm. "This I vow on my brand." He drew the dagger at his belt, his hand clenched so tightly on the hilt that it trembled as he fought the temptation to plunge it into the god's face or his own heart. "This I vow on my blade." The dagger came down, slashing as precisely as a healer's scalpel across his palm. "This I vow on my own blood." He clenched his fist, then slapped his hand down on the altar, leaving behind a bloody handprint.

7

Tavern

Year 410 D.S.: Fifth day of the month of Harvestend

The sound of the wind was rising as Varian prowled restlessly back and forth in front of the fireplace. The great hall was still well populated this evening. Everyone knew a storm was coming; the wind was cold, and earlier, high, thin mare's-tail clouds had scudded overhead. Sensible people preferred to stay warm and dry, and if one could have company as well, why not stay in the hall and let the lord's fires warm them, too?

Ice leopards, however, are not sensible people. The urge to get out, to change to thick, water-repellent fur and a sharper nose to scent the wind, was very strong tonight. The time he must wait for other people to be gone, until he was able to go to his own room and out through the passage, was almost unbearable.

Corven, in contrast, was sprawled comfortably on his belly on the bearskin hearthrug in front of the fire, his head pillowed on his folded arms. Only his eyes moved as he watched Varian pace. When Varian nearly stepped on him for the third time, however, he yawned and pushed himself to his feet.

"If you have that much energy, Varian, why not put

it to good use instead of wearing out the flagstones?''

Varian stopped in his tracks and eyed him sullenly. ''Do you have a suggestion as to 'good use'? Go out and hunt storm spirits, maybe?''

Corven stretched until his joints cracked and then shook himself like a dog. ''I was thinking about going down into the town. The Seven Stars Inn has a new singing-wench. I've heard that she's very good.''

''At singing or in bed?'' Varian jeered peevishly. ''The place will be packed full of traders and people come for the Harvest Fair.''

''We're not going to try to get a bed there,'' Corven explained patiently. ''Just a couple of seats and a mug or two of cider. Come on, the walk will do you good.''

''Please do, Lord Varian,'' Margretha put in from her chair nearby. ''I declare, you're giving me nerves, pacing back and forth like that, like a cat in a cage, and the Blessed Lady knows I need a few minutes to relax in the evening without—''

Varian winced and interrupted her. ''All right, all *right,* I'll go.'' As he stomped off to find a cloak, he muttered, ''Man turns into a servant in his own house, go there, do this . . .''

Once out in the weather, his mood improved. Even a human nose appreciated the fresh air, and he took note without realizing it that the wind in his face now would be at his back on the way home.

It was less than a mile from the castle gates to the Seven Stars, but long enough to chill even men wrapped in warm woolen cloaks. About halfway there, the expected rain started to fall, gusted by the wind into sudden stinging sheets. They ran the last few blocks, startling the town watchman, and let the wind blow them into the dooryard of the inn.

The common room was warm and hazy with woodsmoke. It was nearly full, as Varian had predicted, but they managed to find seats not too far from the fire. They had been in without ceremony often enough in the past that the innkeeper knew of Varian's desire to remain inconspicuous. He pretended not to notice there was a lord present, who should by rights have the best seats the place had to offer.

Corven was squirming back through the crowd with their drinks when a young woman came out on the tiny stage and sat down, cradling a stringed instrument in her arms. She played a few unnecessary notes to quiet her audience and smiled at them. She was red-haired and very slender, but a little too young, Varian thought, for his taste. Her voice was a sweet alto as she began with a quiet love song currently popular.

As she sang, Varian let his gaze wander over the rest of the crowd, idly making mental bets with himself as to which people were local and which were likely traders or merchants. That big man on the other side of the fire, for instance, was probably a Free Trader. He had the look of that people, with black hair and eyes. He was heavily tanned but too well dressed to be someone who worked in the fields. He was accompanied by two pretty young women, either daughters or wives, or perhaps one of each. Daughters, Varian decided, and was pleased when his guess was confirmed as the singer finished and one of the young women addressed the man as "Father."

The red-haired young singer had correctly judged the mood of her audience. The wistful melancholy of the first song brought enthusiastic applause and requests from the listeners for similar tunes. She smiled and shook her head. "I have a new one I'd like to try. This is a song I heard some weeks ago on the shores of the Inland Sea. They believe there that some of the seals are not true seals, but selkies, who can come ashore and take human form by removing their sealskins."

She played a rippling string of notes that seemed to have something in them of the wind's eerie cry and began to sing in a minor key.

Now once on a moonlit night, they say
Three selky-maids swam to the land

And doffed their silver-gray sealskin cloaks
To dance and to play on the sand...

Her voice throbbed as she wept for the youngest
selky-maid, captured by a fisherman who stole her seal-
cloak and kept her for years far from her beloved sea.

There was a moment of respectful silence when she
finished, and the applause broke out again. The girl rose
and bowed, saying, "Good people, I will return in a few
minutes."

Her exit prompted a lively discussion as to whether
there truly were such things as shape-shifters. One elderly man held the floor for a few minutes by declaring
that his grandfather had seen an ice leopard attack his
sheep and shot it; when he got home that evening, a
neighbor had been mysteriously hit by a crossbow quarrel in the very same part of his body and was tried and
convicted of being a were-leopard. A younger man who
obviously considered himself to be the local comedian
countered with a story that he'd heard of were-wolves
and now were-leopards, but that *his* grandfather had
been a were-rabbit, who used to sneak up on innocent,
unsuspecting farmers and viciously attack their cabbages
and carrots.

In the laughter that followed, Corven nudged Varian
in the ribs and said quietly, "She's watching you, Varian."

"Who?"

"That pretty black-haired Trader girl. See, she's
turned her chair so she can see you out of the corner of
her eye."

Varian grinned at him. "Are you sure it isn't you
she's watching? You're the one with the reputation for
the ladies." Nevertheless, the girl was very pretty, so as
he caught her glance, he smiled at her and raised his
mug slightly in greeting. She blushed and looked away,
then turned back to him and smiled slightly in return.

Just then a serving wench moved in to serve the table
between Varian and the Trader's. As she tried to maneu-

ver her tray in the crowded area, she stepped back too far and her skirt brushed into the fire. The thin fabric burst instantly into flames.

The inn's cook came out at that instant from the kitchen, screamed, dropped her tray of food, and tried to rush to the rescue through the crowd. Before the serving girl herself could draw breath to scream, the dark-haired Trader girl reacted. Out of her chair before anyone else, she threw an arm around the server's shoulders, knocking her to the floor. She began to beat at the blazing skirt with her hands, then reached up and grabbed a cloak that was hanging over a chair back to dry. She covered the flames with the damp wool and continued to slap it down until she was certain the fire was out.

Other people near the fire jumped to their feet, either to try to help or to push back out of the way. The cook shoved unheedingly through them. "Rosalia, Rosalia, my Rose, are you all right?" she sobbed, picking the girl up and holding her tightly.

Varian, on his feet with everyone else, heard the serving girl's name with a shock like a blow to his unprotected belly. The words echoed in his head. *"She who snatches a rose from the fire."*

He shook his head to clear it and heard the inn-keeper's voice calling for order and room to see what had happened. The cook was still sobbing. "My little girl, my little girl, she's a true heroine, she saved my little Rose."

And hating himself for what he was about to do, Varian shook his hair back so that the gold rings shone in his ears and pushed through the crowd.

"A heroine indeed. One who should be honored throughout my lands," he said in a ringing voice calculated to cut through any noise people were still making. In the sudden stillness, broken only by someone's murmur, "Is that the *baron*?" quickly hushed, he bowed to the girl who was still sitting on the floor, the deep, reverent bow he would have made to a queen.

"I am Varian, Baron of Leopard's Gard. My house would be deeply honored if you and your family would be guests at my Harvest celebration and feast tomorrow." He added swiftly in a voice of quiet concern, "Are you burned, my lady? Shall I send for a healer for you and the other girl?"

The girl's father helped her to her feet. She looked at her hands in something of a daze and then back up at Varian.

"No. Yes. I mean, I'm not hurt, but see to that poor girl, maybe she needs a healer."

"Oh, miss, she's not hurt but for a few little blisters," said the cook. "You were so quick, and I don't know how to thank you."

The Trader bowed also and then stood tall, with dignity fully equaling Varian's. "I am Alfgar of the Free Traders of Clan Leioness. My daughter is Cathlin, and this my wife is Luned. It is we who will be honored to be your guests, Your Excellency."

Varian smiled slowly. "Then it is settled. I will send someone to fetch your belongings and will come about midmorning for you myself. I will not ask these lovely ladies to stir out of a comfortable inn on a night like this. Until tomorrow then, Master Alfgar, Mistress Luned. My lady Cathlin?" He held out his hand and she slowly put hers into it. He bowed slightly again and laid a gentle kiss on her fingers. With a swirl of his cloak, he was out the door and gone, a startled Corven two steps behind.

Cathlin was not the only one to look wide-eyed after him. The singer smiled to herself and said to nobody in particular, "He may be a lord instead of a performer, but he sure knows how to make an exit."

"I know him, I know I do, but where? When?" Cathlin murmured to herself as she cuddled down into the warm bed later that night. Something in her memory said *summer*. And then, as she thought of his smile and the glint of gold half-hidden in his dark hair, she remembered.

Remembered how she had lost her twelve-year-old heart to a gleam of white teeth and green eyes in the firelight one summer night, remembered how she mourned for days that he hadn't noticed her at all. She had been too shy, had felt suddenly too skinny and clumsy and coltish beside his devastating handsomeness and swordsman's grace.

And now they were invited to be his guests. At his castle? It must be. He had said someone would fetch their things. And yet even the thought of staying in the rumored luxury of a castle was overpowered by the knowledge that she could be near him, could perhaps even get to know him. She wasn't shy or clumsy anymore. And think how much good it could do the clan if her father could get some trade concessions out of him.

Cathlin, that's atrocious. Stop being so mercenary, she scolded herself. Her lips curved in a smile as she pictured instead a wild flight of fancy, that he could be so dazzled by her wit and beauty that he would ask her father for her hand. He wouldn't, of course. She was a commoner, a Free Trader, not an appropriate bride for a lord baron. No doubt he was either already married or betrothed to someone of suitable rank. And the lords only had one wife at a time, not like her people. Perhaps there would be too much strife over their successors if a lord had as many wives and children as her father.

But it was fun to dream, wasn't it?

8

Proposal

Cathlin did not see the lord immediately the next morning, for he sent the young man who had been with him the night before.

"Master Alfgar, my ladies, I am Corven," he said with a smile. "Lord Varian has asked me to fetch you and see you settled comfortably."

"Thank you," Luned said gravely. "The Lord Varian is well this morning, I trust?" Cathlin wished she had been able to ask that, but it would never do to presume to be so familiar with a lord.

"Quite well, my lady," Corven assured them solemnly, then the planes of his face shifted as he grinned. "Actually, he's drowning in Harvest Fair plans. There's only so much you can delegate. When I left, people were three deep around him with problems only *he* could solve. Will I be an acceptable substitute for this morning?"

He wasn't handsome like Varian, but he was very likable, Cathlin decided, and she grinned back.

Corven was also quite willing to talk about his lord, Cathlin found on the way up to the castle. He walked beside her horse, pointing out things of interest and telling her about the changes Varian had made in the last three years.

Their arrival at the castle made them the target of all eyes. Many people watched them cross the outer bailey, for Corven's tale of the young heroine who had captured the lord's attention had already made the rounds.

Corven turned them over to a plump, motherly lady he introduced as Mistress Margretha, the castle's chatelaine.

"Welcome, welcome, Master Trader, and the ladies, too, oh my yes, I see what that rascal Corven meant about how pretty the young lady is to catch our Varian's eye. Now if you'll just follow me, I'll show you to your rooms, don't just stand there, you lazy creatures, pick up these things and take them to the guest wing, surely you can't expect the ladies to carry such heavy stuff." (This last was to the servants, Cathlin assumed after a startled moment.) "I've put you in connecting rooms so you'll feel more comfortable about someone being nearby, and of course if you need anything, just ring for the chambermaid, she'll tend to all your needs, and if she can't, have someone send for me, although I don't know why I have to do everything with a whole castle full of worthless servants who have nothing better to do than stand around eating their heads off at poor Lord Varian's expense, even though I try and try . . ."

The servants following her rolled their eyes and gave Cathlin a look of suffering amusement. Evidently, Mistress Margretha drowned everybody in words.

The room she showed Cathlin was small but well appointed. The bed was curtained and canopied to make a snug sleeping space, and warm down-filled coverlets invited one to pounce in the middle of them just to sink into the feathers. A fire was laid but not lit on the hearth (which was not big enough to roast an ox, contrary to rumor—a rabbit, perhaps, or a suckling pig, but certainly not an ox). Tapestries decorated the walls, and heavy curtains hung at the glassed-in windows. The room for Alfgar and her stepmother was similar but a little larger.

One of the servant girls murmured something about helping them unpack, but Luned shooed her away briskly. "We're not helpless, child. There isn't so much here that we can't unpack ourselves."

Cathlin was delighted to find that Lord Varian himself came to meet them after they unpacked. He gave her a slow smile and a slight bow. "Welcome to my home, my lady. Does everything meet with your approval?"

"Oh, yes, Lord Varian. The rooms are beautiful."

"Not nearly so beautiful as the lady inhabiting them."

Luned interrupted smoothly, "My lord, it is not customary among our people for men to make such extravagant compliments to unmarried girls."

Varian's smile to her was more than a little rueful. "I thank you, Mistress Luned. Is it permissible to make extravagant compliments to married women, or will your husband chastise me in turn?"

Alfgar laughed uncomfortably. "My lord, our women have ready enough tongues to do their own chastising. If you do not mind, I would like to look in on the Fair now. My brother is usually quite competent, but there is no hand like the master's, you know."

"Of course, Master Alfgar. And if you do not mind, I will escort the ladies so that you will be free to tend to your business dealings."

That sounded suspiciously more like an order than a favor or even a request, but Alfgar was not about to jeopardize a possible good deal by refusing something so reasonably in line with his own plans.

Cathlin remembered that Fair as one of the most golden afternoons of her life. Luned's presence was no damper on the attentions Lord Varian paid to her, although he gave her no more "extravagant compliments." They visited every booth at the Fair, the ones where games were played as well as those that sold goods. The baron seemed to enjoy himself as well, with an almost child-like pleasure in playing silly games.

One game in particular amused both of them. One had to thump a mallet down on one end of a small seesaw, propelling a toy frog (stuffed with beans for weight) into one of several half-barrels painted blue to represent ponds. Only the smallest center barrel was a winning jump, however. Cathlin burst into stifled giggles when Lord Varian's first mighty try sent the frog flying not toward the barrel, but back into his face. Luned's frogs never went far enough, for not wanting frogs in her face, she was too timid to whack very hard. When it came to her turn, Cathlin used her first two frogs to judge angle and velocity, then gave her third frog a carefully judged tap. It flew straight and almost true for the center pond, but not quite far enough. It struck the edge of the barrel with its belly and hung half in, half out.

"An' th' lovely lass is a winner!" shouted the booth's owner, with a wary eye to his lord. "What will ye take for yer prize, m'lady? This pretty pendant for yer throat, or these bright ribbons for yer hair? Or . . . I canna offer ye a prince, fair princess, but ye can have yer choice 'f any of th' frogs!"

Luned and Cathlin both burst into giggles at that. "How can I resist, after that?" Cathlin laughed. "If you please—the green one there. Where do you get the fabrics for them?" The frogs that did the jumping were sturdy woolen homespun dyed in bright colors, but a few that sat on the prize shelf were luxury fabrics—brocades, satins, even one or two of velvet. The green brocade one had the most knowing expression in his bulging button eyes.

"M' mother's a seamstress, m'lady. These're scraps left from th' clothes th' merchants have her make for them."

"Thank you," Cathlin said as she accepted her frog. As they walked down toward the next booth, she commented, "Your merchants must be very well-to-do, to wear such fine clothes."

"They tell me they are practically starving," Varian grinned. "Especially at tax time. I'm a cruel, evil lord

who makes them pay their fair share, you see." He
leered at her and twisted his mustache in the stylized
manner of a traveling player portraying a heartless vil-
lain. "Best you be wary of me, fair maiden."

"Help, help!" Cathlin squealed through her laughter.
"I'm being attacked by a ruthless fiend! Defend me, fair
prince!" She raised her frog and brandished him in Varian's face. Luned joined in, clasping her hands over her
heart and declaiming, "Will no one save my poor
daughter?" None of them noticed the occupant of the
next booth until she spoke in their ears.

"Tell your fortunes, children." The voice was low
and cracked, the owner small and bent and wrinkled, the
very image of the half-witch that a fortune-teller should
be. She wore a bright red skirt and presumably an
equally bright blouse, unseen for the number of gaudy
scarves and shawls and beads that covered her upper
body. "Oh, m'lord, be kind to old Granny. Let her tell
the ladies' fortunes, yes, yours and the other young
man's, too. Old Granny knows everything."

Corven had turned up out of nowhere to stand in Varian's shadow. Cathlin hadn't noticed him; perhaps the
old woman had sharper eyes than anybody realized.

"Come along, young man. Not afraid old Granny will
try to carry you away, are you?" Corven looked behind
himself, perhaps hoping that the fortune-teller was
speaking to someone else, then laughed sheepishly and
dug a copper two-piece out of his pocket. The old
woman took his hand and peered closely at his palm.
After a few moment's scrutiny, she let out a cackling
laugh.

"Oh, such a life, my lad. So many lasses in your
palm, those in the past and those yet to come. Ah, but
love's there, too, love unlooked for. Soon, laddie, soon.
After that, another love will lead you into danger. Have
a care when you ride out on that love's trail."

She released his hand and reached for Varian's. He
did not let her take it, but stepped back with a laugh. "I
could have told Corven that, Granny. If there's a bed in

the barony he hasn't been in, it's not for want of trying.''

She gave him a sharp look from black eyes so hidden in wrinkles that they were no more than bright beads. ''Dinna make fun of one man's life, m'lord, until your own is laid open for all to read.''

Varian's posture changed from relaxed indolence to the alert stance of a swordsman as she spoke, and a ripple of anger flowed across his face. ''Have a care, old woman, and remember who I am.''

''Who you are, m'lord, or who you think you are?'' Their eyes met and locked. The fortune-teller broke that stare first. ''Now you, mistress. Yes, you,'' she beckoned to Luned. ''Oooh, now, child. You fear that you are barren, and you have grieved, yes, many nights. But here in your palm I see many children, two, three, four. And see here, the one that you carry now.''

''But—I'm not even sure myself, how can you—?'' Luned gasped.

''Old Granny knows everything!'' the old woman cackled as she took Luned's coppers. ''Now you, pretty miss.''

Cathlin extended her hand as she sat down. Granny grabbed it, and gave a small shriek. ''Ahh, now you, child, must come inside for your fortune. This is not something for all the world to hear, no indeed.'' She tugged the girl to her feet and toward the tent that stood behind her booth. Cathlin cast a puzzled, helpless glance at Varian, who looked angry. He took a step toward her, but the old woman stamped her foot at him. ''She'll not come to harm, my fine lord. What, d'you think I can magic her away out of my tent?''

The gaudy, stuffy interior of the tent exactly fitted Cathlin's idea of a fortune-teller's dwelling, just as the old woman's appearance did. She took a seat as Granny bade her, and held out her hand again.

''Do not be deceived by appearances, Cathlin.''

The voice was not that of the old woman, but deep and soft. Cathlin jerked her gaze away from her own palm to the face of the woman who sat on the other side of the table. The wrinkles and bright, beady bird-eyes were gone. A Lady sat there, gazing at her out of clear blue eyes, a Lady of no more than middle years, with a face that Cathlin had seen only once before. At her dedication to Byela, the face of the priestess had changed in just this way as the goddess possessed her.

"No, My child, do not speak. Listen and learn. We do indeed come to Our people when We have need of them, just as We may choose to help Our own when you call Us. Know you that whatever happens, I will indeed be with you.

"But know you also that nothing is fixed, that every choice you make may lead to another, totally unforeseeable. This is as true for the gods as it is for you. You have looked for love, child, and love may indeed come to you. If you choose to accept it, it may lead you to trials harder than you can imagine. Trust the man you love in that dark time.

"Remember also, Cathlin whose name means innocence, that names have power, power to heal and power to harm. I am permitted to tell you a name now. Guard it well, and do not use it until the right time. *Khahara-fael.*"

Cathlin had never heard that name before. It had the ominous grumble of thunder behind it, and the hidden power of a storm. Speechlessly she stared at the Lady, and as she watched, the goddess shriveled and shrank back into the old fortune-teller.

Granny blinked at her and extended a shaking hand. "Did Granny's fortune please you, pretty lady?"

Cathlin choked back a gasp of surprise that the old woman expected to be paid for just such a fortune as she had told to Luned. Perhaps she didn't know that she had been the mouth of the Lady Herself. "Y-yes, of course. Here."

Lord Varian looked relieved when she made her appearance. "You seem disturbed, my lady. Are you all right?"

She thought she had hidden her feelings better than

that. "I'm . . . the sun is very bright after the dark tent, Lord Varian. It's made me a little dizzy."

His concern at her words was very gratifying. He led her gently to an outdoor table at a nearby inn and sent the serving wench scurrying for cold drinks. The drink's appearance startled her almost as much as the Lady's; there was *ice* floating in the pewter mug. The lord laughed at her look of surprise. "I expect that's the last of the innkeeper's stock, my lady. We get plenty of ice in the winter and store some for summer use." He went on to explain how the ice was cut from ponds in the early winter, then stored in deep cellars with insulating blankets of sawdust.

The rest of the afternoon passed in a dizzy whirl for Cathlin, still wondering why the Lady had come to her. And yet, even through her distraction, she was aware as never before of the man who walked by her side. Varian. She wanted to say it over and over, just to hear it. She had been infatuated with him as a twelve-year-old; now she fought hard to lay that old infatuation to rest. He was being so nice to show her honor. Anything else must be her imagination. Surely it was her imagination that he looked at her with anything other than the polite interest of a lord to a commoner. And yet . . .

Over and over, she noticed how he seemed to be loved by his people. They smiled and nodded when he passed them, and once a small grubby child of indeterminate gender ran up to him with a cluster of wilted kingsgold flowers clutched in its hand. It stopped and peered shyly up at him from under long eyelashes, and he stooped and picked the child up.

"What have you got there, little one?" he asked kindly.

"Flowers!" the child said indignantly. (Surely even a dumb grownup ought to be able to see that!)

Cathlin and Luned smothered amused smiles as Varian nodded solemnly. "Of course. I tell you what . . ." and he whispered in the child's ear. It nodded just as solemnly and wiggled loose from his grasp. With all seriousness, the little one made a very creditable bow to Cathlin and intoned, "From the people of Leopard's Gard, m'lady, with our thanks for yer courage."

She took them just as seriously. "Thank you. They're lovely."

As they watched the child run away, Corven murmured in her ear, "They used to be afraid of him, my lady."

Before she could ask what he meant, Lord Varian turned back to her. "I apologize, my ladies. I've kept you out here in the hot sun all afternoon. You will want to rest and bathe before dinner, I'm sure."

"It's been wonderful!" Cathlin smiled up at him. All her awe of him as a lord baron had disappeared, vanished when he showed his gentle side to the child. "I'll remember it all my life."

It must have been her imagination, too, that his face clouded, as if she had said something wrong. He murmured something polite and led the way back to the castle.

"I'll remember it all my life," she said. Poor girl, when all her life is likely to be no more than a few days. She'll know soon enough what sort of monster you are, Varian. Let her have her little pleasures. Varian sat in his own bath and scrubbed viciously, as if he could remove the Dark God that way. *Making an innocent like that into your sacrifice, you bastard.* His self-hatred grew until he had to push it to the back of his mind so that he could shave. Cutting his own throat would not free his people, only following the dictates of his master. He stared broodingly at the razor and fought down the impulse.

Shaved and dressed at last, he put spurs to his conscience and rang for the chamber servant.

The woman smiled at him. She was the oldest of the former slaves, somewhat simple-minded, and he knew that she would not question or disobey his orders. He smiled conspiratorially back.

"I have a job for you, Lella. You are the chamber-maid for the visitors, aren't you?"

"Aye, m'lord."

"Do you think Mistress Cathlin is pretty?"

"Oh aye, m'lord. Sometimes, when I was young, I wished I could be that pretty."

"You're going to think I'm going soft in the head, Lella. I'd . . . like something of hers as a keepsake, to remember her by after she leaves us."

"M'lord? I'm not sure I understand. Ye don't want me to *steal* somethin', do ye?" Her eyes were vaguely troubled.

"Nothing that she'll miss, Lella, and it wouldn't be stealing at all," he coaxed. "Just a few hairs from her brush, so that I can look at them sometimes and picture all that beautiful black hair. You can do it easier than anyone else. Please, will you help me? So I don't have to sneak in there like a village swain trying to court his sweetheart without her father knowing?" He tried to look sheepish.

Lella smiled happily. "Now, Master Varian, are ye sure ye don't mean like a small boy snitchin' spice-bread? Of course I'll help ye."

He shrugged ruefully. "I can't put anything over on an old servant, can I? Thank you, Lella. And please, don't tell anyone. I don't want any silly stories all over the castle that I'm in love with her."

The feast that night was difficult for him. He kept watching Cathlin and trying to force himself to share in her enjoyment. Her modest blushes when he stood and described to the feasters her courage at the inn struck him through to the heart. She was so sweet and innocent; would her courage be help or hardship when he gave her to the Dark One?

When Varian went to his own room later that night, he found on his pillow a dozen long dark hairs tied with a scrap of thread. He stood looking at them, running them through his fingers over and over, while he gathered enough unwilling courage to do as he had been ordered.

The way to the cavern had never been darker or colder. He lit the candles and herbs with a sullen reluctance and said the words that fouled his tongue. The glow of light that preceded the Evil One reflected his own mood: a dark, angry red that rippled at times into glowing blackness.

"The girl is here, the one You wanted. I have some of her hair here," Varian said bluntly when the face appeared.

The Hidden One's scowl reflected Varian's own. "Is this how you address your master, beast-man? When will you learn that you are My slave, My toy to play with as I desire? Give Me My proper title or suffer the punishment of a slave."

Sweat broke out on Varian's forehead as he stood in stubborn silence. He knew what was coming. Pain streaked along his back, as if a silent, invisible slave-whip slashed down on him. Again and again the lash fell until Varian was driven to his knees in torment.

"Well?" The One's face twisted into a sneer.

"Master," the beaten man forced out, and immediately the pain eased somewhat. He knew from past experience that there would be no pain tomorrow, no lash-marks to scar his back. This whip scarred the soul.

"Are you ready to follow My instructions? Or do we need to drag back one of your people next week to play with? A child perhaps, a lovely little thing like the one today with the flowers."

"I am ready, master," he said dully. "Please, master, why this girl?"

The face scowled again. "My enemy thinks She is laying a clever trap with the pretty little slut. She will learn, aye, They all will, that I am cleverer. Now, beast-man, take out your crystal."

Varian yielded. The crystal dissolved when he put it in the stone bowl, leaving the gray claw dark and slimy. He tried not to think as he followed instructions, reading out the words from one of the sorcerous books that Baird

had hidden here in the cavern. Again he gashed his own
finger for blood to empower the spell that would bind
Cathlin to him and make of his crystal a geas charm to
control her. He hated the thought of controlling her,
making her more helpless even than he was himself, but
he had no choice. Sweet and innocent she might be, but
not stupid. He could not say, "Come along my dear, so
that I can give you to Him as a sacrifice," and expect
to be witlessly obeyed.

The last words of the incantation grated through the
silent, listening cavern, and the contents of the bowl coalesced again into the crystal sphere. Three black hairs
now twisted through the swirls of blood and twined
themselves around the claw.

The next morning, he repeated over and over to himself, *There is no other way. You have to, Varian, for
your people. You have to.* He faced his guests with
dread; surely they would see that the smile on his face
as he greeted them was as false as gilded lead; surely
they would know something was wrong and leave with
hurried, polite excuses.

But the merchant, his wife, and his daughter did not
see anything other than the polite friendliness of their
host as they sat down to breakfast. Cathlin gave him a
brilliant smile when he asked if she had spent a comfortable night. "Oh, yes! I've heard all my life about
how much luxury the lords live in, but I never imagined
that it would be such a snug, homelike luxury."

"We live very simple lives here, my lady Cathlin,
compared to the great lords like my uncle. But as you
are so content, please feel at home and stay as long as
you like."

Alfgar smiled more easily than Varian had seen before. "You will spoil us, my lord, for life on the road.
Inns and wagons will be a disappointment after this."

"I have some idea of your road-life, Master Alfgar,
and I hardly think a few days will make you soft. Some
years ago, I traveled for a day or two with a train of
your people, and I was most impressed with the vitality

of everybody, especially the ladies of the train.'' He smiled ruefully. ''I was too young, I think, to appreciate them fully, since at the time I thought most females were a nuisance. And I see that *that* boyish opinion was wrong. I was impressed by Mistress Cathlin's courage at the inn, and now that I have seen more of you, my lady, my admiration for you is growing.''

The Trader cleared his throat. ''This is very kind of you, my lord. We know our ways are not yours, but it is a good thing, I think, when a liking for each other can be rewarding for both parties.''

Varian smiled slowly. ''Perhaps liking is not the word I want, sir.'' His eyes moved from Alfgar to Cathlin, and she felt something inside her turn over. Her heart, perhaps, although it felt more like her stomach.

''My lady Cathlin, I am a plain man. They tried to teach me courtly speech and failed miserably. But for you, I will try.'' He held out his hand, and she slowly put hers into it. His warm, rough fingers closed over hers, and they felt so comfortable, so right. ''My lady, do you believe in love at first sight?''

Cathlin stared at him in openmouthed astonishment. He couldn't be saying that he loved her! And yet his green eyes were steady on hers, looking so wistful and hopeful that her heart went out to him. She heard the words come out of her mouth almost without willing them. ''Yes. I thought I had it happen to me when I was younger.''

''Then you understand what I mean when I say you have been in my thoughts since I first saw you at the inn. I never hoped to find a woman with your courage and spirit and beauty. I . . .'' His voice failed him, as the self-hatred for what he was about to do almost overwhelmed him. She was everything he had said. Why couldn't the Nameless One want some whining petulant shrew that he would be glad to be rid of? He swallowed hard and focused on the geas charm. ''Cathlin, will you marry me?''

''Yes. I will.'' Cathlin didn't know why she had said

the words she heard coming out of her mouth, but once they were said, she found that she meant them. For years, she had cherished the image of the handsome young warrior lord. Now she had a better idea of the man to put with the face, and she wanted him as she had never wanted anything else. This was a man worth fighting for.

"My lord," Alfgar gasped. "You—you can't be serious. *My* daughter? A lord doesn't choose his bride from commoners like us! I couldn't possibly dower her appropriately."

Cathlin fought down an insane desire to giggle. She could just see the look on this lord's—Varian's—face if Father presented him with the traditional wagon and six horses!

"I am quite serious, Master Alfgar. Nor do I expect a dowry. This lady is dower enough in herself, a gift more precious than anything you could give me." Varian paused as he considered what would best win over the Trader. "I don't want to sound mercenary, sir, but you and your clan will not find me ungenerous in return."

Alfgar harrumphed into his mustache. "Luned, take Cathlin and run along now. Now, now, child," he added hastily at Cathlin's indignant expression, "I've not said 'no' to your, ah, impetuous suitor. I know your stubborn independent ways. Lord Varian has asked and you've accepted; if I said 'no' now, you'd go your way with or without my blessing.

"But you don't want to sit here and be bargained over like a string of beads. Please, child, run along. Go visit your horses. I'm sure Silverbell is wondering where you are."

Varian still had her hand captive in his. Cathlin wondered if she imagined his reluctance to let her go, for his thumb gently brushed her knuckles and he squeezed her hand a little tighter before he released her.

"Please, my lady. You would enjoy the gardens, I'm

sure, or someone can show you the way to the stables if you wish to check on your horse.''

Luned, who had been watching all this with various amounts of astonishment, annoyance, and pleasure of her own, pulled at her stepdaughter's other hand. ''Oh, come on, Cat. You know how your father is at his bargaining. Lord Varian will hardly have a copper griffin to his name once Alfgar's done with him.'' She swept Varian an impish curtsy and tugged a bemused Cathlin away.

Marriage

Cathlin had never imagined that a marriage could be arranged with such speed. Among her people, there was much bargaining and exchange of gifts at the betrothal and for many weeks afterward. She was admiring the gardens with their fragrant herb borders when Mistress Margretha bustled up to her and overwhelmed her with a breathless flood of pleasure, good wishes, advice, and wedding preparations. The ceremony was to be only two days from now, just long enough for Varian to send a message to his kinsman Earl Duer and give that lord time to arrange his coming.

There was hardly time for Cathlin to catch her breath after that, for Margretha swept her away and threw her into a maelstrom of busyness. The wedding gown itself was unearthed from the castle coffers, and the seamstresses began to alter the lovely blue silk to fit her. Her preferences and customs were asked for the wedding feast, and she was moved in state from the small bedroom into one of the larger suites that would represent her father's home.

That evening, she was led with ceremony to the dais for her betrothal. In front of the population of the castle, Varian formally asked leave of her father to take her for his promised wife. In symbol of that promise, he slid a ring onto her finger, a ring that was a smaller duplicate of his own signet ring.

There was a soft spattering of applause and muted praise; then the people of the household, one by one, came to bow or curtsy before her. Varian murmured their names, and with his help, she sorted out at least the major figures: Migael the steward, who walked with a bad limp; Margretha who she already knew, of course; Master Evan, whose wide smile didn't match his grizzled bearlike surface; and Jaelle the kitchen mistress, who made the sketchiest curtsy of all and then hurried back to her domain to supervise the cooking for the upcoming wedding feast. Most of the other names ran together until she despaired of sorting them all out, although there were no more people here than in her own clan-village.

The next day was even busier. Cathlin saw Varian for only a few minutes at breakfast, for that morning the guests (most of them Cathlin's own Free Trader kin, already there for the Harvest Fair) began to arrive and tradition demanded that he must greet them all personally. She had little time to miss him, however, for her day was just as full. The newly altered wedding gown met her eyes when Margretha escorted her back to her room. It needed a few minor changes still, so Cathlin allowed them to help her put it on and stood trying not to squirm while they pinned and chattered and giggled.

Tradition ruled the rest of the day. The groom must wear a shirt embroidered and sewn by his bride, so they brought out one that was nearly finished and she spent two finger-pricking hours stitching tiny pearls over the collar and cuffs and hemming the bottom. The bride must bake a loaf of bread for her new husband, so next they carried her off to the kitchens and she took out her nervousness on an innocent batch of bread dough. When it was pummeled sufficiently and put to rise, she was ravenously hungry and more than happy to sit in the warm kitchen and share their noon meal of bread and cheese.

Luned caught up with her there and accompanied her with the unmarried maidens of the castle to gather flowers and greenery to decorate the great hall.

Flowers were scarce this time of year, for only the hardiest survived the frosts that came early to the mountains. Roses were traditional, but only one wrinkled blossom held stubbornly to the sheltered bushes. Calendulas still bloomed, but she didn't like their acrid scent. After consultation with Margretha and Luned, Cathlin decided to use evergreens for table and hall decorations, hung with tiny apples and studded with dried wisps of a tiny white flower Margretha called swan's down. Amid these decisions, she mourned for her mother again, for one of their last happy discussions had been about the flowers for Luned's wedding. Allara had not lived to see the wedding of her youngest daughter. Luned herself was sweet, but she was not much older than Cathlin and felt more like a sister than a mother.

The bride-to-be was sucking a finger pricked by the holly when a young boy trotted into the room and bowed before her. "My lady, the lord requests your presence to greet his kinsmen."

This simple request created a stir that seemed all out of proportion to Cathlin. Before she knew what was happening, it seemed everybody in the room descended on her to get her presentable. Margretha whirled her around to untie her apron strings, someone else tweaked a bit of leaf out of her hair and hurriedly smoothed it, two girls brushed out her skirt, and the boy was sent running for her embroidered slippers to replace her sturdy boots. He returned with both slippers and a silky white tabard set with gold beads and tiny gold bells. As Margretha dropped it over her head and belted it in front with a blue sash, she wondered what sort of state did these lords keep, then, that she couldn't appear as she was?

Varian smiled in reassurance when she made her shy appearance. He, too, had changed from the plain shirt he had worn at breakfast to one of deep blue, embroidered with gold at collar and cuffs. "You have time to catch your breath. The watchman saw them on the road, and they won't be here for a few minutes." He took her hand and led her to the steps outside the door to the great hall. "Don't be nervous, my dear. Duer isn't nearly as fierce as he looks."

The man who rode into the courtyard at the head of a veritable procession certainly looked fierce enough. His great brush of mustaches would have overwhelmed a smaller man, and the roar of delight with which he greeted Varian was entirely in keeping with his bearlike appearance.

Nor did Lord Duer bother with formal bows and greetings. Instead, he swept his nephew into a bearish hug while he pounded him on the back. "So you've finally found a bride, lad!"

"Aye, Uncle. And if you pound her the way you've just pounded me, there'll be nothing left of her!"

The earl laughed and turned to Cathlin, moderating his voice to a bearable rumble. "I'd not do that to you, child. Only to this boneheaded nephew of mine. And now that I've had a look at you, I can see why he waited so long. Welcome to the family." He held out both great paws and she shyly put her hands into them. "Ah, my Gavriveda will be sorry to miss this wedding, but our son Kieran's wife is too close to birthing our first grandchild to make the trip, and she'll not leave her. She sends her best wishes and this gift for you, Lady Cathlin."

He beckoned to a servant who handed him a box most carefully carried. "My dear sister should be here to do this for her son's bride, but I'm afraid you'll have to accept me in her place."

Cathlin opened the box as painstakingly as she could and fought back the tears that sprang to her eyes. Inside, carefully crafted of silk, was a bride's coronet of white roses.

• • •

The wedding day dawned cold and clear. Varian found that already he missed seeing Cathlin's face at breakfast, for on her wedding day a bride could not be seen by any man until her husband brushed back her veil. *And if I miss her now, what will it do to me when she is gone? Damn You, is this what You wanted to happen? For me to fall in love with Your sacrifice?* He fought the idea down, pushing it into the back of his mind. There was this day to get through first. Let the poor girl have her day, a wedding that she couldn't have dreamed of. She deserved that pleasure, at least.

Cathlin wasn't sure if the day was a pleasure or not. She could eat little of the breakfast they served her, even though Luned and the other ladies of the castle urged her to at least eat the eggs, the necessary tokens of fertility.

The ritual bath was not embarrassing for her, at least. Bathing with a room full of sisters, half-sisters, and cousins cured one of body shyness at a young age. She had a tub all to herself, and reveled in the luxury of rose-scented soap and having her hair washed, rather than wrestling with the length of it alone.

She blushed, though, when someone frankly admired her body and remarked that she would have no trouble bearing or suckling children. Mildly bawdy jokes flew around the room in reference as to how one got those children. It was a little embarrassing, too, to let the bathmaid towel her dry instead of drying herself.

"Oh, dear," she heard the girl murmur. She looked down in puzzlement and the bathmaid pointed tactfully to a pink smear on the clean towel.

So that explained the twinges in her belly that she had been putting to nervousness. There was a moment of discreet silence, then several of the ladies sighed wryly. "There's never a good time for that, is there?" said Luned. "Your husband will just have to learn to wait, my dear. They all do."

"Varian's a good man, he'll not be angry with you,

my lady,'' reassured Margretha as she sent a girl for clean cloths.

"This is a minor mischance that is not going to spoil my wedding,'' Cathlin declared firmly, even though her belly quivered at the thought of having to tell a man who was still a stranger that she couldn't bed him just now, and why. She hoped that Margretha was right, and he wouldn't be upset, for she was annoyed enough herself at having to postpone her wedding night.

They sat her in front of the fire to comb her hair dry. It would be worn loose all day today to symbolize her maidenhood, and several ladies made mention of its silky, raven sheen. She hadn't realized what a nuisance it would be, for normally she kept it braided or bundled into a net, and several times managed to pull it by sitting on a strand.

Cathlin held Luned's hand for one of the ceremonies, for it was not one of her people's and she wasn't sure how much it would hurt. The healer of the castle rubbed a stinging cold liquid on her earlobes, then took a heavy needle and pierced her ears. The tiny gold studs she put in would be there only a matter of hours, for they soon would be replaced by the gold rings of her new rank. It didn't hurt, really, much less than the tattooing at her dedication to Byela, but for days afterward, Cathlin would be aware that she had ears and had never really noticed them before.

At last it was time to put her into her wedding dress. Mistress Margretha, as both the highest ranked lady and substitute for the mother of the groom, laced it up the back with a silver cord, molding it so snugly to her body that nothing was left to the imagination. With two pins of pearls and sapphires, they fastened to her shoulders a white silk train, embroidered with blue and gold and white flowers, vines, and ears of grain. Two little girls, chosen by lot from the castle's children, were assigned to keep it flowing straight and warn away any clumsy feet that might step on it.

They put the lace veil over her head, hiding her from

the gaze of evil spirits, with the rose coronet to hold it
in place, and she was ready.

Musicians played as they led her in ceremony to her
new home's great hall; people called out good wishes
as she passed between them, and showered her with
flower petals. She tried to maintain a serene face and
steady walk, but her hands shook and she wondered
frantically what she was doing here, marrying a complete stranger.

Varian knew why he was marrying her, and when she
appeared in the doorway, looking so small and alone, so
beautiful and courageous and gentle, he wanted to stop
it all and send her back to her father, away from the
harm he would do her. *"One girl, or many, beast-man.
Your choice,"* whispered the voice in his head.

He held out his hand as she advanced, and her eyes
behind the veil were steady and serene and loving when
she looked at him. His voice shook as he said the ritual
words that would make her his wife, as he promised to
cherish and protect her, for he knew that they were vows
he would not keep, and he was forsworn at the instant
of their making.

Her voice was strong and clear and untroubled as she
vowed in turn to be a faithful and loving wife, to tend
hearth and home and children for her husband.

Varian moved the betrothal ring from the forefinger
of her right hand to the ring finger of her left, lifted her
veil, and they were married.

This would have ended the ceremony for commoners,
but for them one thing more was needed. He led her
down the length of the great hall, outside, and up onto
a temporary platform. In the great courtyard, not a fingerwidth of stone cobbling was visible. People crowded
shoulder to shoulder, sat on the ramparts, and spilled out
the gate, with small children held in their parents' arms
or riding their necks. Cathlin felt shy of all the eyes on
her and clung tightly to Varian's hand.

"My people!" he said, not shouting but booming the
words out in a carrying voice. "I give you your new

lady.'' Not a sound came from the courtyard, not even the sound of their breathing, except for a baby's cry, quickly hushed. Cathlin's hands fumbled with the gold posts in her ears, and he waited patiently, smiling down at her. The gold rings were cold and felt heavy when he slipped them into her ears. He smiled again and whispered, ''Now, step forward to the rail.''

She did so, and as her hands touched it, a swelling roar of cheers burst from the crowd, so loud and strong that the impact on her ears was almost that of a physical blow. She hadn't known humans could make that much noise with throats alone. Varian's hand on her shoulder made her jump; his lips moved, but his words were lost in the surge of noise. She didn't expect it, then, when he pulled her into his arms and kissed her.

She had been kissed before, but none of the shy, courting, almost childish kisses from other boys had been like this. His mouth was warm and demanding and tasted of sweetened wine, the smoothness of his lower lip in sharp contrast with the tickling dark mustache. His tongue brushed her lips until she opened her mouth for him, and the tingle that spread through her body when their tongues met was like nothing she had ever felt before. She couldn't tell if the crowd was still cheering or if the roaring was only in her ears.

Varian released her and stood looking down at her, shaken to his soul. He wanted her as he had never wanted any woman before, wanted to hold and cherish not only her body but her heart and soul. None of them were his, nor could ever be. His master had already claimed her.

The wedding feast was long and tiring, for it seemed that everybody in the barony had brought food or gifts to be ceremonially presented, or wished to perform something in honor of their new baroness. She praised and admired and smiled until her face hurt. All through the hours she clung to the memory of his face when he kissed her as she wanted to cling to his hand. She had little time to wonder at the shadow in his eyes.

Suddenly there was a shout, and a group of young people, men and women, rushed the high table. Instantly, Varian was out of his chair and scooped Cathlin into his arms while Corven drew his sword. Shouts and laughter and cheers rang like sword blades as the newlyweds retreated down the hall and up the stairs to the bride's chamber, their pursuers not at all frightened by the mock battle Corven waged to protect his lord and lady. Someone started a bawdy song traditional to weddings, and everyone joined in the thumping verses.

Cathlin was flushed and laughing when Varian dropped her on the bed, and everyone who could crowded into the room. Now it was the turn of the ladies to pursue and threaten the young men until the last of them was out, even the bridegroom.

The women stripped her wedding gown off to the thunder of even bawdier songs coming through the door, and dropped a sheer silk bedgown over her head. Oddly, this made her feel more exposed and naked than plain bare skin, for she was intensely aware of the way it covered her body without hiding it. Cathlin had never felt silk next to her skin before, for plain linen was appropriate for one of a merchant's many daughters. She shivered and they bundled her into the great bed, but she was not allowed to pull the covers up to her chin. She must wait for her husband to join her.

The opening of the door for the women to exit was the signal for more cheers and shouted advice for the entering bridegroom. The young men had been working their way with their lord as well, for Varian's shirt and boots were gone and his breeches clung precariously to his hips, half the buttons undone or missing. He struggled to close the heavy door and threatened to lop off any hands or feet that still remained in the room. The bolt slid closed with a solid thump, although the noise outside did not abate appreciably.

Varian stumbled wearily over to the fire and dropped into one of the chairs, his hands running distractedly through his hair. He pulled the cork on the waiting bottle of wine, poured two goblets, and swallowed half of his own before bringing the second one to Cathlin. She blushed bright pink as his eyes traveled over her body, clearly visible through the transparent gown.

"Are you tired, my lady?" he asked quietly. "I'm sorry, but you'll get no sleep for a while, I'm afraid. They'll keep that racket up for hours. At my cousin's wedding we caroused outside their door all night."

"Only a little. I don't mind. My lord . . ."

"Varian," he corrected with a slight smile. "I know we are strangers yet, but I do want to hear my name on your lips."

"Varian, there is something I must tell you. You can't . . . I can't . . . my woman's flow started this morning." She stared up at him, flustered and embarrassed.

His shoulders slumped, and his eyes closed briefly. *Blessed Byela, thank You! She won't expect me to consummate this marriage, not now.* "Are you afraid I would be angry, Cathlin? I'm not. Waiting won't hurt me."

He was disappointed, she knew, for she had seen his body sag when he sighed. She was sorry, too. The silly bawdy songs and jokes were meant to help a newly wed couple, to leave them blushing and aroused, with half their shyness overcome already. She ached to feel his arms around her again, to run her hands over his muscular body and feel it molded to her own. If his kisses were so intriguing and exciting, how would it feel when he covered her body with his and took her virginity? "I'm sorry, Varian. I want to love you the way a wife should."

He sat on the edge of the bed and leaned down to kiss her gently. "I don't suppose I'm the first man to spend his wedding night alone. My room is through the door there. If you need something, just call me."

Cathlin took his head in her hands and kissed back. "Later, my love. We have all our lives."

Varian slid quietly through the connecting door, and

she frowned after him. He could still have spent more
time with her. But maybe it would be too difficult for
him, seeing her body when he couldn't bed her. She had
heard that a man's arousal could be painful for him if it
was unsatisfied. Cathlin burrowed down into the covers
and thumped the pillow into the shape she preferred.
Outside, they started another bawdy song; maybe a quiet
wedding night next week would be preferable after all!

Varian stood before the cavern altar and stared balefully
at the face of the Dark One. "It's done. The girl is my
bride, and still virgin."

The face smiled unpleasantly. "Very good, beast-
man. I will have you bring her to Me when I am ready."

"I've done Your bidding; now keep Your side of the
bargain!" Varian shouted in angry frustration. "How
many more of my people will You kill until You feel
like sending for the girl?"

"Tsk, tsk. What a way to speak of your bride, boy.
The Lady Cathlin must have a chance to see and be seen
by her people. Would you selfishly deny them that?"
The Nameless One vanished.

He stared after the god in agonized frustration; then,
with a curse, ripped off his clothes, forced the were-
change, and went leaping out into the night.

Justice

The morning after her wedding, Cathlin woke with a start. She could clearly hear a man's laugh, Varian's laugh, and it contented her down to her toes. In a few days he would be in her room, in her bed, and she would hear that laugh close at hand. She slid out of bed, wincing a little as her bare feet touched the cold floor, and pulled on slippers and a thick plush robe that someone had laid out near her fire. She tapped on the connecting door, then opened it and walked through to find that her husband was laughing at the antics of a litter of tiny kittens in the middle of his bed.

"Oh, what darlings!" she exclaimed. "So you didn't sleep alone after all?"

He shook his head and grinned. "I guess not. I found them here when I woke up this morning."

"Gmrf!" said a voice outside the door to the corridor.

Cathlin hesitated as she reached for the prettiest of the kittens; would a servant announce his presence in such a peculiar manner? Varian rolled his eyes and huffed through his mustache, then headed for the door.

"Gmrf!" insisted the voice. "MRGOWGMRF!"

"I hope you realize I'm not your doorman, little sister," he said firmly as he opened the door. "If you hadn't left that horde of ruffians in the middle of my bed, you wouldn't be on the wrong side.''

''MRgrf,'' the big calico cat asserted through a mouthful of feebly wriggling mouse. ''Mrrrf.''

''Oh, no. Not on my bed, you don't. You teach them to hunt on the floor.'' He began to scoop kittens up and deposit them on the floor; Cathlin took that chance to pick up two of the soft, buzzing balls of fluff and cuddle them next to her cheeks. The black one struggled to get down, sticking her with tiny needle-claws, but the orange-and-white one went completely limp in her hands and its purr increased.

The smile she turned on her husband was brilliant. ''He likes me! Look, he thinks he's a baby!'' She turned the kitten on its back and cuddled it in her arms. A smug look spread over its tiny face and its paws drooped languidly as she scratched under its chin.

''Mummmrrrf!'' the mother cat demanded.

''I think she wants to get on with her hunting lesson, my dear, and I don't think you want to watch. I'll send Maggie to help you get dressed and see you at breakfast?''

''Couldn't you help me get dressed, my husband?'' Cathlin asked, smiling flirtatiously.

His smile disappeared. ''Not today, Cathlin. I'll send Maggie to you.'' He left, leaving the door ajar and Cathlin's feelings a little hurt. What was wrong?

At breakfast a little later, she began to think she had imagined the coldness in his eyes, for he was all affable politeness. ''No rest for the weary,'' he said cheerfully as Corven snorted. ''I have to start on the fall circuit of my lands, Cathlin. Do you want to come with me?''

''Circuit?''

''Leopard's Gard is a lot smaller than, say, Sundare or Riaza, but it's several days' ride from one end to the other. Once a quarter, I make the rounds of all the towns and larger villages to check on things and see if there are any problems the local steward or provost can't handle, or any lawbreakers that must be tried. I know there are people in the farther villages that didn't get here to our wedding; I'd like for them to see their new lady. Unless you aren't well enough to ride?''

"The day I'm not well enough to ride, you can bury me," Cathlin said firmly.

"Then do you wish to change for riding? What you have on is very pretty, but it doesn't seem very . . . ah . . . practical?''

She looked down at the old-fashioned morning gown Maggie had unearthed from the castle coffers and insisted was appropriate for a new bride. The flowing sleeves of the silky, dark blue undergown were so long that they covered her hands well past her fingertips and had to be turned back to show the brocade sleeve lining in order for her to eat anything. Her overgown, trimmed in the same red and gold brocade, trailed on the floor to fall in heavy, graceful, wine red folds at her feet. The picture that came to her mind sent her off in a fit of giggles.

"If I add a cloak and manage to climb onto Silverbell's back, how long would it take to arrange everything properly? And then there Silverbell would be, covered with fabric from ears to tail, with my head sticking up in the middle.''

Varian rewarded her with the wicked grin and mischievous green eyes that she already loved to see. "What, no velvet hat with feathers and a jeweled pin?''

She pushed back her chair to stand, then dropped him an impudent curtsy. "I cry your pardon, my husband. I forgot all about the hat with feathers. I will go and fetch it immediately.''

"Please do, my lady. We will be waiting outside the east door, in the inner bailey.''

Although Maggie fussed and fretted that it wasn't proper for a great lady to wear such simple garments, she had to admit to herself that Cathlin was not unattractive in her riding clothes. The high collar of the soft green blouse drew the eye to her delicate jawline and pretty face, framed on one side by the fluffy feathers in her hat and on the other by her sleek black hair, woven into a long, smooth braid that was pulled forward over her shoulder to fall past her waist. Her darker green skirt fell to her ankles in such rich folds that it was difficult to tell that it was split for riding astride. Someone had polished her black boots to the glossiest perfection she had ever seen.

After being guided by a small child to the east door to the inner bailey, she found Varian and Corven waiting. Corven and one of the stablemen were holding Silverbell's bridle, and Varian was holding out his hand for her to sniff, all the time talking to her in a low, soothing voice and stroking her face and neck. Silverbell was sweating and shifting uneasily from foot to foot, although there was nothing Cathlin could see that should alarm her.

Corven, who was the only one in a position to see the door, turned his head and said something quietly to Varian as Cathlin approached.

"There, little one, it will take some time," Varian said in the same soothing voice. "Joss, take her and walk her a bit. Lady Cathlin is here. Much better for riding, my dear." And he smiled at Cathlin as his eyes swept her up and down, pausing only slightly at the hat with feathers.

She tried to look past him at her horse. "Is something wrong with Silverbell? What will take time?"

Varian shrugged slightly. "Horses and dogs don't like me for some reason; I frighten them, so it takes some time for most horses to get used to me. The stablemaster thinks it is the way I smell. I wish I knew that mythical 'horseman's word' that is supposed to make them obey you."

"Not mythical, Varian. Watch." Cathlin beckoned for the stableman to bring Silverbell closer. As the mare tossed her head, the young woman caught her muzzle with both hands, blew into her nostrils, and said a single inaudible word.

Immediately Silverbell's laid-back ears pricked forward and she began lipping contentedly at Cathlin's sleeve.

"That's my girl, that's my baby, see, nothing to frighten you, silly creature." She took a small apple out of her skirt pocket. "Here, Varian, you feed it to her."

He looked doubtful but took the apple from her hand, then blinked in surprise as the gray mare took a step toward him, stretching out her neck to reach for her treat.

Corven laughed softly. "Well done, m'lady. I knew you were more than a pretty face to catch Varian's eye. Magic when you least expect it, hm, Varian? Do you also know a lord's word to make him obey you?" and he winked at her, then ducked in mock terror as Varian pretended to reach for his sword.

They and their entourage of a few horsemen and a baggage wagon did not leave through the town but out the east gate of the castle itself. The road descended gently at first, then dropped in staggering switchbacks across the face of the steep slopes. Cathlin thought that if they were wooded, it would make a wonderfully beautiful place, especially with the frequent streams and standing springs, but only low grass spangled with late wildflowers covered the hillsides. Twice they passed mixed herds of sheep and goats, and the goatherds greeted them with shy waves. Once, too, she saw a group of men scrambling carefully up the slope; every once in a while one would reach for the ground, and she realized that they were pulling up some sort of vegetation. One of the castle guardsmen watched them, not helping with whatever they were doing, just watching.

She tipped her head back to see the castle high on the rocks above them, and thought how strong it looked, like its master, and almost without her willing it, she turned her head to find him watching her.

She shouldn't blush under his steady regard, surely! He was her husband, and he would be seeing much more of her than the avid curiosity on her face.

"Questions, my lady?" he asked genially.

"What are those men doing? It looked like they were pulling something up."

"They were. Tree seedlings, low brush, anything that could grow high enough to be used for cover in an attack. And if you noticed that they didn't look too happy, they're probably not. Remin doesn't let any of them slack." At her quizzical expression, he explained further. "They're being punished for minor crimes. Drunk and disorderly, mainly. They don't do anybody any good just standing there in the pillory, and I've never liked flogging. That can just leave a man meaner and more resentful than ever. This way at least they are doing something useful."

"Oh. That's why it looks so bare around the castle. I missed trees and wondered if something had killed them all."

"Remind me to show you my mother's private garden when we return. There's a weeping willow there Maggie says she planted with her own hands."

They chatted of trees and gardens, among other things, as they rode, and Cathlin discovered that her husband was interested in almost everything. Nothing that could be turned to helping his people was ignored. Farther into the valleys he showed her orchards of tiny trees, and when she frowned in puzzlement, he broke off a small twig for her to smell. Its spicy sweet scent took her straight back to the family warehouses where she had helped take inventory as the wagons were unloaded from their trading ventures.

"Kuta bark? Is that why you have such big pots of kuta tea every morning, even for servants?"

Varian laughed to himself. That was the trader speaking there, scandalized that so expensive a luxury should be dispensed so lavishly. "We don't trade much of it, most of what we get is still collected in the wild. It needs lots of cold and snow for the flavor to develop properly. I guess that's why nobody's ever thought of trying to cultivate it. You know what it brings; if we can meet the demand with orchard-grown bark, think what a market we'll have."

"But still, I'll bet even the king doesn't give kuta to his servants."

"I'd rather give them all a cup daily than have half of them so sick with scurvy by spring they can hardly walk."

Cathlin only nodded, distracted now by the sight of several people at a cluster of cottages. All were armed with bows, men and women alike, and they seemed to be involved in a friendly archery contest, for there was a lot of laughter and chaffing to be heard. "That reminds me," she said to her husband. "I brought my bow, but I haven't had a chance to practice yet. Where in the castle are the butts?"

"Aha, a warrior woman! Are you sure you're safe with her, Varian?" Corven said in a stage whisper.

The baron ostentatiously ignored him. "Master Evan holds practice three times a week. The butts are in the north outer bailey; I'll show you when we get back home. Do Free Traders train all their women as archers? I don't think many ladies have much interest in it."

Cathlin shook her head. "Not usually. When I went to the Sanctuary of Byela, the mother-priestess insisted that some of us girls should have training in it. And once I gained some skill, I found that I liked it." Briefly, she wondered if she should tell him how strongly Mother Illyana had insisted that she learn.

Her husband's attention had wandered, however, for his horse had chosen that moment to decide that it was frightened at the sight of a bird flying in front of it. He brought it swiftly under control, muttering good-natured curses under his breath. "You'll have to teach me that horseman's word, my dear. This idiot creature is determined to have its own way. What were we discussing? Ah, archery. The bow isn't really my weapon, but I'm sure someone will be happy to shoot with you when we return home."

They continued to talk as they rode, although some-

times Cathlin was content to observe the countryside as
they passed. This was not the rolling farmland of her
home, but valleys of rocky fields edged in dry-stone
walls, mostly given over to cattle or sheep. Here and
there in more fertile pockets, grain had grown, harvested
now so that only the golden stubble showed. High, rocky
slopes rimmed the fields, the angle varying from steep
to impossible; not far away, the true cliffs of the Barrier
Mountains loomed over everything. Trees grew in thick,
second-growth forest, mostly evergreens, aspen, and
young oaks, though occasionally an ancient oak thrust
its green-and-russet head above the others. Squirrels
bounced from branch to branch and scolded them as they
passed, and once Varian stopped the entire procession
to show her a flight of swans migrating southward, their
whistling calls oddly clear in the still air.

Late that afternoon, they came to the large walled village of Kendalwood, dominated by the small stone castle
in its center. The few guardsmen manning it and the
steward who welcomed them seemed to expect the visit
of their lord and his entourage, for there was no frantic
scurrying to attend to their needs. All was in readiness,
from the bedchambers to the food.

The next afternoon, the Lord's Court of Justice was
called in the village square; not only the population of
Kendalwood, but that of all the smaller neighboring villages attended. Two heavy chairs had been brought from
the castle and set under a canvas awning. Varian escorted Cathlin with all ceremony to one of them and
presented her as the new baroness to their people. Again,
she blushed at the enthusiastic cheers, which were cut
off only by the brassy squawk of a trumpet opening the
court.

Many of the things brought before the lord were minor disagreements that could have been settled by the
local steward, but it seemed that these people trusted
their lord to deal with them more fairly. Or perhaps,
Cathlin thought, they believed that he had less intimate
knowledge of the details and so could possibly be de-

ceived into making a judgment in opposition to the steward's ruling.

That happened only once, though, in the matter of a boundary dispute, and Varian showed that he had a very good recall for the details of his own lands. He gave a judgment for the defendant and ordered compensation for him for the loss of grazing for his sheep.

After a brief break, more serious things were brought to his attention. A group of men asked for relief from their taxes for the year, for they had suffered a grievous loss. Nearly the entire female population of their tiny village had disappeared the week before. The women and girls had gone on a berrying party and had not returned; the steward had ordered out his men in conjunction with the village peacemen under the local provost, but no sign of them could be found. Only a few trampled berry bushes and a single scrap of cloth caught on the thorns showed that they had struggled against their mysterious captors, but no trail led away from the clearing where the berries grew thickest.

Varian asked many questions, but it appeared that all the things that could have been done were done properly. The grief on the faces of the men was real; this was not an elaborate trick to get out of paying taxes. He willingly gave consent for the tax relief and organized a special guard for the village for the next few months. A few women were persuaded to return to the village to care for the motherless children, but beyond that, there was little anybody could do. As the villagers departed with grief-stricken thanks, the steward cleared his throat. "We have kept the most serious cases for last, Your Excellencies. These are both criminal cases. Bring them out!"

Two men, hands bound behind their backs, were brought from the dungeon cells of the keep where they had been kept awaiting trial. One was a stocky man of a little more than medium height; he fought against the bonds and had to be held by the provost's men. The other was very young, perhaps no more than sixteen. He stood quietly and held his head proudly. The stocky man was brought before Varian first.

"The first one of these, my lord, is an outlaw. He was captured when a train of Free Traders was attacked, and one was badly injured. This man was left behind by the band, wounded slightly and unable to run because one of the Traders had her horse standing on his hand." This brought malicious chuckles from the assembled crowd.

"Did the Trader die?" Varian asked.

"No, my lord. His arm was badly slashed and the healers say he will have little use from it. The Traders have gone on their way, but they have left a sworn deposition."

"Were the bandits pursued? Where did this attack take place?"

"On the pass between Wayland and Bradby, where the road narrows and there are rocks and trees to cover an ambush. The Traders captured this man and reported the attack when they came into Bradby, and the village peacemen brought me the reports," said the provost. "I raised a hunt, and we flushed out a band of about a dozen. Five more were killed and the others have apparently fled; there have been no more attacks. The dead outlaws were displayed in both Wayland and Bradby, as the law requires. No one came forth to identify them."

"Baltair, make a note about that pass, it should be cleared. Have those two villages who were squabbling about goats do it. Provost, has this man given you any information about the outlaw band?"

"Nothing, my lord. He refuses to give even his name. Do I have your permission to put him to the torture?" The provost's voice held an edge of eagerness, and Cathlin felt slightly squeamish.

Varian frowned but was clearly considering the idea. "When was this attack? You say there have been no further raids by these same outlaws?"

"This was several weeks ago, the fifth day of Yellowgrain. It is true, they have not been seen since," the provost assured him.

"No torture, then. It seems likely that they have changed their base of operations. Torture will not reveal information this man does not know. Have it cried to the shire that if any more attacks take place, I am to be informed immediately so that I can deal with it."

Varian stood up and, in a voice calculated to carry to all the crowd, commanded, "Bring the man forward. You, who have chosen to remain a nameless bandit, are you ready to defend yourself before you hear my ruling?"

The outlaw, surly and silent, refused to meet Varian's eyes and stared sullenly past him. When it was clear that there would be no reply, Varian continued with the long-established ritual of the trial. "Are there any here that would speak for this man?"

Again there was silence.

Varian spoke again. "It does not matter that neither the injured party nor the accused is one of my people. Trade with the neighboring lands is the lifeblood of this barony. Any who would prey on it harms, therefore, both my people and my lands. If the Trader had died, you, outlaw, would have been chained to a stake in the middle of the village square, wounded in the same way, and left hanging there until you died. As he lives, hear you my judgment now.

"Tomorrow, you will be mercifully hanged at the neighboring crossroads, and your body left there as a warning to others who would seek to harm my people. So it is judged, so let it be done!"

The bandit was dragged away, and the young man for the next case was brought forward. He walked without compulsion to stand in front of Varian, meeting his lord's eyes squarely and without defiance.

"This, Your Lordship, is a clear case of murder. This young man challenged his victim in public and stabbed him to death."

"Are there witnesses, Provost? Murder is not usually a public spectacle."

"There are many, my lord. The victim, one Traherne,

was standing with a group of his friends in the village square when this one, Leonarel, came at him with a dagger. They fought, and Traherne was killed."

"Call the witnesses," Varian ordered.

The first, a weedy, pimply young man, was clearly afraid of his lord. He refused to meet Varian's eyes and muttered to the ground about two feet in front of him, "Well, m'lord, we was all jus' standin' an' talkin' an' Leonarel ran up an' hollered, 'I'll kill ye for that, ye boghart,' an' they fought an' he killed him."

Other witnesses agreed in the general details, arguing only about whether Leonarel had said "boghart" or "bastard."

"Leonarel, you have been accused of the crime of murder, deliberate and unprovoked. Do you have anything to say in your own defense?"

"No, my lord," said Leonarel clearly, and clamped his mouth shut.

"Nothing?" asked Varian skeptically. "No reason, you just felt like killing him?"

"Many people felt like killing him, my lord. He was a braggart and a vicious bully. My reasons are my own, and I will not reveal them."

The steward, standing behind Varian, gave an annoyed huff through his mustaches. "The man is dead, my lord, and the boy admits it. What further do you need to pass judgment?"

Cathlin, sitting silently and listening, thought, *Why is he trying to hurry this? What reason does he have for wanting the boy dead? Because murder in one of his villages looks bad, and "Well, my lord, here's the murderer, all nice and neat and tidy" ends it?* She resolved to speak to Varian as soon as she could.

Varian continued grimly, "Are there any here that would speak for this man?"

For a breathless moment, there was silence. Then a stir in the crowd became a young woman pushing forcefully through to stand in front of the lord and lady. The prisoner made a convulsive movement toward her and cried, "Leonadra, don't!" He was restrained, none too gently, by his guards.

The girl threw him a swift, compassionate glance and then curtsied reverently to Varian. "My lord," she said, "I come to ye for justice. I know why my brother killed Traherne. I—he—please, my lord, my lady, may I tell ye in private?"

Varian shook his head, regretfully, Cathlin thought. His voice was gentle but firm as he said, "No, Leonadra. Your brother has been accused in public, and he must be defended in public."

For a moment, the girl looked as if she would cry, then she visibly straightened her body and her chin took on a firmness very reminiscent of her brother's. "Leonarel killed him because he raped me," she stated clearly.

A murmur ran through the crowd and the pimply young man protested loudly, "She be lyin', m'lord. Traherne said as how she wanted it, she was askin' for it." Leonadra flinched as though he had slapped her.

Cathlin quickly touched Varian on the arm and whispered, "Please, my husband, may I ask them some questions? That poor girl is afraid of either you or the steward and might be more inclined to tell me the truth." He looked at her curiously for a minute and then gestured that she was to proceed.

She thought rapidly, then said clearly, "You, boy, did Traherne say how Leonadra was 'asking for it'?"

The boy didn't answer but looked indignantly at Varian. Why should he answer an impertinent woman, even if she was the lady?

Varian fixed him with a cold, steely stare and said in a voice that held deliberate menace, "You, boy—all of you—" and his eyes traveled through the crowd, "will answer my Lady Cathlin's questions as you would my own. Is that clear?"

Pimples blanched. "Aye, m'lord!" he answered, and the assemblage quickly echoed him.

"Fear has its uses, my dear," Varian said in a voice

meant only for Cathlin's ears. He raised it when he added, "Continue, my lady."

"Well, boy?" she asked.

"M'lady, he—I heard him say that she was jus' too prissy an' standoffish, that her mother taught her to pretend she din't want it, so's she could lead a man around by th' balls, beggin' yer pardon, ma'am, but ye said—"

Cathlin cut him off angrily. "So when a girl ignores or repels a man, she really wants him to force his attentions on her, to rape her, is that what you are saying?"

"No, m'lady," he muttered, and looked at the ground. "But it's still jus' her word, bein' that he's dead an' can't defend hisself." There was an ugly mutter of assent from the people.

She considered this, then looked back at Leonadra, who had stepped over to stand as close to her brother as she could. "Leonadra, you said Traherne raped you. Afterward, where did you go, what did you do? Did you tell your mother?"

"Our parents are dead, but I went home, my lady. I . . . was so ashamed and embarrassed, I didn't want anyone to know. But I can't let my brother die because I'm embarrassed."

"Leonarel, when your sister came home, did she tell you she had been raped?"

"No, my lady. She jus' cried. But I could see that she was all scratched up an' bruised, an' she was . . . she was bleedin' down there, so I ran for th' midwife."

"Is the midwife here?"

A tall, thin woman came forward. "I am Camiola, the midwife for these villages, my lady, my lord." She did not curtsy, but instead inclined her head slightly. Cathlin thought that this was a woman to trust, and she spared time for a thought that she would wish for such a woman at her childbed.

"Camiola, have you been a midwife long? Have you ever treated a woman who was raped?"

"I have been a midwife twenty, no, twenty-one years,

Your Excellencies, and treated many more women than I would have liked who were raped. Leonadra showed bruises and injuries that are very common in such cases, injuries that a willing woman does not incur." She dropped her voice to a confidential level. "I would spare the poor girl at least some embarrassment, my lady, my lord. Need I go into detail about her injuries?"

"Thank you, no, Camiola," Cathlin answered her in the same tone, and glanced at Varian for his agreement. In a carrying voice, she asked, "Is it your professional opinion, then, that Leonadra was raped?"

"It is, my lady," the midwife replied in a carrying voice of her own. "It is also my fault that the boy went running out in a rage. I was quite angry myself and did not watch what I was saying."

"There is no blame attached to you," Varian said firmly. "Is there any more to be said?"

The crowd was silent, although this afternoon's events would be the subject of juicy gossip for many months.

Varian stood again. "Leonarel, are you prepared to hear my judgment?"

"Aye, my lord."

"By the king's laws, rape is a crime punishable by death. As it seems clear you were punishing the rapist of your sister, you are cleared of the charge of murder.

"In doing so, however, you have committed an equally grave offense: that of usurping the privilege of sentencing and retribution that is mine and mine alone. It is also clear that you are guilty of this crime. The penalty is, by custom, the choice of the lord of the dominion.

"Can you use a sword?"

Leonarel blinked at him and opened his mouth, but was so surprised that no words came out.

"I am giving you a chance to fight for your life, boy," Varian said impatiently. "You have proven yourself as a dagger fighter. Can you use a sword equally well?"

"I . . . have some trainin', m'lord, but no' much," said the young man cautiously, clearly so unsettled by the unexpected question that he slipped back into the mountain dialect.

Varian turned his head sharply and ordered, "Corven, two shields and swords. Evan, clear these people back and give them room. You there, cut his hands free."

"Your Lordship, do you think this is wise? The boy is a killer. If you give him a sword . . ." protested the steward.

"What's the matter, Baltair? Afraid that the provost's men and I can't protect you from a sixteen-year-old?" Varian baited him. "Should I ask my lady to fetch her bow for additional protection?"

Leonarel had indeed had some training. He held the shield well, and easily caught the sword Corven tossed to him. As Corven approached, he fell into one of the standard defense postures. Corven sparred easily with him for a minute or two, and noted with approval that the young man was trying to maneuver the fight so that he would have the lowering sun at his back, directly in his opponent's eyes. It was clear also that he had forgotten the waiting mob, staring breathlessly as they waited to see blood spilled.

Suddenly Leonarel pressed to the attack, landing a flurry of well-aimed blows in an attempt to quickly defeat his adversary. Corven watched carefully, giving ground slightly and feigning injury to draw the younger man into a precisely laid trap. Leonarel fell for it, tried to press too hard, and laid himself open just for an instant, an instant that was long enough for Corven's greater skill to drive through his defense and neatly flip his sword out of his hand.

"Hold!" Varian called sharply, and the fighters turned to face him. Cathlin was certain she saw a signal of some sort flash between her husband and his sword-brother, but she could not interpret it.

"You fought well," Varian continued, and smiled to himself as he watched Leonarel force himself to stand proudly, determined to meet his end with courage and not give in to the cold fear Varian could see in his eyes.

After all, his lord had said "fight for your life" and he had lost.

"Leonarel, it is my sentence for your crime that you be taken from this place and brought to Leopard's Keep, there to be given over to Armsmaster Evan, to be trained as a guardsman for my household." He chuckled wickedly and broke off the youth's stammering thanks as he realized that he would live.

"Be assured, boy, that this is not a reward, but a true punishment. Think about thanking me again in two weeks, when you have a nice collection of bruises from Evan's training. You may wish I had just ordered you a flogging so that it would be over and done with."

Cathlin poked Varian in the arm again and hissed, "Don't leave Leonadra alone in this village. She may still be held to blame or even shunned."

He pretended to ignore her; respect they must give her, but he could not afford to let the populace think that she ruled him through female wiles.

"Leonadra, you may accompany your brother if you wish, and we will find you a job, also. One without bruises," he said.

She looked surprised and then glanced uncertainly at a young man who had moved over to stand near her. "I . . . may I have a little time to think about it, m'lord?"

"Until tomorrow morning. Is there any other thing to be brought before me?"

There was no answer from the buzzing gathering. Varian waited for a short while, then signaled Baltair to announce that the Court of Justice was over.

Over and over, in the next few days, Cathlin noted her husband's sense of responsibility and justice. When he spoke of "my people," she could see that he did not mean it in the sense of "people I own" but "people I am responsible for." As well as administering justice, he checked with both stewards and people about their welfare: their homes, crops, children, animals. Nothing was too insignificant to overlook.

Except, perhaps, his bride.

Though he spoke politely and amiably to her, showed her honor and deference when he presented her to the people, and occasionally rode at her side, it seemed there was growing coolness between them. At the keeps and inns, and once even when of necessity they set up tents and camped overnight, he escorted her respectfully to her own quarters and left her there. Never did he treat her as a lover, even when her woman's flow stopped. She was too shy to tell him so, but hinted as best she could. She tried to tell herself that of course he wouldn't consummate their marriage in a tent where every guardsman with them would know what they were doing, or in an inn room, where somebody might hear them; he was too considerate of her possible embarrassment. But drat him, he could give her real kisses, couldn't he?

Slave

A few mornings after their return from the circuit of Leopard's Gard, Margretha came bustling up to Varian as he and Corven came into the great hall for breakfast. "My lord," she began, uncommonly formally, and as Varian turned toward her with some surprise, she dropped a curtsy and repeated with a slight frown on her face, "My lord, I must speak to you on a matter of some concern."

"It must be of great concern if you 'my lord' me, Maggie. Is there a problem that can't be solved by your great wisdom and excessive patience?"

"Yes, er, no, my lord Varian," and she smiled slightly as she caught the teasing look in his eyes. "It concerns my Lady Cathlin. Of course, whatever household staff Your Excellencies wish to have is completely up to you, and I've never been one to complain of the lack of decent help, hard as it is to find good, conscientious people, but you see, even though the Lady Cathlin says she doesn't want or need one, she has no body-servant, and none of these lazy, good-for-nothing serving girls will admit to knowing anything about being a lady's maid. Well, I have been helping her myself, and you know as well as I do all the other work a chatelaine

must do, so I don't really have time, what with keeping
this staff properly doing a day's work to earn a day's
pay, and besides, it doesn't look right and all, the lady
of the castle not having a body-servant or any compan-
ions as she should, so if you would do something about
providing her with a proper lady's maid, it would go a
long way to being the proper staff a lord's castle should
have. Sir.''

She scowled at Corven who was trying to hide a laugh
behind an exaggerated cough, for Margretha's verbal
barrages had always amused him greatly. ''And don't
bring home another impudent rascal like this one. We
don't need two of them, so we don't.''

She wondered at the sudden tightness in Varian's
face, even though he said mildly, ''Well, then, as it is
proper that my lady have a body-maid, it seems as if a
visit to the slavemarket is in order. Thank you, Maggie,
for drawing this to my attention. If you will have breakfast brought in, please?''

Another one to ask questions and grieve at her death,
he thought. *Already, Corven and Maggie are taken with
her.*

''And you are not, Varian?'' whispered the tiny voice
in his head, and it seemed to him that it laughed unpleasantly.

A rustling sound of skirts and Cathlin's soft voice
came to his ears. ''What was that about a slavemarket,
my husband? I thought I heard that there was no slavemarket in Leopard's Gard.''

''There is not, my lady wife,'' answered Varian, and
explained their errand. ''Corven, order the horses around
for after breakfast. We will be riding to market across
the river at Roskear Ford. Do you want to come with
us?'' A look passed between the two men that Cathlin
could not interpret: absolute blankness on Varian's face
and an odd shadow in Corven's eyes, like an unhappy
memory.

''I can take one of the other guardsmen, if you would
rather not,'' Varian added gently.

Cathlin watched Corven's face change as he drew himself up into a grave, formal salute, as if he flourished a sword in front of his lord.

"I rode at your side into battle, my lord. That is my place. Should I flinch at a morning's ride?"

"Your place is where you wish it to be, Corven. We have been swordbrothers since we first stepped onto the training grounds, and I don't doubt your courage. I but wished to give you a choice."

"Then I will ride with you, my lord Varian. Should I tell Master Evan that we will not be at sword practice?"

"Yes, please. Too bad, I was looking forward to pounding the stuffing out of you this morning." Varian grinned.

"Why do I need the stuffing pounded out of me, my lord?" Corven parried.

"You keep calling me 'my lord' instead of 'Varian,' and it is entirely too much this morning. The horses and the message to Evan, if you please?"

"As you wish . . . Varian."

As Corven trotted out to deliver his messages, Cathlin asked Varian, "What was that about? He hid it under all that formality, but why was Corven upset?"

" 'What' is that he doesn't like slavemarkets. 'Why' is his story to tell you, if he chooses.

"Have you been finding enough to do to keep yourself entertained? I don't know what sort of things ladies do for amusement, except embroidery, and Maggie has the chatelaine's job that should be yours by right."

"So she tells me, but I think it would break her heart to be superseded. I have no training in running a castle anyway, since it's not something I ever expected to do. Would Mistress Margretha be offended if I asked her to teach me?"

"She would probably be delighted, even though she complains that she is dreadfully overworked. She has run the castle since before my mother died. Maybe she would like to slow down and let somebody else cope with some of it. I'll talk to her tomorrow; we'll be gone most of today.''

''Varian, why is there no slavemarket here? Why make such a long ride?''

''I don't like slavemarkets, either. When my father died and I became baron, it was one of the first things I changed.''

''Then why are you buying a slave for me? Why not hire a freeborn girl?''

Varian smiled. ''You will see this afternoon, my lady. I see breakfast is being served. Shall we leave some for Corven, or try to eat it all before he gets back?''

Over breakfast, Cathlin pondered the things he had told her and tried to analyze her own uneasiness at the thought of owning a slave as she would own a dog or horse.

Free Traders did not have any slaves. Her father always said he preferred things of value that would not try to take themselves away in the middle of the night, and that all people should be as free as they themselves were. Consequently, she had never had much to do with any slaves or thought much about them. Some she had felt sorry for; once, on a trip with her father, she had seen an inn-slave stumble and drop a tray of dishes, and the terrified look on the boy's face made her think he was in for a dreadful punishment. She never saw him again, even though they had stayed at the inn several more days. She had tried to forget it; the memory made her feel sick.

Now she wondered what had caused her husband to apparently hate slavery so much that he would ban slavemarkets in his lands. And if he hated it, why did he keep slaves? She looked at the people who were beginning to fill the hall, collecting their morning meal and drifting about talking, or sitting in small groups at the lower tables. None of them wore a slave collar, nor did any of the men have the shaved heads that by law marked a male slave. Now that she thought about it, she did not recall seeing any of the castle's people who did wear a collar. Were there no slaves here then? If there were not, why was he buying one for her?

There was so little she knew about him, even though sometimes it seemed as if she had known him always. When he laughed over some silly happening, a joke told by Corven or the cat pouncing on his toes, he seemed to be a different person from the serious young man who sometimes treated her so formally.

Did all the great lords and ladies treat each other so? Was that why he did not come to her bed?

And now we're back to that problem, she thought sadly. *Maybe when we have been married awhile, we will feel easier with each other and I can find out what is wrong. But if he didn't want me for myself, why did he marry me?*

Varian's voice interrupted her musings. "Are you finished, my dear? We should be going soon."

They rode out over the drawbridge some time later, carefully threading through the people entering the castle grounds from the town that clustered at the foot of the walls. Cathlin looked about her as they rode, for one of her joys in traveling had always been to see something new.

She recognized the Seven Stars Inn from her first nights in Leopard's Gard and shook her head in wonder at the changes in herself since she first saw it. From being a merchant's daughter to being the lady of even a small domain such as this still seemed to her something out of a children's nursery tale.

The town looked prosperous, and most of the people happy. These were the men and women that Varian meant when he said "my people," the ones that had crowded the courtyard and cheered at their wedding, when he put the rings in her ears.

His people, she thought. *If they are "his people" to serve and protect, are they my people, too? How could I serve them? I always thought it was the people's job to serve the lord and lady, even their slightest whims.*

And yet Varian works hard all day, judging their disputes, ordering his lands, even fighting to safeguard them. I wouldn't want to have to be a warrior, but it seems I have just as hard a job to learn how to be a lady.

They were well along the road through the still bright forest, gleaming with red-gold leaves accented by the dark green of pines, when they drew near a cluster of small houses by the side of the road. A small child broke away from his play to disappear inside one. The riders were just past the last of the cottages when a woman's voice called breathlessly, "Varian! Corven! Oh, please, stop!"

Cathlin turned and saw a small, fat woman waddling as quickly as she could after them. To her surprise, both men drew rein and slid off of their horses, delighted smiles on their faces. She was even more surprised when her husband picked up the woman and kissed her soundly.

"Mally, is everything going well with you then? Do you need help?"

"Put me down, you idiot. I wanted to see your new bride, and now what she must think of me!"

Varian carefully set her on her feet, and now Cathlin could see that she was not fat but heavily pregnant.

"Oh, yes. Cathlin, my dear, this is Mistress Mallena, a childhood friend. Her mother worked at the castle."

"I'm so happy to meet you, milady. Var—Lord Varian has needed a wife for such a long time now, and I'm so happy for both of you!"

Cathlin smiled coolly and murmured something polite as Corven came up and caught Mally's hands in his. They moved out of the road and proceeded to catch up on each other's news, talking so fast that Cathlin, still unfamiliar with the northern dialect, could scarcely understand a word.

Varian had watched the meeting of the two women with some puzzlement. Why did Cathlin not seem to like

Mally? *Who can tell with women?* he thought. *They hide behind pretty smiles and don't seem to know that their bodies tell a different story.*

As he watched Mally and Corven, for a moment he allowed himself to remember a summer day from their shared childhood, a rare free day for all of them that they had spent climbing trees and playing in a creek. He had caught a frog and put it down Mally's dress to make her squeal, and they had spent the rest of the afternoon making frog-noises, "ribbit, ribbit," and laughing.

"Corven, we have to go now," he called regretfully. "Mally, do you want to come back to the castle for your birthing? You'll be safer, I think, with us than a village midwife."

She smiled wistfully and shook her head. "I can't, Varian. Garek's parents have been so nice to me, and with Garek . . . gone, I can't take their only grandchild away. But it was sweet of you to ask." And she stood on tiptoe and kissed him quickly.

He didn't know that Cathlin had been watching him and wondering jealously about the half-smile on his face. A fiendish voice was asking pointed little questions in her mind: *"Whose baby is it, that your husband is so anxious to take care of her?"*

It's her baby, and he said she's a childhood friend, she thought firmly at the voice.

"Oh, yes. A 'friend.' I see."

You shut up, and she walled it away solidly and refused to listen.

It was market day in Roskear Ford when they crossed the bridge, their horses' hooves echoing hollowly on the planking. If the bridge guards did not recognize Varian himself, they knew his badge and eyed his sword and did not presume to demand the usual toll.

Varian pointed out the black flag that was flying from the castle battlements, with its black eagle displayed on a gold sun.

"Lord Duer is still in residence. He must be intending

to stay in the North for the winter. I know you remember
him from our wedding, Cathlin.''

"Certainly! He frightened me half to death. I've never
seen such a big man, and he looks so fierce.''

Varian laughed. "He frightens a great many people.
I lived with his household for two years, and I thought
he would kill me with arms practice. We turn left here.
Is there anything else you want to look at in the market
here, my lady?''

"I can't think of anything, but—oh, *no*.''

Cathlin's first sight of the Street of Slaves had
prompted her unconscious protest. Although it was as
clean as any of the city's market streets (and cleaner than
some) she thought she had never seen a place with a
more dismal atmosphere. She thought even Varian
flinched at it, and Corven had gone from his usual half-
smile to a blank, almost stony face.

She was right, for just as she was sensitive to ambi-
ence, Varian was sensitive to smells. The place stank
with the smell of misery and the sharp reek of human
fear. There were only two slavers' chains on display that
day, as this time of year the market for slaves tended to
be slow. As they rode down the street, the calls from
the slaves, "Please, master, mistress, buy me,'' sounded
at best half-hearted.

Corven and Varian slipped off their horses and tossed
their reins and a small coin to a young boy who seemed
to appear out of nowhere. Cathlin shook her head as
Varian reached to help her dismount.

"No, thank you, Varian. This is awful. Are you sure
we can't just go home and hire a free girl for me?''

"I have my reasons, my lady. Stay mounted if you
wish.''

Both slave-dealers, scenting a prospect on this slow
day, took notice, calling out, "Good lord, gentle lady, I
have fine stock for your delight and interest!'' and "Do
not deal with that cheating scum, my lord, I have much
better servitors than the dregs he will sell you!''

Varian ignored both of them and surveyed the slaves

ranged up and down the street. None of them looked particularly promising, for most seemed to have had the spirit beaten out of them long ago. He had turned to speak to one of the slavers when he heard a soft hiss of anger from Corven.

A tall, heavyset man in the uniform of the city guard was pawing at a girl who was fastened, wrists braceleted behind her back, at the far end of one line. As Varian turned, the guardsman reached into the front of the girl's low-necked tunic and began to fondle and pinch her breasts. She closed her eyes and tried to fight back tears as Corven strode angrily forward.

"Leave her alone!"

"And who will make me, little man? You?" The guardsman smiled, displaying broken teeth as he noticed the leopard's head badge on Corven's jerkin. "Run away home and play with your kitties, sonny." He turned back to the girl, viciously pinching her nipple, and ran his hand up under her skirt.

The metallic *shhhf* of Corven's sword leaving its scabbard jerked him around in the next second, stepping away from the slave girl and pawing for his own sword. The girl, wide-eyed with fright at two men suddenly fighting over her, tried to pull away and fell as the chain on her ankle hauled her up short.

The two swordsmen began to circle warily, each watching the other closely for a break in attention. The guardsman, taller than Corven by a head and with longer arms, tried a quick disabling blow to Corven's sword arm, only to find it skillfully blocked with a return that jarred his arm to the shoulder.

"Hold!" rang out two voices in unmistakable command-tone, freezing both combatants in mid-stride. Varian and another man, also in a city guard's uniform, moved quickly forward to separate them.

"Corven!" Varian snapped furiously. "Do I have to tell you Lord Duer doesn't allow brawling in his streets, any more than I do in mine?"

The tall guardsman whined, "But, Captain, I was only

defending myself, I was doing my job and he—''

''I saw what you were doing, Malik,'' interrupted the guard captain. ''Your job doesn't include mauling slave girls in the market. Get back to barracks. I'll deal with you later.''

The guard captain turned a sharp look at Varian, noticing without seeming to both the gold in his ears and the unmistakable aura of command.

''You are Lord Varian of Leopard's Gard, sir?''

''I am, and I assure you my guardsman will also be disciplined.''

''Well, that's your right, m'lord, but Malik's always been a troublemaker. We'll see what a month of cleaning out the sewers will do for him.'' The captain took off his helm, ran a hand through his hair, and wiped the sweat off his forehead. ''Maybe I should have let your man go after him, teach him a lesson. I saw both of you in the fighting last year at Kaden's Pass, and I never saw any man move so fast as you two.''

''Best they didn't fight, Captain. Corven's not armored.''

''Wouldn't have mattered; I don't think Malik could have touched him. If you're up to the castle for a few days, I'd like to see you visit our arms practice.''

Varian shook his head regretfully. ''Not this time. I— we, my lady and I, will be visiting over Yearsend; maybe then.''

''Well, ask for Vardon, then. Good day, my lady, Lord Varian.''

Varian turned back to Corven with a sigh compounded of half relief and half exasperation. ''Dammit, Corven, that was a fool hotheaded thing to do. He would have been well within his rights to toss you in a cell and hold you for the next city court.''

Corven was standing at attention, stiff as a pikestaff and his stone-face firmly in place. ''No excuse, sir.''

Varian sighed again. ''All right, if that's the way you want it. You'll spend the next week with the brush-clearing crew outside the walls, and you can thank whatever gods you like that *we* don't have sewers to clean."

He looked about for Cathlin and found her crouching in the dust next to the slave girl, helping her to sit up. The girl's cheek was scraped and oozing blood, and her face was streaked with dirt and tear stains. Cathlin had sparks of anger in her eyes, and she was issuing rapid orders to the slave-dealer in what sounded very much like a command-voice of her own.

"Get these repulsive shackles off this girl *now,* and I want a clean cloth and some hot water and wound-ointment. Can't you see she's hurt? The very idea, tying up a human being so she can't fend off any man who wants to come along and paw at her!"

The startled slaver hastened to obey, sending a small girl running for the water and cloth, and unsnapping the leather cuffs that confined the girl's hands. They were designed so that the wearer could not reach the fasteners, and as Cathlin had found out, needed a man's hand-strength to unfasten.

"Varian, I want to talk to you in private." Cathlin turned aside with a soft "Thank you" to the little girl who was shyly holding out the things she had demanded. Cathlin shoved them abruptly into Corven's hands. "Here, Corven, you are partly responsible for this, help her get cleaned up. Varian?"

They walked quickly around a corner, so as to be out of earshot. Cathlin spoke rapidly as if to keep Varian from interrupting. "My lord husband, this is the girl I want. I can't leave her here, Byela alone knows what will happen to her. I don't think you or Corven saw, you were too busy, but the slave-dealer was furious with her. If he'd had a whip within reach, I think he would have beaten her. Please?" Her voice faltered as if she feared that he would be angry with her as well.

To her surprise, he smiled at her. "I see, my lady. Don't ever be ashamed or afraid to show me your tender heart. I won't scold you for it. Or do I seem that grim and fierce a man to you?"

She sent a relieved smile back to him. "No, Varian.

Just a puzzling one, but what man is not puzzling to a woman?''

He laughed and grabbed her hand to lead her back to the Street of Slaves. As they rounded the corner, he made a soft shushing noise at her. "Shh, will you look at that? Oh ho, he's been hit hard this time, and from the looks of it, so has she.''

"What, Corven's hurt? But I thought . . . Ohh, I see,'' she said as she spotted what Varian had seen.

The slave girl had her now-clean face trustfully turned up to Corven, and he was carefully dabbing ointment on her grazed cheek. Both of them appeared to be blissfully unaware of anything or anybody around them; they had eyes only for each other.

The slave-dealer hurried up to Varian and Cathlin, still anxious for his prospective sale. "Yes, my lord baron, my lady, how may I serve you?''

"We wish to interview this girl. My lady has need of a body-servant.''

"Of course, of course, great lord. She is fully trained and would make an excellent body-slave for a lady, and quite reasonably priced too, only—''

"I said I wished to interview the girl, slaver.'' Varian coldly cut him off in midstream. Cathlin looked up at him, startled. She had never heard him pull rank on anybody before, and he still sounded angry.

Varian did not need to feign anger to put the slaver in his place. He had never liked being pushed into a corner, with only one course of action open to him. Now he was committed to buying this particular girl, it seemed, suitable or not. That he had brought this situation on himself by insisting on buying a slave in the first place did not make him like it any better.

She looked frightened at his approach. Corven said something softly to her, and she cast him a quick, grateful glance before looking down. To Varian's surprise, Cathlin spoke before he could.

"What is your name, lass? Do you have any experience with helping a lady?''

"My name is Ame—" She faltered and threw a swift, frightened glance at the slave-dealer. "Ama, mistress. I— my stepfather ran an inn and sometimes I used to help any ladies that were traveling, if they didn't have their own servants. Is—is that all right, mistress?"

"It's all right, Ama. Don't be frightened, we'll get you out of here. Nobody will mistreat you in our home."

Corven spoke quietly from her other side. "See, I told you we wouldn't leave you here, even if I have to buy you myself."

Varian mentally raised an eyebrow at this; Corven usually spent his money on gambling and occasional tavern-crawling. Did he have the price of this girl saved up, or was he willing to go into debt for her after only a few moments in her presence? Well, no matter.

He turned to the slaver hovering at his elbow and asked bluntly, "How much?"

"For such a lovely young girl, your lordship, and so skilled, the usual price is sixteen gold griffins."

Varian did raise an eyebrow at the outrageous price. "The girl is too young, only half-trained, and timid as a rabbit. Five."

"*Five*, your lordship? A poor man like myself must make a living. You are asking my wife and children to starve on such a paltry price. I might be able to lower it slightly to thirteen for such a grand lord as you. Your guardsman, there, I think would give me fourteen."

Varian let out a short bark of derisive laughter. "Him? He hasn't got two coppers to rub together. You won't get anywhere trying play one of us against the other."

The slave-dealer shrugged wryly and switched to a different tactic, dropping his voice to a confidential whisper. "She has just turned fourteen and is a virgin, lord. Picture her waiting trembling in your bed for your taking—*urk!*"

Varian had wrapped both hands in the front of the slaver's shirt and jerked him off his feet to glare at him. "Do I look like a man who would enjoy raping children, slaver?" he hissed. "My offer just dropped to four."

"Please, great lord, I meant no offense! Perhaps I was too hasty in my judgment—surely we can discuss this like reasonable men. If you would put me down, please?"

Varian set him back on his feet, none too gently, and smiled grimly, showing his teeth in a manner that seemed suddenly threatening to Cathlin.

"Perhaps I should have Lord Duer's magistrates look into your business dealings, slaver. I believe the laws on enslaving His Majesty's subjects are quite strictly enforced here."

"My lord, I purchased her from a slaver in Ardesana, who bought her from her father in a legitimate transaction," protested the slave master. "I believe he needed money to pay his debts, or something of that sort.

"However, since your lady has taken such a liking to the girl, I can see my way to selling her for, oh, say ten? Er, eight gold pieces?"

"Are you hard of hearing, slaver? I offered you four," Varian said in a chilling voice.

The slaver looked into Varian's face and blanched. "Yes, yes, your lordship, certainly, four griffins will be quite adequate. If you will come inside please, while I fetch her papers? No? Certainly, I will be glad to bring them out here, here is the key to her ankle-ring while you wait," the man babbled as he disappeared inside.

Corven neatly caught the key tossed in his general direction and smiled up at Ama as he knelt to unlock the shackle around her ankle. "There, my sweet, you see? Nothing to it."

" 'Nothing to it,' Corven? I ought to take those four griffins out of your worthless hide. 'Your guardsman would give me fourteen,' " Varian mimicked pointedly. "I'm sorry about the two coppers comment. I hate bargaining with a slimy bastard like that."

Cathlin looked speculatively at her husband. "Varian, we'll need to go to the market after all. Ama can't ride that distance in nothing but this thin tunic; she'll freeze, and her legs will be rubbed raw. We'll have to get her some clothes.''

The slaver came bustling back out with the bill of sale and registration papers. "If you will sign here and here, lord. One must do the legal paperwork, after all. Here is the key to her collar, no extra charge, consider it my gift to you. Thank you for doing business with my establishment, good day to you, sir.'' And he vanished back into his shop, clearly anxious to have done with customers who were likely to turn violent.

"I think we've been insulted, my lady. I believe I will have someone look into his dealings.''

"The market first, Varian? This poor child is all but naked.''

"As you wish, my dear.''

At the market, Cathlin's spirits rose, and all of them managed to enjoy themselves, watching a dancing bear and throwing coppers to it as it begged, and buying food at various stalls and stuffing themselves. Varian watched with amusement as his lady put all her trader's knowledge into use. She bargained, critically examined the clothes she wanted, threw up her hands and called upon the gods to witness that she was being vastly overcharged, and bargained again. She finally concluded the bargain by clasping hands with a beaming merchant who was clearly delighted that a noble lady was willing to play the game with him.

In the end, Ama was outfitted with a simpler version of Cathlin's riding garb. Corven teased her into admitting she liked blue, and bought her a blue ribbon for her hair. She was still very shy and seemed fearful of Varian, even when he lifted her into place behind Corven for the ride home.

Amethyst *was* afraid of her new master, too afraid to even try to use the strange "seeing" that sometimes came to her. She had hoped that the young guardsman would buy her; he was so brave and kind to rescue her from that horrible man. He had promised, and then the lord had bought her instead.

The last few weeks since her mother died had been a nightmare. Mother was barely cold in her grave when a group of merchants, accompanied by the magistrates' representative, had called on her stepfather. She didn't know what he had done to incur such debts, gambling, maybe. All she knew was that when she had fetched them some food and wine, they were demanding money from him. The inn that was her mother's legacy must be sold, the magistrates' man said, if Jared couldn't raise the money any other way.

He had gotten roaring drunk after they left. It was all her mother's fault, not letting him run the inn that was his by right as her husband, and then dying on him. Amethyst had tried to run away, but he caught her by the hair. An evil leer came over his face, and the air around him turned an ugly blackish green. He would teach her mother a lesson, all right. She and her brother were legally his now, and he would sell them instead.

She didn't know where her brother Farris was now. She had last seen him beaten to his knees by the slave-dealer, his back oozing blood as he submitted to save her from the same fate. They had been separated after that, and she had been sold north here to Roskear Ford.

Most of the other slaves had ignored her, but two of them had enjoyed tormenting her with brutally graphic descriptions of what a master would do to her when he claimed his rights to her body. The slavers had done nothing beyond verifying that she was a virgin; she would fetch a better price so.

So now she was sold like a horse or hound, and with no more rights. Her new master could do what he liked with her. Amethyst wondered what the slaver had said to him to make him so angry. His anger had been strong enough to break through the barrier she had tried to erect against her ''seeing''; it had boiled around him like a dark red cloud. And he was going to punish his guardsman (what was his name—Corven?) for trying to help her.

At least her new mistress seemed kind; maybe she could intercede.

"Ama?" Corven's voice broke into her thoughts and she realized, with a sinking feeling in her stomach, that he had called her slave-name several times.

He was twisting in the saddle to try to look at her, but thank the little goddess he didn't seem to be angry at her inattentiveness.

"Your name isn't Ama, is it?"

"How did you know, m-master?" she gasped.

"Not master, never master to me," he corrected her swiftly. "Just Corven. Never mind how I know. What is your name, then?"

"Amethyst. The slaver said that it was a free name, too good for a slave, and that my name was Ama. I'm sorry I didn't answer at first, I'm still not used to it. I am trying, truly I am." She fought to keep the fear out of her voice and tried to lean around him to see where the master and mistress were.

Did they hear me claiming a free name? When will I learn to think before opening my mouth in front of a free man? she thought in dismay.

"Don't worry," he said comfortingly. "They can't hear us. I just wanted to tell you to hang on to my belt if you need to. I can tell you aren't used to riding. Tell me if you get too tired, and I'll put you in front of me so you can lean back. It's a long ride back home."

Home. Home was her mother's face in the firelight, and a tiny attic room in an inn far to the south. Home was gone, and getting farther away every step the horse took.

It was dusk when they rode up to the gates of the castle, and in the last fitful light, it seemed to Amethyst to be crouching like a great beast, swallowing her down as they passed over the tongue of its drawbridge and through the passage in the walls. She could hear the message being passed that the lord and lady were home, and a tall, sour-faced man who walked with a limp (the steward?) met them as they dismounted.

"Supper has just gone in, Lord Varian, Lady Cathlin. This is the new girl? She's to sleep in the alcove in the lady's rooms? I will have Margretha come and fetch her as soon as you are finished with your meal."

"Thank you, Migael. Will you have the bell rung to assemble the rest of the household in the hall, please? I want to get this done now, not wait until morning."

"As you wish, my lord."

Get what done? Amethyst wondered uneasily. She followed Corven into a large, open room that was filled with tables and benches. She could smell bread and meat, but oddly enough, she wasn't hungry. Her stomach seemed to be a hollow filled with apprehension.

She could see her master standing on a raised platform at the head of the hall, and as the last few people entered, the bell she had just been aware of fell silent.

His voice rang out loudly in the empty stillness. "Corven! Bring the new slave."

Corven caught her hand to lead her forward. Was this some sort of ceremony nobody had told her about? What was he going to do? *Blessed Mother, no, he can't, he wouldn't claim master-rights on me in front of everybody, would he?* Her panicked thoughts went around and around, but came back to the same point. *He owns me, he's a lord, he can do anything, beat me, rape me, anything he wants to and nobody will stop him.* She couldn't feel Corven's hand leading her or her own legs moving, but suddenly there she was in front of him on the platform.

"Kneel, and hold your hands out in front of you, wrists together," Corven quietly prompted her. She heard him add, just as softly, "Her name is Amethyst, Varian."

She was too terrified to do anything but obey and bow her head. Through the roaring surge of her own heartbeat in her ears, she heard her master say sternly, "This girl submits herself to me as a slave." He stepped forward and then his hands were at her throat, his fingers twisting the tiny key in the lock of the collar that marked her as a slave.

"This woman, Amethyst, is a slave no longer. From this moment, I renounce all claim to her body and service. She is free. Is it witnessed?"

She heard Corven's voice, and a heartbeat later the voices of the assembled people: "It is witnessed!"

Slowly she raised her head to meet the lord's eyes. "F-free? Truly, m-my lord?" she stammered.

"There are no slaves in Leopard's Keep, Amethyst. Hold out your hands." And he laid the slave collar in them as he helped her to her feet.

"Why were you so frightened?" He looked at her for a moment with intense curiosity until Cathlin pounced on him from behind.

"Varian, why didn't you tell me this was what you had in mind? Do you always try to spring things like this on people?" she demanded as she pulled his arm to make him turn.

"It's more fun this way."

"Fun! Amethyst didn't think it was fun. You scared her to death. Are you all right now? You're shaking, poor child."

Free. She was free again. All at once, the confidence that was her normal behavior came flooding back. "Silly girlish fears, milady. But if I'm free, what do I do now? Do you not want me as the lady's servant after all?"

"Yes, we still want you," Varian said softly, smiling at her for the first time. "But you'll work for wages, now. Or you can go home, if you want to."

She studied his face carefully, for the first time trying to see the aura around him without blocking it in panic; she found only the ordinary emotions of a tired man who wanted his supper. There was nothing to be afraid of. She'd let her imagination run away with her. Finally, she shook her head.

"There's nothing—nobody—for me at home now. I'd like to stay." She looked down and realized she was still clutching the slave collar. "What do I do with this, milord?"

Corven answered before Varian could. "I threw mine in the moat."

Amethyst looked at him, astonished, and realized the Lady Cathlin was mirroring her expression. "You? You were a slave, Corven?"

"I was born a slave. Lord Varian freed me, and a lot of others, when his father died."

"Tell her later, Corven. Take her out to throw that thing away, if that's what you want, and let everyone get on with their meal. My lady, if I may escort you to your place?"

Seducтion

Amethyst rapidly became Cathlin's friend as well as her maidservant, for Cathlin did not know how to treat another human being with the cool indifference highborn ladies generally gave their servants. Accustomed to the company of many other females in the communal life of a clan-village, she treated the younger girl as if she were a sister or cousin, for and from whom mutual help could naturally be expected. She had not realized that part of her unhappiness was the result of being separated from that sort of support system until Amethyst came into her life to replace it.

Together they discovered the life of a lady of the nobility as interpreted by Mistress Margretha, for that worthy lady was indeed delighted to have a pupil to learn the intricacies of running a castle. Cathlin discovered quickly that Varian's remark about ladies not doing much but embroidery must have been completely uninformed, for the chatelaine's job was as extensive as that of a clan-village Firstmother. If she had married into her own people, Cathlin would have had years, decades per-

haps, of gradual learning before she reached that exalted
state.

Now she was trying to learn everything at once: over-
seeing chambers, kitchen, dairy, larder, bakehouse, brew-
house, stillroom, weaving room, and storerooms. Outside on the castle grounds there were orchards, the
kitchen garden and herb garden, and the living larders
of doves, chickens, rabbits, and pigs. Though each of
these had people to attend to them, it was the duty of
the mistress of the house to see to it that the jobs were
being done correctly.

Cathlin's days were full, and through them all, Amethyst was her shadow. Frequently, the girl surprised her
with an astute comment and once or twice a shrewd
criticism. She discovered that Amethyst had not been a
serving maid at the inn that had been her home, but the
daughter of the innkeeper. She had learned in miniature
all the duties that were now Cathlin's to learn, and at
times her support seemed to be the only comfort Cathlin
had to lean on.

It was late in the month when events in the outside world
ripped through the smooth pattern of those days.

Every day Cathlin made time for archery practice; that
day, she had finished and was walking back across the
inner bailey when she heard the shouts of the men at the
gate and the hurried drumming of hooves across the
drawbridge.

A horse so lathered with sweat that it was impossible
to tell what color it was came to a halt in front of her.
The man who tumbled off its back was not in much
better shape. "Message for the lord baron," he gasped.
"Vital, m'lady."

What sort of message could be that important, to ride
a horse into that condition? Migael appeared at her elbow and summoned stablehands to deal with the horse,
while Cathlin sent Amethyst scurrying to find Varian.
She herself led the messenger to the great hall and sat
him down on the nearest bench. A serving girl went

running for a mug of ale while he caught his breath.

Before the serving girl returned, Varian himself appeared. Wordlessly, the messenger handed over his pouch.

Cathlin caught her breath at the sight of the griffin badge stamped on it. It was from the king.

Varian fumbled the paper open and scanned hastily down the page. "They're certain?" he snapped at the messenger.

The man nodded and said hoarsely, "Aye, m'lord. I don't know Tiorbran's sources, but he's dead certain."

If they didn't tell her, she would go crazy! "Varian, what is it?"

"Corleon is making noises about his 'ancient land-right' again."

Corleon? Why would the king of the neighboring country say something like that, if he didn't mean . . . "War?" she whispered, her lips almost too stiff to say the word.

Varian turned swiftly to her and took her hand. "Nothing to worry about, my dear. Border skirmishes, most likely, here in the North. Ah, Evan, there you are." He gave her a smile that must have been intended as reassuring, squeezed her hand, and turned away.

She watched him go, too stunned to call him back and not at all sure what else she could say or do if he did return to her.

Amethyst's hands trembled on the brush as she smoothed Cathlin's hair preparatory to rebraiding it. "Will they all go off to war, do you think? Even—even Corven?"

"I wish I knew," Cathlin said bleakly. *My Varian, going away, maybe to war, and I've never had anything from him . . . Byela, what do I do?*

"He—I'm—oh, please, help me, Cathlin," Amethyst begged. "I know Corven likes me, he said he wanted to see me this evening, but he's so much older than I am, I'm afraid he thinks I'm just a little girl. And I love him.

What can I do to make him see me as a woman?''

Poor baby, Cathlin thought. *Dear goddess, do both of us have to be unhappy over these men?* Her eyes filled with sudden tears. "I don't know," she blurted. "My own husband won't . . ."

Small strong hands came down on her shoulders and she sat stiffly, hardening her jaw and widening her eyes in an attempt to keep the treacherous tears in their place.

"Won't what?" Amethyst asked gently. "He loves you, I can tell. Anybody can see it when he looks at you." She didn't say how she knew; even Cathlin would probably think she was crazy if she said she could see people's emotions.

"Won't come to my bed." There. It was said, but she couldn't tell yet if sharing her misery was going to make it easier or harder.

Amethyst's mouth dropped open as she stared at her mistress. "You mean to tell me you—he hasn't—how long have you been married? *Three weeks?* Well, if he was my husband, I'd go right in and have it out with him. He has no right to treat you that way, lord or no lord!"

"Lord or no lord," echoed Cathlin. "Maybe that's it, Amethyst! Maybe with lords and ladies, the lady has to make the first move, to tell the lord he is welcome in her bed, so he knows she's not frightened of him! I mean, think of having to bed a stranger in an arranged marriage, someone like Lord Duer. Oh, that's right, you never saw him. He's twice Varian's size and has these enormous mustaches." And Cathlin gestured with her hands, miming a mustache two feet wide on either side.

Amethyst burst into giggles and Cathlin, enormously relieved to have solved her mystery, joined her. They both fell on the bed, dizzy with laughter and anticipation, and fell to discussing plans how best to seduce their men.

Later that night, Cathlin smiled good-bye at Amethyst as the girl slipped out the door to keep her tryst with Corven, and turned herself to the door that connected her room with Varian's. It moved silently on its well-oiled hinges, and Cathlin padded softly on bare feet toward the window. The moon was just rising, and the fire still glowed on the hearth. He would see her outline against the window, she thought, and the fire would reveal her actions.

"Varian?" Her voice was a breathy whisper. "I . . . would like to have your company, my husband. I'm cold, and lonely." And in a pretense of maidenly modesty, she looked aside as she turned to face the bed and pulled the laces of her bedgown loose, allowing it to settle in a shimmering silky puddle at her feet.

There was no sound from the direction of the bed, not even a creak of movement.

"Varian?" And she looked up appealingly.

The bed was empty.

It had been slept in, or at least occupied; the fur coverlet was pushed back to the foot. The clothes he had worn that evening in the hall were folded neatly on the chest. As she turned to survey the room again, she noticed that a tub of hot water steamed in one corner, and two buckets of fresh water waited near the hearth. There was no sign of where Varian might have gone.

A wave of red anger flowed from her belly up to burst in her brain. She wanted to scream and throw something to watch it shatter. Her husband dared to leave her alone while he chased some serving maid or tavern slut, did he? Well, she would follow Amethyst's first suggestion and have it out with him. She might not be one of his highborn ladies, but a daughter of Clan Leioness was not someone he could kick in the face like this! And then tomorrow she would take her horse and the things she had brought and leave, return to the clan-village and go back to her old life.

She still wanted to scream. It would serve him right if she did scream, loud enough to wake the whole castle and lay everything out in the open. Only the remnants of her pride stopped her; instead, she grabbed a pillow

from the bed and screamed into that, then sank down on
the bed and wept out her broken heart.

She was not aware that she had slept until a soft click-
ing noise jerked her back into wakefulness. A panel
beside the fireplace swung open, and she opened her
mouth to berate him as he came sneaking back from his
tryst . . . and left it open as her jaw dropped in fright. It
was not Varian. The biggest cat she had ever seen slid
through the opening; the moonlight through the window
threw it into sharp relief. Was she dreaming? She could
see now the dappled silver fur and the ivory fangs; the
ice leopard's eyes gleamed as it turned its head toward
her. She saw its claws emerge briefly, then retract into
the huge paws. It seemed to be in pain as it crouched,
with shoulders hunched and fur spiky. And as she
watched frozen and breathless with fear, its silhouette
seemed to shift and shrink.

No, it can't be, this is some insane dream, her
thoughts screamed. But it was, it *was* Varian who
crouched there naked on the floor in front of her. As she
snatched the bed-fur up to cover her own nakedness, he
looked at her again, looked at her with a leopard's
gleaming, yellow, slit-pupiled eyes, until they darkened
and became the familiar green.

Still he didn't speak as he pulled himself shakily to
his feet, only studied her with a still intent gaze that
reminded her of a cat waiting at a mousehole. Then he
nodded and smiled to himself, as if he had reached some
satisfactory judgment.

"More courage than I had thought, my lady. Why did
you not scream?"

"Why didn't you tell me?" she countered. "They
told stories at the inn about shape-shifters, but I thought
they were only wild tales."

"How could I? 'Speaking of hunting, Cathlin, I'm a
were-leopard. Will you run the night with me?' " He
turned aside, started to run his hand through his hair in
the familiar distracted gesture, then stopped and stared
at it in distaste. There were streaks of dark red on his

hands and arms, she noticed now, and another ran along his jawline.

"Varian! Are you hurt?" and she started to scramble from the bed, only to be stopped by an even more horrible thought. "That is . . . blood? On your hands?"

"Blood, yes, my lady. Deer blood, this time."

The words he did not say, *Not human blood,* seemed to hang in the air between them. The silence stretched out, finally broken by Varian's sigh. She thought she saw him wince as he turned stiffly away.

"You *are* hurt," she said accusingly and slid out of the bed, unmindful now of her own nudity, to look more closely at the long gash that ran from his side to just under the shoulder blade, clearly visible in the center of a growing bruise.

He gave her a somewhat sheepish look and nodded. "I misjudged my leap and caught a hoof in the ribs. I think I broke one."

"You didn't break it, the deer did," Cathlin said absently. "The skin is gashed and you're bleeding a little." She ran her fingertips carefully over the bruise, trying to feel the outline of his ribs. "It doesn't seem to be broken, but it may be cracked. Try not to do anything else to hurt it, like letting Corven hit it at arms practice."

Goddess, she thought, *I'm babbling like an idiot. I am an idiot. This man is a were-leopard and I'm not running and screaming, I'm about to help him take a bath, of all things.*

"Into that tub I saw over there, and get that blood off," she ordered briskly and frowned at the bemused smile he gave her as he carefully obeyed her commands.

Varian sank back in the small tub as best he could and relaxed, closing his eyes and letting his head drop back. She knew, and she wasn't afraid. She didn't hate him for deceiving her. He had thought he would have to use the geas charm to control her and keep her quiet, but she seemed still to trust him. She was a brave woman, he mused. The ladies of his acquaintance, few as they were, would likely scream and faint at the sight of a tiny mouse, much less a full-grown ice leopard.

The sting of a wet cloth slapped across his chest made his head pop up and eyes fly open the next second. His wife smiled sweetly at him.

"You can wash yourself, my lord, I presume? Where do you hide the soap?"

"In the metal box in the clothes chest, there. Soap is a luxury we don't see much of, my lady."

"You will. I know how to make it and will start your people . . . our people on it tomorrow."

She handed him the sliver of soap and watched him start to scrub off the bloodstains. *I could have killed him just now,* she reflected, appalled at herself even as she thought. *I could have put a dagger through his heart, instead of smacking him with a wet washcloth. He trusts me. If he is truly a monster, I should have . . . but he* trusts *me.* "Give me that soap," she said briskly, "so I can clean that cut properly. Sit up and lean over, so I can see it."

Varian twisted his head to try to watch her soap his back, her fingertips gently sliding over his ribs. He could not remember the last time anybody had done him such an intimate service; the touch of her hands seemed to leave trails of fire on his body, more painful than the scrape to his ribs, for her touch was kindling a desire that he knew he had to resist.

Cathlin's hands moved even more slowly as she fought to keep her feelings under control. *Why do I love him, even now? Sometimes I think he loves me, but then he turns all formal . . . why did he marry me? I want him so much . . . I want him to love me . . .*

Varian could feel her eyes on him; as if spellbound himself, he lifted his head to meet her gaze. Her eyes were enormous, dark pools that reflected his own image, brimful of unshed tears.

He stood up abruptly, shedding water as he stepped out of the tub, reached for a towel, and extended a hand to her. "Cathlin . . . don't. Don't cry, please. I'm sorry you were frightened, I can't help what I am."

"It doesn't *matter,*" she said fiercely and threw herself into his arms. She reached for his head and pulled his face down to hers, searching for his mouth, ignoring what might have been the beginning of a moan as his resistance collapsed. She found his lips with her own and kissed him deeply.

Instinctively, his arms went around her and pulled her closer, ignoring the dripping water as his hands caressed the smoothness of her back and stroked through the silky dark fall of her hair, as he had wanted to do all these weeks. Her mouth was warm and sweet and welcoming, as he knew her body would be if he swept her up and put her on the bed. The feel and scent of her was intensely female to his still-heightened senses; he wanted to kiss and caress all of her, he wanted to—and then the part of his brain that was still ice leopard, that was always ice leopard, told him why her scent was arousing him so. It doused his ardent desire as effectively as a bucket of ice water.

His body stiffened in her arms and she felt his hands slide from her buttocks to her upper arms as he pushed her away. "No, Cathlin, I can't, I *won't*—for the love of your goddess, listen to me!"

"But I love you, I want you, I know you want me, you can't deny it," she sobbed, as she stared at him with bewildered wet eyes, and she tried to reach for him again. "I don't care if you're a were-leopard. I wouldn't care if you're the Dark One himself! I love you!"

"Cathlin, not half an hour ago you saw what I am, what I am cursed to be as my father was before me. I will not sire a child on you tonight to be cursed the same way. *I will NOT!*" and he dropped her arms and pivoted away from her, slamming his clenched fist repeatedly into the stone wall, as if physical pain would distract him from the anger and frustration she could see gripping his body.

For a long moment, they stared at each other; Varian was certain that she would break and run away in tears. But again he received unexpected proof of her courage.

She scrubbed her face with her hands and said in a gentle voice, "I understand, Varian. Maybe someday . . . I'm sorry, too, my love." Then she turned and slipped quietly through the door to her own room, leaving Varian staring after her in wonder. He hadn't said he was sorry, he was sure. How had she known?

Battle

Varian sat his warhorse with Corven next to him, waiting as they all were. He had never decided if the battle-nerves that quivered through his belly were the worst part of fighting or not. As experienced a fighter as he was, they still hit him hard. Even harder was hearing the noise of battle and having to hold back, to wait for the proper time.

This was no border skirmish that Varian waited to join. This was all-out war. Corleon, King of D'Alriaun, marshaled his armies just on the other side of the valley. The hills were black with warriors, and the unmistakable outlines of catapults and other war machines were clearly visible. Corleon had come in force to lay claim to Sundare, anciently part of his lands. So he said.

Varian knew his history. One of Earl Duer's Swordguard could not help learning. Long ago, a D'Alriaun princess had brought these lands to her bridegroom, a prince of Dur Sharrukhan. They had been Sharrese ever since, and Corleon had no vestige of claim to them. He held even less claim to the eastern valleys of Leopard's Gard. Those were Varian's.

King Tiorbran, though old and arthritic, had taken the field in defense of his lands. For two weeks he had led his forces through minor skirmishes and clashes. Now, however, the weather seemed to choose sides. It was cold and rainy, typical for late autumn, but disastrous for the king. Yesterday he had forced his aching joints to bear him through the halls of Roskear Keep to attend the council of war; today not even the strongest of his aides had the heart to pry the old man from his bed. Now the Crown Prince Gardomir wore the royal armor and fought under the king's banner; his younger brother Alnikhias commanded the reserves.

Varian didn't know whether to be glad or sorry that he and his men were under nominal command of Prince Alnikhias. King Tiorbran's younger son was reputed to be a master strategist, young as he was. It was his strategy in use today. The center there, under command of Gardomir, was fighting fiercely, but would soon seem to crumble and turn to run. If Likarion was on their side, the enemy would give chase and be sucked into a trap as these hidden wings would sweep out and catch him in a classic pincer move.

So Varian waited for the signal to lead his people into battle. The summons to war was, in its own way, a relief. Here was an enemy he could fight at last. There would be no frustration in sweeping down off this hilltop, nothing to hinder the building battle-lust.

The signal came, and with it a sweet and heady jolt of release. His own voice screaming his war cry was drowned in the booming roar of the men around him. Rowan under him was an extension of his own body as he sent the horse into the thick of the battle. Training so bone-deep that it felt like instinct took over as he slashed and stabbed, and the whirling maelstrom of noise and bodies fragmented into brief pictures: the gasp frozen on the face of a mercenary warrior as Varian's sword slid into his throat; the banner of one of Corleon's nobles toppling as its bearer was cut down; the flight of stones from a D'Alriaun catapult and the screams of the men they crushed.

A flash of blue and red in the distance caught his eye as the cries intensified. The sudden surge of bodies around the horse of Prince Gardomir increased as a flung stone sailed unstoppably through the air. It plowed directly into the pack of men struggling to get out of its way. Gardomir's horse went down with a sickening crackle of broken bones, and the prince flew off its body as if the saddle were a catapult, too.

The thud as he landed must have been in Varian's own mind. Surely no man could hear such a noise over the din. The few men of the prince's bodyguard left standing rallied around his fallen body in a desperate attempt to defend him. A wave of D'Alriaun fighters flowed over the place, and the blue of the royal tabard was drowned in the spurts of red that followed.

A sickened Varian wrenched his attention back to his own part of the battlefield. Prince Alnikhias had seen his brother fall; all the cool precision of his fighting was gone now as he charged forward in his turn, still trying to wrap the tail of the reserves around to trap the D'Alriauns. "To me!" he screamed and the trumpeters picked it up and blared their signals through the noise.

The Sharrese fighters responded. Varian's own Leopard's Gard troops fought their way to the prince's side, until Varian could nearly have touched him. They drove the D'Alriauns back and back, until the fighting swarmed over the already contested center of the field.

Alnikhias' sword swung again and again as he faced the last mounted warrior opposing him. He broke through the other's defense and sent his sword into the D'Alriaun's chest just as a blood-dripping figure rose under his horse's belly with a broken spear clutched in its hand. Nobody was near enough to stop it as the spearhead sliced deep into the horse's unprotected belly. The animal screamed the terrible scream of a creature that sees its own death coming and twisted away. Prince Alnikhias, his sword jammed in the D'Alriaun's chest armor, lost his balance and fell as his dying horse went down.

Rowan's hooves pounded the life out of the spear-wielder a heartbeat later. Varian threw himself off his horse's back at the same instant, for a number of bloody figures sprang from their hiding places among the dead. They laughed, terrible high-pitched shrieks as Varian straddled his downed prince's body and prepared to die in his defense. A shout in his ear was all that prevented him from whipping around and taking out the man who plunged off his horse behind him. It was Corven, and the wave of relief that surged through Varian forced a shrill, defiant scream from his throat. They were back to back, fighting like madmen, the whipping steel in their hands forming a deadly circle about them.

Varian was aware as he fought that the prince still moved and gasped for the breath that had been knocked from him. One of the foemen fell and threw his sword like a spear as he went down. It did not reach the prince but stuck quivering in the ground. Alnikhias snatched at it, coming to one knee. Corven, who had fought so far in deadly silence, bellowed a warning and took off the head of the man who tried to reach the prince.

Shouting and the pounding of hooves broke into their awareness as a detachment of warriors in the blue and red of the King's Elite fought their way through to them. One of them pulled Prince Alnikhias onto his horse behind him as Varian and Corven scrambled onto their own mounts.

The tide of the battle turned in their favor as the D'Alriauns realized that they had fallen for the feigned retreat. The King's Elite bore the prince away, and soon the wartrumpets signaled again. The jaws of the pincers shifted and opened, leaving the D'Alriauns a way out if they chose to take it, a way out that would lead them straight to the river. Perhaps their warleader saw it and knew it for what it was but also knew that to stay would mean slaughter as the armies of Dur Sharrukhan avenged their crown prince's death. Retreat, even into the river, might save some of his troops. And retreat he chose.

The reserves of the Sharrese, somewhat fresher than the main body, rode to harry him on his way.

The aftermath of a battle was always a time of aching weariness, for a field commander could not drop down and rest wherever he chanced to be. He must see to his men and insure that they in turn saw to their mounts. The moon had risen on the battlefield, throwing the twisted bodies into sharp black and silver relief before Varian could at last ride up to his own tent and drop wearily off Rowan's back.

Good, someone was in there already, for he could see the glow of a lantern. He hoped it was his orderly and that the lad had had sense enough to rustle up some food and wine. How he would summon the strength to eat it, Varian did not know.

There was bread and cheese and wine on the table, but the man who sat there was not his orderly. It was Earl Duer. He greeted his nephew with only a nod of his head, poured a cup of wine, and waited until Varian had swallowed some of it.

"Bad news, lad. Very bad." Duer looked more solemn than Varian had ever seen him.

"About Prince Gardomir? I know. I saw it." He propped both elbows on the table and leaned his face tiredly into his cupped hands.

"No. Not just that. The king is dead, too."

For a moment he couldn't take it in. It was just words, and he looked at Lord Duer in silent puzzlement.

"When they brought the news to him of his son's death, they say he looked stunned. His face turned white and then red, and he fell over as if he had been poleaxed. He died an hour later. Godstruck, they say."

"Oh, gods," Varian murmured prayerfully. He had met the king once and liked the elderly monarch. But the grief of a loyal subject must be nothing compared to the grief the young prince must be feeling. "Does Alnikhias know?"

"He was the one who told Tiorbran about his brother's death. Poor lad, brother and father both taken at once. The Council of Nobles has already proclaimed him as the new king. We felt it couldn't wait, since we're still at war."

Varian wiped both hands wearily down his face. "Yeah. I can see you couldn't wait. My vote wouldn't have changed anything, anyway. I've got no quarrel with Prince Alnikhias as king, even though I've never met him."

"Never met him? Who was that baron who rescued him this afternoon, then?"

He gave a tired chuckle and reached for the bread and cheese. "That's hardly a formal introduction."

Lord Duer laughed softly, too. "He still wants to see you, tomorrow about midmorning."

"His Royal Majesty will have to wait till I wake up, then. I'm about to fall asleep right here, and an earthquake won't move me once I'm gone."

It was nearly noon before Varian was admitted to the suite of rooms in Roskear Keep that had been set aside for the new king. "His Majesty has pressing business, you understand, my lord," an officious steward had said, and kept him kicking his heels and waiting for nearly an hour.

He entered the rooms warily. Varian knew how many people attended on even a duke, and he expected to find at least that number of stewards, bodyguards, slaves, lesser nobles, and whatnot cluttering up the place. He was surprised to find only one man in the room, slumped on a bench, staring tiredly at the fire.

He turned his head as the door closed quietly, and smiled at Varian. "So," he said quietly. "It's been a long time, Varian. You haven't changed much."

The eyes and the set of the mouth told Varian who

he was, even though it had been a long time. "Niko?" he asked guardedly.

"Yeah. Changed some, haven't I?" For a moment, as he smiled, he looked like the boy he had been, then his face drooped wearily again and he stretched his shoulders as if to relieve a cramp. He looked much older than the eighteen that Varian thought he must be now.

"It's good to see you again," Varian said awkwardly. "Are you Swordguard now for the king, or what?"

"Or what. Grab a chair, I've been wanting to talk to you."

Varian heaved a doleful sigh as he sat down. "I'd rather talk to you than to the king, but Duer said *he* wanted to see me. Where is His Royal High-and-Mightiness, by the way? In the privy?"

Niko laughed mockingly. "Hey, kings have to use the privy just like anybody else, you know. Relax, nobody's going to force you into 'Yes, Your Majesty, no, Your Majesty.' The king has good reason to talk to you. You saved his life yesterday, like a good subject. Who was the other swordsman, by the way?"

"Corven. He's a freedman now."

Niko's mouth curved in a reflective smile, and he began to laugh helplessly. "Of course," he sputtered. "It would have to be, wouldn't it? It's lucky for all of us that he still has a sword hand."

"Lucky for the prince, anyway. And if you wanted to know, yes, I still hold to the fealty I swore to you for his life. Do I ever get to know just who you are? There's no reason to keep it secret anymore."

A knock on the door interrupted Niko as he opened his mouth to answer. "Come in!" he barked, clearly irritated at the disturbance.

Lady Gavriveda swept in at the head of a small procession of serving slaves bearing trays, one of whom almost ran into her as she swept abruptly into a deep curtsy. "Your Majesty," she said reverently. "The noon meal as you requested it, although we can show you much more choice foods than this. May I know of your pleasure for dinner tonight?''

''Whatever you choose will be my pleasure, my Lady Gavriveda. You may leave the food and retire.''

Varian sat frozenly watching the serving slaves as they put the trays on the table and scuttled away, the lady sweeping along behind them much more smoothly now that there was no danger of collision from behind. Nor did he move, except for turning his head to find Niko watching him closely. ''Your Majesty?'' he asked quietly.

Niko shrugged expansively. ''Stranger things have happened, Varian. I expected to be no more than plain Prince Alnikhias for the rest of my life. That was why I wanted your fealty. It never hurts to have a friend on your side. In time, I suppose I would have commanded Gardomir's warriors; he preferred not to take the field.'' Suddenly his jaw muscles clenched as he forced his voice into steadiness. ''I just wish he hadn't taken it this time.''

If this had been the old Niko, the twelve-year-old, Varian might have moved to comfort him for the loss of father and brother both in one day. But now this young man was his king, and he was sure that Alnikhias did not want a shoulder to cry on, even if that was what he needed. Even so, he felt he should say something.

''All of us will grieve for both of them, Your Majesty.''

''Please, Varian, I don't want to be 'Majestied' by you. Not when we're in private.'' Alnikhias stood up and abruptly began to pull covers off the food. ''Bread, cheese, apples, what's this? Ah, chicken. The Lady Gavriveda is trying to make me eat the sort of food a king should. No doubt she'll have spiced peacock tongues at dinner.''

''But you won't have to serve them, Niko,'' Varian said, drawing another smile from Alnikhias as the young king tore off a chunk of bread, cut himself a similarly sized piece of cheese, and pushed the food toward his friend. "The reason I asked you here, Varian, and the reason I cleared out all the bootlickers and toadies is so that we could talk in private. Fealty or no, I trust you not to fawn over me in order to advance yourself. I want you on my Council of Advisors."

"The senior nobles won't like that, Niko. You may trust me, but they don't."

"And should they trust you, beast-man?" whispered the demonic voice in his skull. *"How intriguing. Not only your lands in My grasp, but the kingdom as well."*

He gave a sharp jerk of his head, as if to shake loose the malevolent deity. But the Dark One refused to be dislodged. *"Choose, beast-man. Choose now. Your lady . . . or your lord."*

"Varian? Is something wrong?"

"Sorry, Niko. A sudden memory of something I left undone at home." His stomach roiled, and the thought of eating the bread and cheese in his hands made him feel queasy. He put it down carefully. Now, of all times, he couldn't do anything to cause suspicion. "I will have to consider your request carefully, Niko. I know you realize that this is not the time to leave the North undefended, as I would have to if I attended on you as a councilor."

"Corleon? I think he's learned his lesson for now. And even if he has not, it's not likely he'd try to make his way through your lands."

"No, not Corleon. There are worse things than D'Alriauns to fear in Leopard's Gard." Varian wanted to say more, to warn his king of suspicions that were now almost certainties, but he kept a lock on his tongue. It would serve no purpose to expose himself as a possible traitor.

No. Not a possible traitor, a certain one. He must betray either his oath of fealty to the man who was now his king, or the woman he cherished more than life itself.

"Have I your leave to go, my lord?"

Alnikhias studied him carefully. Something was upsetting his friend greatly, something more than the events of the last few days. Should he try to pry it out of Varian or let it ride and see what came of it? Or had he made a mistake so soon? This man was not the merry, down-to-earth young warrior he remembered. This man was . . . what? *Haunted* was the word that came to mind. He would bear watching. "You may go, and luck go with you."

14

Sacrifice

Varian spurred Rowan through the growing dusk,
Corven a length behind. It was full dark when they arrived at the castle; even then, Varian gave his friend no
explanation when they pulled into the stableyard, merely
curt instructions to take himself off to bed.

Corven stifled the protest and demands for explanation that he wanted to make. For the first time in his
life, he saw the lord and master looking out of Varian's
eyes, eyes as cold and hard as jade, colder than his father's had ever been. As he followed his lord through
the halls, he heard Varian's abrupt snarled orders and
watched everyone scurry in fear to obey.

In the solar that the ladies had made their own, Cathlin and Amethyst greeted their returning warriors with
cries of delight. Varian braced himself, breathing deeply
to control his raging revulsion and despair. His greeting
to Cathlin was correct and formal, with not even the
sparks of warmth he had shown her earlier. She, too,
saw the coldness in his eyes, and more, something of
the deep nightmare that was haunting him.

Too innocent to realize that he looked on warfare as
a necessary evil, she thought that the battle just past was
the cause of his distress and exerted herself to soothe

him with a picture of pretty domesticity. She sent Amethyst to fetch some wine, knowing that the girl would snatch some time for a brief kiss and cuddle with Corven.

"What news is there, Varian? We haven't heard anything," she asked. "Is there no danger of invasion then, since you and Corven are home?"

"Invasion?" He shook his head wearily. "Corleon's forces were crushed. He won't bother us again for years. But we lost so much, Cathlin, more than you could imagine." In a few blunt sentences, he told her the events of the day before.

She watched his eyes as he talked, and wished she could take him in her arms and comfort him. But when she moved to touch even his hand, he abruptly pulled away.

"I'm sorry, Cathlin, I—please don't touch me. I'm going to bed. I'll see you in the morning." He took the pitcher of wine from Amethyst as she entered, knowing that only by getting sodden drunk would he be able to sleep at all, and disappeared.

Amethyst watched Cathlin's shoulders droop as he left, and she wondered if she should reveal her own secret. The lord's emotions had been running very fierce tonight, the deep violet-blue of despair chief among them. That she could understand, but what was causing those spikes of black-edged red that meant hatred? Why did they spike the hardest when he looked at her mistress, when always before his emotions toward her had been the sky-blue of love?

Cathlin's despair was as dark a violet-blue as Varian's. She cried herself to sleep, as she had not while he was away. Her sleep was restless and unrefreshing; when she woke, she had vague memories of nightmares, nightmares in which she was menaced by Varian in his ice-leopard form.

The gray sky that was revealed when Amethyst pulled back the curtains exactly matched her mood, and she snuggled down sulkily into her blankets, not wanting to face a day that she pictured as a repetition of last night.

"Come on now, Cathlin. You'll feel better if you get up and drink some of this kuta that smells so wonderful. And just think, we can have all that we want without having to worry about how much it costs!" Amethyst coaxed. She turned toward the bed with a cup in her hands, determinedly cheerful.

Cathlin didn't want cheerfulness, real or faked, or kuta. She couldn't face it, not then. What good was she doing here? He didn't love her, he couldn't, not when he acted that way. She had been fooling herself all along—

Varian slammed through the door, his face cold with anger. "Get up. Get dressed, in that." He threw a bundle of clothes on the bed, strode up, and ripped the blankets back.

"Varian, what . . . ?" Cathlin asked in bewilderment.

He reached for her wrist and jerked her out of the bed. "Do as I say. Or do you need help?" His fingers clawed out and caught in the neckline of her bedgown, ripping it to her waist. She stared at him in sudden frozen terror, the nightmares suddenly becoming real. Her tongue was too thick and clumsy in her dry mouth to speak.

"No! You leave her alone!" Amethyst's worst nightmares were being reenacted, too. The rip of fabric might have been that of her own blouse as the slaver tore it off her, Cathlin's terror her own as the slave collar locked on her neck. Varian's anger boiled around him hotter than it had the day he bought her from the slave-dealer. She forced herself to move, throwing herself at his arm in a reckless attempt to pull him away from the woman who was not only mistress but best friend.

He turned on her, his hand flying out to strike her aside. Amethyst lost her balance and fell heavily, and Cathlin leaped to her rescue. "Don't touch her!" Terror was replaced by cold, hard anger of her own as she stared up at him. "You need not hit people, my lord, to have your orders obeyed."

"Then obey them, woman."

Wordlessly she stalked over to the bed and shook out the bundle of clothes he had thrown at her. It was a man's shirt and breeches. She had never worn men's garb, but there was nothing difficult to figure out as she stripped and put them on. They were a little too large, but she did not suppose Varian had ordered her to wear them for the purpose of displaying her body.

"Now your boots," he ordered levelly.

Again she obeyed and looked up at him icily. "If I am now dressed to your satisfaction, may I know the reason for this barbaric behavior?"

His heart cried out in anguish as he stared at her silently. For one instant he almost broke and told her. Then, with a wrenching that nearly made him sick, he hardened his soul and replied, "I will tell you at the proper time." He focused on the geas charm, took her hand, and led her unresisting from the room.

Amethyst watched them go, unable to believe her eyes. Anger, hatred, despair, grief—never had she seen such a roiling of emotions from one man in the space of just a few heartbeats. And then something had blocked Cathlin's fear and anger out completely, just as if someone had put a pewter mug upside down over a candle. She hadn't been able to see *anything,* and somehow that frightened her more than any other event of the morning.

Cathlin's emotions were there to herself, terror foremost. The man she loved was gone, and a cold hard stranger looked out of his eyes. That her body followed this man powerlessly, not of her own will, frightened her even more.

She had thought she knew her way around the great castle now, but the way he took her was unfamiliar, narrow and dank and deserted. When they went through a passage and broke into familiar territory, she was even more bewildered. Why were they going to the stables?

She was left to stand silent and alone while Varian saddled Rowan and ordered a terrified stableboy to put a saddle on Silverbell. Her husband caught her eye and answered the question she couldn't force her lips to ask. "We're riding north, Cathlin. Mount up."

She obeyed and followed him through the outer bailey. At the north postern gate, the guard challenged them and Varian drew rein. It was Leonarel, who looked up at his lord in honest puzzlement.

"M'lord! Ye're home? Why . . . ?" His question died on his lips; not even at his trial had the Lord Varian looked at him so chillingly.

"Open the gate, boy." His voice was as cold as his eyes. Behind him, Cathlin made a convulsive movement to turn Silverbell and run as his concentration wavered. Varian slammed back into control, freezing even her face into a frightened mask.

Leonarel was so scared that he could do nothing but obey. The armsmaster had appointed him one of the lady's bodyguards, but surely a bodyguard did not need to defend her from her own husband. And yet she looked so frightened, poor girl—what was he doing to her? Should he try to stop him? But how could he disobey the lord who held life and death over him?

Lord Varian and Lady Cathlin rode north into the waste, unaware that a young man torn with indecision followed them for almost a mile before he turned back.

They rode without pausing through the cold, gray day. Cathlin found it was entirely possible to be scared silly and heartily bored at the same time. One grassy hill followed another. Only rarely did they pass a stand of scruffy trees. Once they came to a ruin that might have been the remains of a farmhouse, now reduced to one barely visible stone wall and the stump of a chimney. If any animals or birds lived in this remote, empty landscape, they hid as the two riders went by.

Though she was unaware of it, they were gradually

climbing all morning. As the sun reached noon, Varian stopped his horse on the crest of a final hill, and a valley that might once have been beautiful spread out beneath them.

Rowan and Silverbell began to graze as soon as they stopped, and Cathlin found that her compulsion had waned somewhat. She ventured a small complaint. "Varian, is there any food for us? We can't ride for who knows how long on empty stomachs."

At first he didn't seem to hear her, only stared ahead with eyes as empty and wide as the sullen land around them, then he gave a start as if he awoke and was aware of her again.

"I'm sorry, Cathlin, what?"

"Food?" she repeated gently. "We can't eat grass."

"Field rations in my saddlebag." He dismounted, it seemed to her reluctantly, and began rummaging in his saddlebags, bringing her some dried meat strips and leathery dried fruit. He ate only a few bites, still looking around him with haunted eyes.

He walked away from her to stand looking out over the valley. She watched him, as troubled by his behavior as by the odd compulsion she had ridden under all day. First he was angry and brutal, now tormented. Was he being driven by the same thing? Were his actions no more of his own will than hers?

At last she sighed and went after him, planting herself right in front of him so that he had to see her. "All right, Varian. What is it, my love? What's wrong, and why are we here?"

He refused to meet her eyes for a long time. At last he licked dry lips and began to talk, dragging the words out of his own private hell. He told her of being given to the Evil One by his own father, of all the rest. She listened in silence, growing more and more afraid.

Only one thing he did not touch on: their marriage and her place in his plans. When at last he fell silent, she said a quick, quiet prayer to her Goddess and drove her fading courage out of hiding.

"And me, Varian? Where do I fit into all of this?"

"Look around you, Cathlin. Long ago this land was much like Sundare or the low valleys of Leopard's Gard. Then He conquered this land and made it what it is now." She made a wordless sound of protest and he went on grimly, "I—there's no kind, easy way to say this, Cathlin. When I became baron of Leopard's Gard, I made a solemn oath to keep my people and my lands safe. Months ago, I bargained with Him for my own freedom. His price was . . . you."

She stared at him, eyes wide with shock, and yet in a part of her mind she was relieved. Now she knew why he was so haunted. He had been forced to choose between his people and his honor, and his people had won.

"I'm sorry, Cathlin. I took some of your hair and made a geas charm to control you. I never thought it would make you fall in love with me. All I wanted at first was control over a pretty young woman that I had to sacrifice, whether I wanted to or not. But then, after we were married and I came to know your sweetness and your courage, I came to hate myself and what I had to do even more. That night you came to my bed, I was almost ready to take you, to keep you for myself, to keep you safe. But I can't now, because of the king."

"The king? But what . . . ?"

He hushed her quickly with a fingertip to her lips. "I swore fealty to him when we were boys, when he was only the old king's second son. I didn't even know then who he was. It wasn't till yesterday, after the battle, that I saw him again and knew.

"And now the Evil One knows, too, that through me He can get to both king and kingdom. I can't let Him, Cathlin. I have to have my freedom, and that means giving you to Him."

She stood in silence so long that he wondered if he had pushed her over the edge into madness. *Maybe that would be best for her. She wouldn't know what happens to her.*

Finally he saw awareness come slowly back into her

eyes, and oddly enough, what seemed to be quiet seren-
ity. She reached out her hand to clasp it over his
clenched fist. "I understand, my love. If it must be done,
let's go and get it over with."

She walked away toward her horse, and he stared after
her in tormented awe. For a long time, he seemed to feel
the place where her hand had rested on his, burning with
a cold fire.

They had been several more hours on their way when
Varian, in the lead, stopped and turned Rowan to speak
to her. Suddenly, a horrible screaming burst on her ears,
and she saw Varian jerk as though he had been hit by
an arrow and then slump over. She fought to control
Silverbell and reach for Varian's reins, but couldn't as
Rowan, rearing and kicking as a warhorse was trained
to do, threw his suddenly unresponsive rider. Two ugly
brownish gray *things* chased after Rowan, and then more
of them were all around her, grabbing at Silverbell and
at her own legs. She was desperate to get to Varian, but
even more terrified to get down where the things could
reach her.

They pulled Silverbell to a trembling halt, and Cathlin
heard the creatures making noises at each other. Were
they *talking*? She could hardly bear to look at them, they
were so horrible. They were short and stocky, perhaps
not quite as tall as she was, and covered with bristly
hair. Their hands had short, stubby fingers; their faces
were long, with forward-jutting jaws and yellow tusks,
like a wild boar. The largest one wore a sheathed sword.
It was the only thing he (definitely a he) wore. The others carried spears and clubs.

They *were* talking. She could make out a word here
and there in the grunting animal sounds. The one with
the sword seemed to be the leader. He looked at her and
said, "Who you, woman? You come master's lands, you
die."

For a moment she was too shocked to answer. The

leader shrugged and turned away to look at Varian's body. "Who kill?"

"Me! Me! Me kill!" insisted one of them, waving a sling.

"Good. You eat first."

One of the other creatures nudged Varian's body with his foot and brandished a club. "Hey, look. Meat not dead. Bash 'im?"

"No!" Cathlin shrieked, and slid off her horse to try to run to him. The leader grabbed her arm, almost casually, and made a horrible face that she realized was meant to be a grin. "Bash meat later. Use woman first."

A cold fury surged into her brain. She put all the command and haughtiness she could muster into her voice. "Get your filthy paws off me. You touch either of us, and you will die. Your master wants us. What will He do to you if you hurt us?"

He looked puzzled. "Master wants?"

"Yes. The man belongs to your master." Something her father always said snaked its way out of her memory. *"If you have to bluff, bluff big."* "I belong to the master. Do I have to tell you His Name?"

She thought the creature flinched; it was hard to tell under all that hair. He said sullenly, "No. No tell hurting Name. Me take you to master, He kill you."

"You will take us both to the master, me and the man."

He growled and turned away. "You, you, put man on horse. Tie hands. We take to master."

The following hours were not ones Cathlin liked to remember later. They threw Varian belly-down over Silverbell's back. She had only a moment to examine his head before they jerked her away. He had a lump over one ear, but she thought the skull was unbroken. She winced inwardly when they tied his hands, brutally pulling the cords tight. The beasts hustled her along places that seemed to have no paths fit for humans. The long, tangled grass caught at her feet and tripped her constantly, but she made no protest at either their speed or their choice of terrain. If they were taking her to their master, let them get there as quickly as possible.

When they finally pulled her through the gates of a castle very much like Leopard's Keep, Cathlin, grimly occupied with keeping up, finally had time to realize that her legs were shaking and her chest was on fire. She wanted nothing more than a drink of water and a place to collapse, even if it was a nice quiet dungeon somewhere.

There had been no guards at the gates and she saw no other humans at all. Her captors huddled together uneasily in the open forecourt, seeming to be as unhappy here as she was. She took the opportunity to check Varian again. He was still unconscious. She was too tired to remember, but she thought it had been too long. Maybe hanging head down over a horse's back was making it worse.

When she turned around, a man was watching her with amusement. She hadn't heard his feet on the cobblestones, or was she just too tired to pay attention? He gave her a mocking bow and asked, "May I be of service, lovely lady?"

Cathlin fought back tears of exhaustion and fear. She could not let them see weakness, not now. Or would it be to her advantage to appear to this man to be a helpless, sniveling female? With a cold chill she met his derisive eyes and realized who and what He was.

She licked her dry lips and said, "Please, can you help us? They've hurt my husband."

"And your husband is . . . ?"

"V-Varian. Lord Varian of Leopard's Gard. I'm Cathlin."

The man smiled, not pleasantly. "And I am . . . call Me Rafel. Welcome, Lady Cathlin. It will be a pleasure to have someone to talk to who can speak words of more than one syllable." His eyes swept up and down her body, and she blushed, feeling exposed and immodest in her male garb.

He turned to the gang of creatures. "Good boys. You bring strangers; master is happy."

Perhaps the master was happy, but the "boys" weren't. They looked pointedly at Varian's body and slurped long red tongues over their snouts. "Meat, master?" the leader hesitantly suggested.

Rafel frowned at them and one or two backed hastily away. "No. Not this one. You go hunt meat now. Go!"

They went, quickly but still hungrily.

Rafel watched them leave. "Bogharts are so stupid. You can't even housetrain them, like a good dog." He raised His hand in some sort of signal. A tall being, not a human but not as ugly as the bogharts, appeared from the shadows. Under Rafel's direction, it untied Varian from the horse and carried him away as if he were no heavier than a child.

Rafel led Cathlin to a small room inside the castle, something like a solar but furnished only with a table and several delicately carved chairs. A soft light from no obvious source dimly filled the room. Thick, soft fabric like heavy velvet covered the stone floors. She had heard of things like this, called carpets, but had never seen one. Rafel walked across it as if such luxury was inconsequential.

As soon as they were seated, another of the servant beings appeared with a tray of filled goblets and covered silver dishes. The aromas from them set Cathlin's stomach to growling. When one of them was put before her, it was all she could do not to knock off the lid and wolf down the contents. She set her jaw and looked down at her hands clenched in her lap.

Rafel took her chin between thumb and forefinger, raised her face to His, and smiled His smooth smile that never reached His eyes. "You're not eating, dear child. You know, they tell such awful tales of Me on the outside. I'm sure you are thinking of the one that says anyone who eats My food is put in My power."

Cathlin looked at Him, startled. Could He read her mind?

"Not your mind, darling. Your face. You have a very easy face to read. Think, child. You are already in My power, evidently of your own free will. How will eating My food change anything? Ah, well, your choice if you miss a few meals." He began to eat His own food, savoring it quite ostentatiously.

Was He right, or lying to her? She was here in His power, but if she couldn't eat or drink anything, she wouldn't be here much longer. She would die of thirst. Well, whatever came, she had to be strong to face it.

She began hesitantly to eat, playing the lady and taking dainty bites and sips of the most heavenly cold, clear water.

Rafel watched her speculatively but in silence until her plate was empty. She tried to watch Him out of the corner of her eye. To an impersonal viewer He might be considered handsome, with a classic profile that might have been carved from marble or ivory. Was it this entity that they meant when they said "a fair hide may cloak a foul heart?" She still preferred Varian's rugged good looks.

"Thank you. It was delicious," Cathlin said softly. She dabbed at her lips with the napkin and hoped He hadn't heard a tremor in her voice. "Please, may I see my husband now?"

"Ah, yes, your husband. Don't you think, my lady, that you could come to prefer Me over him? A brute like that doesn't appreciate a fair flower like you. I've known and dealt with his line for generations: boorish, uncouth brawlers that flatter themselves they are warriors. This one of yours may be a little prettier than the others, but nonetheless, he's only a hill-country bandit—and a traitor."

"He is not!" she flared, then realized that she had walked straight into His obvious trap.

"Is he not, lady? Then why are you here?"

"You know why. You tricked him; You forced him into it."

"Did I, My dear?" he said silkily. "I seldom force

anybody to do anything. At most, I give them a way to make excuses for the evil that they wish to do.''

As she looked down at her empty plate and stubbornly clamped her jaws shut on the fiercely loyal response she wanted to make, He leaned comfortably back in His chair and chuckled nastily.

"How sweet. Of all My sister's pretty inventions, I think this one called love is the most amusing. You think you love him, so anything he does is justifiable.

"What lovely games we will have, the three of us. Until tomorrow, My pretty." He snapped His fingers, and the tall servant creature materialized at her elbow. "Show this lady to her room."

The room she was taken to was an ordinary bedroom, easing at least one of her minor fears, that she would be thrown into a cold, wet dungeon. It was furnished with only an ordinary bed and, in one corner, a heavy, fastened-down box that contained a chamber pot. The heavy door, as she expected, was locked behind her.

A quick survey of the room turned up nothing useful. The same odd lighting as the eating room was here, too, so there was no candlestick, nothing that could be used as a weapon. The bed was too solidly built to take apart and didn't have the usual ropes supporting the mattress; she pulled back the single coarse felt blanket to find the straw-filled bag rested on another low, wide wooden box. The heavy, elaborately carved headboard was pushed right up against the wall. Of the walls themselves, one was stone, the other three plain wood paneling. There were no windows.

The sound of the key in the lock sent her into a watchful, wary stance, although she had no hope she could overpower the servant creatures and escape. The person who entered was the last one she expected to see. Propelled by forceful shoves from two more of the servants, Varian all but flew into the room. Only the conditioned reflexes of his warrior's training kept him on his feet. For a moment, he did not notice her as he swung around to face his captors. They ignored him and slammed the door, the click of the lock putting an end to his spark of defiance. His shoulders slumped as he dropped his guard.

She must have made some noise to betray her presence. His head whipped around, and his eyes widened as he stared at her as if he had seen a ghost. *"Cathlin?"* He took two stumbling steps toward her as she flew to him, nearly knocking him off his feet again. He put his arms around her and held her tightly. After a few heartbeats, or an eternity, he stopped crushing her ribs enough to move her back to see her face.

They both spoke at once. "Are you all right?" "Are you hurt?" Cathlin squirmed her right arm loose and carefully brushed the swelling over his ear with her fingertips.

"I thought you were dead. They hit you with a slingstone."

"Who?" he demanded. "Where are we?"

"I think . . . Dread Keep. We were ambushed by bogharts. They said they wanted to *eat* you." She burrowed her face into his chest again.

"They said? The bogharts? They *talked?"*

She nodded. "Not very well, about like a small child. Why, is it important?"

He frowned. "They were just sly animals, before. Could he be breeding them for intelligence, I wonder? If he can get them as smart as people, they'd be nasty fighters to meet."

She went utterly still in his arms and her face paled. "Oh, no!" she whispered. "Varian, do you remember at that court of justice with Leonarel, they told you about a group of women that disappeared picking berries? Could He have taken them for . . . breeding stock?" And her voice broke on the last two words.

"I remember. I hope you are wrong, but I'm afraid you aren't."

He reluctantly released her and looked around. "How

long have you been here? Is there anything we can use as a weapon?''

''No. I can't even get the chamber pot loose.''

''I didn't think there would be. I wouldn't leave a prisoner a nice heavy object for a club. With luck, though, the servants don't know I have weapons they can't take away. Are you all right? Have they fed you?''

Cathlin shivered, cold now that he had taken the warmth of his body away. Kicking off her boots and crawling up into the bed, she pulled the blanket up around her shoulders and turned on her side to face him.

''I had dinner with Him,'' she admitted. ''He pretended to be nice, but I could see how cruel He was underneath.

''Varian, I . . . understand why you have to do it. And for you and our people and our kingdom, I will be a willing sacrifice,'' she said in a low tone. Then her voice broke, though she made a heroic attempt to keep the quaver out of it. ''But I'm so s-scared. Please, *please,* will you hold me?''

''Cathlin—'' he said hoarsely. *Dearest gods—how can she still trust me like this?* His voice failed him and he nodded wordlessly.

She lifted the blanket as he slid in beside her. Varian pulled her close to pillow her head on his shoulder; she wrapped her free arm around his body in an embrace as desperate as his.

For a long time, he held her in silence and pretended to ignore the hot tears that leaked slowly onto his shoulder and burned like acid into his heart. At last her body relaxed, and he thought she had fallen asleep. Her hair tickled his nose and he dared to brush his lips in a soft kiss along her hairline. She stirred slightly and murmured, ''Varian?''

''I'm still here, love.''

''I have to know. Do you love me?''

His answer was so long in coming that she was afraid he was trying to think of a kind way to tell her ''No.''

Finally, he moved slightly and tipped her face up so that she met his eyes.

"Tell me what love is, Cathlin. The ladies at Duer's court were always chattering on about silly things they called love, flowers and favors and treating a man like a lapdog. If it means that you want me to write sentimental poems about your eyes and flatter and court you, I can't. I'm a plain warrior who always feels stupid and tongue-tied even to try.

"But if it means that I want to hold you like this forever, that I want to keep you safe and happy and give you our children, then yes, I love you. I want you with me all the time. When you aren't there, it's like I'm missing half of me, and the thought of you in danger is like a dagger in my heart. It's been ripping me apart that I've done this to you.

"I know that the bargain I made with Him was evil; I've known it all along. But at first I thought it was a small evil in order to prevent a much larger one. And again and again, I've wanted to back out, and then something happens to force my hand. Now there's only one thing I can do. If you want me to, I will stay here and try to protect you as long as I can, even if it means my own death."

Cathlin closed her eyes and gave a soft ghost of a laugh. "And you said you didn't know how to court a woman." She gave a deep sigh and relaxed into sleep. Varian lay for a long time staring into nothing, trapped in his own anguished thoughts, before he followed her.

15

Corven

Amethyst ran to find Corven, searching frantically through the castle, always, it seemed, just missing him. After a time that to her seemed like hours, she finally tracked him down. He was in the great hall, frowning and looking about for his lord. She stammered out her tale, knowing even as the words left her mouth how utterly fantastic it must sound, how unbelievable her claims of seeing emotions must be.

Corven listened in silence, his eyes intent on her face, his own face growing whiter and more pinched with every word. Abruptly his taut stillness erupted into action. He ran with Amethyst at his heels through the corridors and rooms of the main keep, and out to the inner bailey and the passage that led toward the stables.

Silverbell was not in her stall, and Rowan was gone from his, a fact that shrank Corven's whirling thoughts down to one clear point. Wherever Varian had gone, he had felt the need to ride his warhorse, a need that must have been a final act of desperation.

He stood frozen in a moment of indecision, then turned in his tracks and headed back the way they had come with long, purposeful strides.

"Where are we going? Aren't we going after them?"

Amethyst demanded, her voice cracking a little as she fought to keep up with him.

"Yes, but I can't do it alone. Whatever this is, it's over my head. Something has been eatin' at his soul for months, and I couldn't get it out of him."

Back in the great hall they found chaos. People were crowded about three men who were arguing loudly.

"Look, boy, I don't care what yer imaginin's are. Th' lord and lady have a right to ride out any gate they choose without bein' second-guessed by a tyro guardsman," insisted Master Evan.

The young man who stood his ground stubbornly was not going to back down before his superior. Leonarel's voice was equally loud. "Master Evan, please, *listen to me!* They weren't goin' out for a mornin's hawkin'. Ye assigned me to th' lady's own bodyguard, and I tell ye she was terrified. He dragged her out that gate like . . ."

"Leonarel!" Corven barked. All eyes turned to him, but he ignored them. "What gate?"

"North postern. Please, sir, will *ye* listen to me?" Leonarel begged. "Yes, I admit it, I deserted my guardpost to follow them. They went up toward th' pass into th' wastelands, and both of them were movin' like they were drugged and I can't make anybody else see that there is somethin' horribly *wrong*!"

"I believe you. Run to the stables, tell Dusan that I want Hazel and Falar saddled and any other two horses with war trainin', and have him leash two of his best trackin' dogs.

"Evan, Leonarel's story confirms what Amethyst has told me and what I've been seein', that Varian is either bein' compelled by an outside force or has gone mad. Ye've seen him these last few weeks. D'ye think that he's been *normal*? We're ridin' after them. Migael, send a rider down to Roskear Ford and have His Majesty informed immediately."

Leonarel dashed off; both the armsmaster and steward stared at Corven with astonishment. The quiet young man who was their lord's shadow had no rank or authority to make decisions of this sort. Nevertheless, the power and logic of his demands impelled them to obey. Even Amethyst subsided meekly when her demand to accompany them was denied.

Leopard's Pass was the only gateway for many leagues from the civilized southern lands to the wide expanse of blighted, empty country that was called the wastelands. On either side, sheer rocky escarpments and deep water-gashed gorges formed nearly impenetrable barriers between the two. Leopard's Keep had been deliberately placed as it was to be a cork to that bottleneck. This was the reason that the barons of Varian's bloodline had been granted so much power and freedom; they had to be strong, independent, dangerous men to resist the forces of evil that periodically swept down from the waste.

But now that cork was crumbling. It had been more than a hundred years since the last battle had strewn the bones of warriors defending the kingdom of Dur Shar-rukhan from the armies of the Nameless God, fifty since that same god had gained control over the ambitious lordling who had been Varian's grandfather. Fifty years—not too long for an immortal deity to wait patiently until He could spring His trap.

Four men were a small force to ride into what might be enemy territory; Corven trusted to luck and speed to catch them up with Varian and Cathlin. Only Leonarel had no war experience; Corven, Evan, and Dusan were hardened veterans, and Dusan was the castle's hunting master as well. Once through the pass, Corven trusted Dusan and his dogs to pick up any possible trail.

After they crossed over the bare rocks of the wide cleft that marked the pass, they found few signs of the two that they were trailing. A single hoofprint that Dusan judged to be between one and two hours old was the only indication of human presence. Even the dogs were fussing and whining; it seemed that they could find little sign or scent in these lands.

After an hour or so, Corven made a decision that would have much farther-reaching consequences than he knew. "We can't catch up to them like this. Do you agree, Evan, that they're headin' due north?"

"Aye. No swervin' aside for better goin', nothin'. Like they're bein' pulled by a rope. And the ground they're travelin' will get much worse for ridin'. We may have to dismount and lead the horses."

"That's as I remember it, then. If we swing northwest, we can push on faster through this river valley and make better time, then angle back once we've cleared the bad-lands, maybe catch up to them that way."

The search party was five or six miles farther on when the dogs, as one, yelped and refused to go any further, even on commands from Dusan. He dismounted and roughed up their coats, patting and trying to soothe them, to no avail.

"Corven, Evan, I don't like this," he said apprehensively. "Maybe m' mother's tales are true about m' family havin' the Sight; I know there's somethin' uncanny just ahead. My dogs feel somethin' other than their dislike of Lord Varian, ye've seen how they've been all mornin', and now I'm gettin' it, too."

Corven dismounted also and came to stand beside him. He looked at their trail ahead, his eyes haunted with worry and consternation. "I know, I feel something, too. Maybe we've been fools to ride so openly. Scout tactics, everyone, until we see clearly what's out there."

They went up the hill ahead on foot, crouching as they neared the top and dropping to their bellies to squirm the last few feet. Screened by only a bush or two, they gazed out on a heart-freezing sight.

Rumor had it that humans were gone from the wastelands, that only a few bogharts and other foul beasts roamed the sickened lands.

Rumor was wrong. The Dark Lord made use of many puppets, some more ensnared by Him than others. He

kept only a light rein on these; Avakir tribesmen enjoyed
spreading terror and destruction quite enough on their
own. They needed little command or urging from Him
to invade the soft lands to the southwest.

An immense encampment filled the river valley. Men,
horses, and supply wagons stretched as far as the eye
could see. There were other things that were not human;
small grayish figures could be seen in groups here and
there. Leonarel nudged Corven and pointed. The distinctive shapes of enormous Avakir wardrums could be
dimly seen in the distance.

There was no sign or smell of campfires or privies,
and it appeared that the tents they could see were going
up, not coming down; it seemed that they had stumbled
upon this army setting up camp.

"Likarion! If we'd skylined ourselves up here . . ."
Leonarel whispered, his voice trailing off in horror.

"Aye, lad, we'd be dead. Evan, ye've the most experience with troops. How many d'ye think are down
there?" Corven's mountain accent was stronger, a sure
sign of his agitation.

"At least two, maybe not quite three thousand. And
there are packs of bogharts, too. They'd not be doin'
this much settin' up for a noonin'. They're settlin' in
here for overnight, at least."

"And this may be a stagin' area for even more,"
Corven agreed. "Have we seen enough?"

"No. But the king has to be warned *now* of what's
doin'. I'll stay with Dusan and keep watch. You lads
go."

Corven hesitated for a long moment. The pull of loyalty to his lord, the need to find his friend, was very
strong. But the common sense that had served him as a
slave was stronger. Varian was out of their reach now,
perhaps had been pulled by that strange compulsion into
that very encampment. There was no way to get to him.

They pushed the horses to their limit on their way back
to Leopard's Keep. King Alnikhias had not arrived nor

responded to the message. It was no matter now. Corven carried more important tidings than news of a baron who was either mad or renegade.

He took enough time to tell Migael to order up the fyrd, those men of fighting age who had been left to guard the barony when the main body of the levied fighters had gone off to war with Varian. And time enough, too, to grab a piece of bread and cheese and change horses. As far as he knew, Alnikhias was still at Lord Duer's castle in Roskear Ford. If he was on his way to Leopard's Keep, Corven would intercept him. But as his horse covered the miles through the increasingly overcast day, he saw no sign of other movements on the road.

When he came to the River Sythyan, the bridge was easily passed. The guardsmen, both of Leopard's Gard and Sundare, reported no unusual activity. The gate to Roskear Keep, however, was another matter. These guardsmen, mercenaries from their appearance, refused him admittance until he insisted on seeing their captain. This man listened with grave courtesy to Corven's tale that he was a messenger from Baron Varian of Leopard's Gard, and that he had imperative information for the king.

"I know he's still here," Corven insisted. "You can't miss the royal standard on the battlements."

"What's imperative for you isn't imperative for him," said the captain imperturbably. "I'll send a messenger, but till then, you can just cool your heels right here in the guardroom."

To Corven it seemed an endless time until the man returned. Even so, the captain did not call him immediately. The two mercenaries had their heads together for at least a minute, talking in tones too low to be heard. Then the messenger left again.

"You know, you're not the first messenger out of Leopard's Gard today," the captain said conversationally. "Some garbled story about your lord going crazy and kidnapping his own wife. Now all these lords here are all stirred up, and I advise you not to move.''

At his last words, Corven felt the prick of a sharp knife in his ribs and a hand grasped his shirt collar from behind. The captain continued, ''Now, you're going to stand real still while I take your sword and dagger, or your lord will have one less guardsman. Is that clear?''

''That isn't necessary, captain,'' Corven protested quietly as the captain relieved him of his sword belt and both daggers, not missing the one in his boot.

''Maybe, maybe not. I decide on what is necessary security. Now strip. I want to see bare skin, so I know you don't have anything concealed.''

He bit back an even sharper protest; although it made him feel like a slave again, he obeyed. Clearly, something had happened to make Alnikhias so deeply suspicious.

The captain checked his clothes before Corven was allowed to dress again. ''So you're clean. Now we'll go to see the king, and you remember that dagger in your back.''

His escort was clearly that of a prisoner, not the honor guard that would have been given to Varian himself, nor even a guide. He hadn't forgotten the maze that was Roskear Keep; he could have found his way alone to the little hall.

He recognized Lord Duer first, then a number of other lords. The youngest man there, then, must be King Alnikhias. He had Niko's eyes and firm mouth, but the face had thinned and become sterner. Corven gave him a guardsman's salute to his lord and waited.

''Corven. I thought it must be you. What further news do you have on Varian?''

Corven let out the breath he hadn't realized he was holding. ''I don't know any more than the first messenger brought, that he has ridden into the waste with Lady Cathlin, apparently under some sort of compulsion. What I've got to tell you is much worse. There's an army of two to three thousand men, mostly Avakirs from the look of them, massing half a day's march on the other side of Leopard's Pass. We need to gather all the forces we can before they break through.''

''And is that where your lord has gone? To take command of that army?'' asked one of the other nobles.

Corven's jaw dropped in astonishment. The hostility in the room was palpable, although none of it came from Alnikhias.

''Do you believe that of him, Your Majesty?'' he asked quietly.

''I don't know now what to think. The Varian I knew wouldn't, but what other reason would he have for bolting like that? How do you know of this army?''

''I saw it. We rode after him and tried to head him off by taking a different route. As far as I could tell, he would have missed meeting it by several miles.''

Alnikhias' face was as impassive as a slave's. Whatever he was thinking, he gave no sign of it. When at last he spoke, his voice, too, was cool and unemotional. ''You're asking me to risk everything I've just gained on a story that could very well be a falsehood, concocted with who knows what scheme in mind. Perhaps to lure me and my forces away so that Corleon can come in behind me and occupy the disputed lands when I leave the borders undefended.

''I hear you're a gambler, Corven. Have you ever bet everything you had on one throw of the dice?''

Corven took a deep breath and met the young king's eyes squarely. ''Aye, m'lord. I gambled my life that a twelve-year-old boy would take an oath of fealty as seriously as the man who gave it to him.''

There was no flinching in Alnikhias' face, but Corven thought that he had hit him hard anyway. That was the soft underbelly of most of these nobles: their honor. He pressed to the attack again. ''I know, it's not the place of a freedman to remind a king of his obligations. But if you think my story of a massing army is a trick, consider this, sir. Varian and I fought back to back to protect a fallen man we knew only as the new crown prince. If he—and I—are the traitors such a story would make us, *why didn't we step aside and let them take you right then?"*

Alnikhias' face clouded and he seemed lost for a moment in his own thoughts. Then his head snapped up and he began to issue commands in a clear, decisive voice. "You, slave, fetch me a scribe. Duer, Govert, you are my senior nobles. Will you go on an embassy to Corleon? I'm proposing a truce and a temporary alliance with them. We can't take on an army of three thousand with twelve hundred men; a battle like Kaden's Pass happens once in a lifetime."

The two nobles exchanged bemused glances. The forcefulness of the young king could not be denied. Young he might be, and new to his responsibility, but already he had firm hands on the reins of his kingdom.

"Your Majesty, we've just fought a battle with D'Alriaun, and you want us to ally with them on the word of one man?" protested the same noble who had asked about Varian's motives.

"Yes, Launart, I do. We haven't the troops now to go it alone. We'll have to join forces. Whether Varian's gone renegade or not, this is a threat to both of us that has to be faced."

He continued, "Corven, sit. I want to know everything about this army. With Varian gone, I'm putting you in charge of Leopard's Gard troops, and don't think about arguing with me. Do you think I didn't see you listening in on Duer's command training lessons all those years ago?"

"You didn't miss anything, did you, Niko? I mean, Your Majesty," said Corven admiringly. "We thought a body-slave in attendance on his master would be overlooked."

"That's long ago and far way," said Alnikhias dismissively. "Now, about these forces, how are they drawn up, where exactly, what is the terrain like?"

Although they made plans as quickly as possible, it was well into the evening before anything was settled. Corven knew how ponderous massed troop movement was; even if their own men were ready to move on the morrow, who knew how long it would be before D'Alriaun troops joined them. His instincts told him to get home immediately, to be there to protect his home and loved ones, but when he asked permission to do so, he was refused.

"I'll need you as liaison later," Alnikhias explained. "When we hear from Corleon, then you can carry the message back to your Master Evan about what to expect."

16

Death

The *chunk* of bolts being drawn back brought Varian instantly awake, out of the bed and facing the door warily before it swung open. One of the servant beings stood watchful, silent guard while another put two bowls of food and two mugs of water on the floor. Then they quickly withdrew.

"Aha, breakfast is served, my lady," announced Varian cheerfully to Cathlin as she sat up in the bed. He was pleased to see that she was alert and ready for trouble also, not muzzy-headed and slow. He scooped up a mug and bowl and brought them to her, then fetched his own. "They're still taking no chances, look. Can't make weapons out of these!"

The food that they ate ravenously was cut-up bits of meat and fruit, served in bowls of hollowed-out, dry bread. The mugs were some hard, very lightweight, translucent substance neither could identify. They were also unbreakable, even though Varian tried to shatter one against the bed and even stomped on it.

It was then that it registered with Cathlin that he was barefoot and clad only in shirt and breeches. "Varian, where are your boots?"

He smiled ruefully. "That's part of what I mean by

no weapons. They're probably with my sword and dagger. The first thing I remember since we topped that last rise is coming about half-awake in some sort of guardroom and having a very nasty potion poured down my throat. It woke me up all the way, and then they put me in a holding cell. After a while, they hustled me up some stairs and shoved me in here with you.''

"I wonder why," Cathlin mused. "I would have felt much more frightened and alone if I didn't know where you were."

Varian shrugged. "Who knows why He does anything? He's not human, with human reasons."

"He looked human enough last night. Do you think He can make Himself into a human, or does He wear a human body, like we wear clothes?"

"I don't know that, either. My question is, do we make plans to fight Him or wait here like fish in a barrel?"

Cathlin looked stubborn, and her head went up proudly. "I will fight Him tooth and nail and never give my soul to Him."

That she showed a fighting spirit to match his own warmed him in a place deep inside that he hadn't known was cold and dying.

"*Vivat*, my lady! We will fight." He gave her a fierce, feral grin, and the approval in his eyes further stoked her courage.

He stripped off his shirt and tossed it to her. "Tear some strips off that. Can you use a garrote?" She nodded as she used her teeth to start a rip in the hem of the shirt. "Good. If He's wearing a human body, maybe He can be hurt like a human."

"What did you mean last night, weapons they couldn't take away?"

"Fight Him tooth and nail you said, my sweet, and mine are sharper than yours." He smiled at her again as he began to pull off his breeches, and she noticed again how white and sharp even his human teeth seemed.

"Why are you undressing?" she asked curiously,

even as she admired his lean, muscular body.

"Old tales aside, my love, clothes don't change into fur, and even if I don't split out of them during the change, they hamper me."

"Oh. I was just thinking, I wouldn't like to have to face Him naked."

"How can I resist an entry line like that, My pretty?" Rafel's deep voice seemed to fill the room, and then suddenly He was there.

Varian whirled to face Him and crouched in a fighter's stance, wary and protective, in front of Cathlin.

"Oh, how touching. Having delivered your lady over to Me, now you love her enough to protect her. Don't you think it's a little late for that?" Rafel smiled lazily and moved toward her. Varian didn't move, although Cathlin could see the tension of the muscles on his back.

Rafel continued, "You see, My dear girl, your lord doesn't know that here in My own place, I can control his human body just as I control his leopard one in his own lands." He walked carefully around Varian's frozen figure and stopped by the bed. "Turn around, beast-man. I want all of us to participate in our game session today."

Varian turned. She saw the struggle in his eyes as he fought for control of his own body and failed.

The Hidden Lord smiled His cold smile again. "Very good. Now!"

And Varian leaped, not for Rafel but for Cathlin, crushing her body beneath his as he pinned her to the bed. She struggled to squirm out from under his punishing weight, but he grabbed one wrist and moved to restrain her even more securely. Rafel negligently tossed a handful of silken cords within reach of Varian's other hand. "Tie her hands to the bed."

Cathlin fought desperately, forgetting that it was Varian's body that she was biting and scratching and kicking. Her free hand caught his cheek, and her nails scored three deep gouges down his face. He did not appear to feel it but slipped the looped cord over her captive wrist and pulled it tight. The bed's carved headboard provided numerous places to bind the other end. In spite of her struggles, she was no match for his warrior's strength and soon her other hand was tied as well.

She gasped for air as Varian's body moved off her. Rafel tossed a dagger to Varian, who caught it with one neat, graceful motion. He held it before her eyes and turned it in his hand so that the light ran like a silver river up and down the blade. Sweat ran down his face to mix with the blood on his cheek, and a look of agonized fear was in his eyes as he put the point in the hollow of her throat and pressed lightly. A bright bead of blood appeared as she felt the sting and froze.

"That's a good girl," approved Rafel. "Hold very, very still or My puppet might slit you from throat to crotch. I would hate to see blood on your lovely body— at this point."

The blade moved from her throat, and Varian began to cut her clothing off. When she was naked, he viciously thrust the dagger into the headboard of the bed, missing her face by a scant inch as she bit back a cry of terror. His eyes were afire with hatred as he backed away from the bed and stood still.

"You see, My pet, I control him as easily as a child her doll. Has he ever shown you what he truly is?" Rafel loomed over her, still standing at the side of the bed. She tried to sit up and spat defiantly up at Him; He casually raised one hand and slapped her hard enough to make her ears ring. Half dazed, she heard Him say, "Such spirit, little one. I can break it, and eventually I will, but for now I want you to fight Me. Rape is so much more enjoyable when the woman thinks she has a chance. I said, has your beast-man ever shown you what he is?"

He took her jaw brutally in one hand and wrenched her head over to look where Varian had stood. Now there was no man there, but a massive ice leopard, crouched as if to spring. Only its tail moved, slashing like a maddened snake. Rafel released her and took a step back. "Forget him, lady. I will have a use for him later, but for now he will stay there and watch Me while I take your precious virginity. I intend to enjoy your lovely body again and again, My pet. One of My creatures is no defense to you from Me."

"You promised You would release him!" she snarled up at Him.

"He defaulted on that bargain, little one. He did not bring you to Me, you brought yourself when you ordered the bogharts to take you to the master. You will learn, I am indeed your master."

She watched as He dropped the long, fur-lined robe He wore. He was naked underneath, and she stared at Him in fascinated horror. His body had the same classic marble beauty as His face, hideously marred by hugely swollen genitals. He moved onto the bed to kneel above her legs, and His face turned ugly. "Fight Me, girl," He purred. "Struggle. I want you to taste the bitterness of defeat when I force your legs open and ram into you. This body is human so that I can enjoy it, but no man born of woman may harm it." He closed His eyes as if to savor His victory.

Words in a woman's voice broke into her mind. *"Now,* Cathlin!"

She pulled her knees to her chest and kicked out with every ounce of her strength. Her feet caught Him squarely in the groin as she yelled, "Khaharafael!" His eyes bulged out and He made an abortive grab at His crotch, as the ice leopard, released from His control, leaped. The last things He saw were nine long, needle-tipped claws driving themselves into His human eyes as Varian pulled Him into position for a killing bite to the back of His neck. The leopard shook the unresistant body, clamping his jaws ever tighter until the head was nearly severed. Then he carefully backed off the bed, dragging the body with him.

(And in some nebulous place that was neither space nor time, a goddess smiled at Her opponent as She removed a piece from an equally nebulous shakarr board, amid murmurs of approval from other watching deities. "No man born of woman, Brother dear?" She smiled. "When has that ever worked? Cathlin is not a man, and at that point, neither was Varian."

He turned what might have been purple with repressed anger and studied the board intently, abandoning His carefully laid out tactic and turning His concentration to another area . . .)

Cathlin dropped her head back to the bed, closed her eyes, and spent a few moments having quiet hysterics. She thought she owed it to herself. *After all, how many times have I had to face a near rape by the God of Evil and seen Him torn to death by a wild animal? A wild animal who is sitting there washing his face like a housecat.*

After she had indulged herself, she felt greatly relieved and lifted her head to look for Varian. He was still in ice leopard form and padding around the room; he seemed to be sniffing at the walls. The circuit worked him back to the bed, so that she could see only his ears and the end of his tail as he examined the foot. "Varian?" His tail flicked at the tip in answer, so she knew he heard her.

"In case you've forgotten, I'm tied up here," she said with some astringency noticeable in her voice. His head appeared unexpectedly, and he gave her a scratchy lick on her toes. "Varian!" He squeezed his eyes at her, shook his head until his ears made a flapping noise, and disappeared again.

After another few minutes, his human body sat up at the foot of the bed. He shook his head again before he got carefully to his feet. "I'm sorry to leave you like that, love, but I had to find something out before I changed back."

"I'll forgive you if you call me that again."

Varian made an effort to smile at her and she reached up to kiss him as he pulled the dagger loose. "Love," he said softly. Moving slowly and carefully, he cut the cords that held her, dropped the dagger, and fell onto the bed beside her.

As she moved over to give him room, it seemed to Cathlin that except for returning her spontaneous kiss, he was careful not to touch her. He was lying on his belly with his face buried in his folded arms. After a few moments, she leaned over him and gently touched his shoulder. "What is it, Varian, what's wrong? We're safe, you killed Him."

The guilt in his soul made her light touch burn like a white-hot brand, and the nearness of the woman he wanted to hold and cherish and love was unbearable. He deserved her hatred, not her love, deserved whatever punishment she chose to inflict on him, if there could be a punishment worse than the loss of her love. She also deserved an honest answer, his conscience reminded him.

Abruptly he sat up and reached for his breeches. "I don't deserve your forgiveness, Cathlin. Not until you are out of here and truly safe. I brought you here, I must shoulder the blame for your ordeal."

"You did what you had to do, my love," she said gently. "And I do forgive you."

"I should have cut my own throat, instead," he growled roughly. "I should have run headlong into a hunter's net or let my people hang me like a bandit."

"And then who would have cared for them or killed this foul monster?" Cathlin challenged. "He was worse than you will ever be as a leopard, and now He's dead because of you, don't you see?" she pleaded. "This is what was meant to happen. We just . . . got dragged into it."

Varian only shook his head. "You don't understand," he said bluntly. How could he tell her that as Rafel's body died, he had heard His voice whisper through his head, *"You don't escape Me that easily, beast-man. Nobody does."*

After he was dressed, Varian explained what he had

been looking for. "I can smell fresh air coming from somewhere, and it seems to be under the bed. If this place is anything like Leopard's Keep, there are secret passages all through the walls."

Cathlin used the rags of her clothing to wipe the blood off her body, then pulled on her boots and, with a shudder of distaste, Rafel's discarded robe. She joined Varian at the foot of the bed, poking and prodding at the wooden box that supported the mattress.

At last, one of them touched the right place. They heard a click and the lower edge of the foot panel moved out a fingerwidth. Varian wedged the point of the dagger under it and lifted; the whole panel swung up on concealed hinges to give access to the box. Varian dropped to his belly and squirmed underneath. Cathlin heard him swearing under his breath, and then a scraping sound.

Crawling under in her turn, she found he had hauled away a block of stone from the wall, leaving a hole just big enough to admit a human body. A definite draft of cold air poured from the hole, strong enough to make a chill crawl up her arms.

Varian had to pull his shoulders in to fit through the hole, but once in, he found a passage on the other side of the wall, just high enough for him to stand and a little more than a body's width. Dust was thick under his bare feet; could he trust from that, that nobody knew about this passage? Cathlin joined him a moment later, touching his arm in the darkness.

Either there were fewer spyholes in this passage than the ones in Leopard's Gard, or the other rooms were not lit or windowed. They moved by feel slowly down the tunnel, each with a hand to one side, Varian probing ahead with his toes at each step. It was in this way that he found the steps going down. Their progress slowed even more as he carefully felt for each one.

Cathlin would remember for years, after that, the endless time of creeping through the silent darkness. Her heart was pounding again, so loudly that she could hear nothing else. She kept a firm rein on her imagination; it would be all too easy to believe that this way was endless, a trap cleverly designed by the Evil One to give them hope, only to trap them in this sinister gloom forever.

The steps changed from a straight run to a spiral, still down and down. At the bottom was another long, straight corridor. They turned a corner and there, finally, was a shaft of light.

It was a spyhole, too high in the wall for Cathlin to use. Varian reported that it looked into a large room, apparently stone on all four walls. He pulled back far enough for Cathlin to see his face, and grinned. ''Fortuna is with us, my love. That's the guardroom they had me in. Feel around for some sort of catch here, there must be a door somewhere.''

There was not. Varian muttered curses in a whisper until Cathlin tugged him away. They worked their way down the passage, this time sweeping up and down the walls. Around another corner Cathlin caught her fingers on some sort of rough protuberance and pulled on Varian's arm to make him stop. She guided his hand to it, heard him hiss in satisfaction, and a soft click.

It took both of them to force open the long unused door. Every noise they made caused Cathlin to wince with apprehension. Surely the servant things could hear; they had responded to Rafel—Khaharafael's—voice. How could the two of them hope to fight them off if they were discovered?

Cathlin need not have worried. Varian slipped first out the door, flattening himself to the wall, armed and ready for trouble. Left behind in the darkened passage, she waited breathlessly, expecting to hear the noise of battle or a soft hiss to tell her all was clear. Instead, she heard her husband *laugh*. ''Come on out, Cathlin. Look!''

The servant things were there, three of them, sprawled loose-limbed across the floor. ''As if they were puppets with their strings cut,'' she mused aloud.

''I think so. They weren't living things at all, but golems. The old people in the villages tell tales about this

place, that a sorcerer lived here who could make mani-
kins out of clay and give them the semblance of life.''
He was crossing the floor as he spoke, and gave a soft
cry of pleasure as he caught up his own sword and brandished it.

Sword first, Cathlin noticed, then boots and dagger.
''Then that wasn't the Dark One at all, but a sorcerer?''

Varian shook his head and shuddered. ''No. Well,
maybe He took over the sorcerer's body for His toy, but
that was Him, no mistake.''

''Then all we have to do is walk out of here?''

''It can't be that easy.'' His face hardened. ''And I
want this place destroyed, every rock of it, and the
ground sown with salt.''

In the guardroom they found a dagger for Cathlin and
several dusty bows and a few quivers of arrows. Only
one bow was light enough for Cathlin to pull. She
checked it over dubiously. ''The upper limb's a bit
warped, and I don't know how long that string will last,
but it's better than nothing.''

Warily, they explored the rest of the castle. Surely the
sorcerer had some sort of workroom they could find.
Only magic, Varian felt, could bring down a castle of
this size. If such a room existed, however, those same
magic arts must have kept it well hidden.

Cathlin did find a few more useful things. In a room
much like the one in which they had spent the night, she
found a skirt and blouse, not too much too big for her.
She gladly shed the Dark One's robe and pulled them
on.

The kitchen showed signs of recent use. Several more
of the servant beings lay collapsed in an untidy straggle
of limbs. The day's bread baking was stacked neatly on
trays on the big tables.

''What could they want with so much?'' Cathlin puzzled.

''The logical answer, my dear, is that someone eats
it. Human guards, maybe, or some other minions. I

rather doubt that it's alms for homeless bogharts."

Cathlin grinned. "Lunch for lost nobles."

"What's that?" Varian's head went up sharply.

"What?"

"I thought I heard a baby cry."

"A baby? Here?"

"It wasn't a cat. Cats I do know, my love."

They tracked the crying to a corridor just off the kitchen. A heavy oak door barred the way, bolted at top and bottom. Varian looked quizzically at Cathlin, who shrugged back. Drawing his sword, he pulled the top bolt as she shot back the bottom. He burst into the room, ready for battle.

Twenty or more pairs of eyes were wide with terror at his abrupt entrance: huge eyes in dirty female faces. There were only women and young girls in the room, clustered about one lying on the floor. The smell of blood and human waste hung sharply in the air.

One of them, taller and slimmer than the rest, took two long strides away from the group, planting herself protectively before them. Her bruised face twisted into a snarl. "You touch that baby, you heartless bastard, and I'll kill you with my bare hands!"

Varian didn't quite ignore her as he whipped a quick glance around the room, looking for armed foes. Then his eyes came back to her as he sheathed his sword. "I know you, don't I? You were part of the garrison at Kaden's Pass Keep. Mirada, if I remember right."

"Mirad. And who are you?" Her eyes were still wary and her body still tensed and ready.

"Likarion, woman! I took your fealty oath, and you don't know me?"

"I know who you look like. But the lord I swore to would never be on *His* side."

Behind her a baby cried again in a newborn's sharp wail. Cathlin could no longer keep silent. "He *is* Baron Varian. We were ensorcelled and pulled away from Leopard's Gard. And *He* is dead! We killed Him."

Mirad still looked as if she didn't believe her. Varian

gave a sigh of exasperation, pulled the daggers from his belt and boot, and dropped them on the floor behind him. He unbuckled the sword belt and held the sheathed sword out to Mirad, hilt first. She made a dive for the blade, jerked it out in one clean pull, and stood ready. Varian made no move to defend himself, letting the sheath drop to the floor.

"I can't blame you for what you were thinking," he said quietly. "If you distrust me that much, go ahead and kill me."

For a long moment, she studied him; then her shoulders relaxed and she brought the blade up in salute. "Your orders, m'lord?"

"These are the kidnapped village women?" Varian asked as they watched the women and girls tear ravenously into the fresh-baked bread. "How did you wind up with them?"

Mirad nodded. "I was home on leave. It sounded like a simple, pleasant day, picking berries and having a picnic. I didn't even take my sword. And then they hit us out of nowhere."

"Bogharts?"

She nodded again. "And Avakirs. After they brought us here, the Avakirs took the three prettiest women away with them and left the others for the bogharts. *He* watched while they raped us, day after day. The only ones to escape it were those too old or too young to bear children, and Brianda there." Her hands tightened into fists as she pointed with her chin at the new mother.

Cathlin looked sick. "Oh, Blessed Lady! Then . . . He *was* using you for breeding stock."

"Yes. At least a dozen of us are pregnant. I did what I could to keep us sane . . . and I wonder now if I did right. Madness would be better than knowing that you are going to birth a monster . . ."

"Mirad!" an older woman said sharply. "Of course you did right. We're alive, we're ready to fight back, and when we get home, I can abort most of them."

"Yes, Mama," Mirad muttered grimly. "What now, m'lord?"

"We'll get you home, gods willing." Varian gave a sigh and massaged the tight muscles on the back of his neck. Even if the gods were willing, how? It was a full day's ride here from Leopard's Keep. How long would it take women and young girls to walk it? And what about the new mother?

Cathlin was the practical one. "Varian, we can't stay here any longer. What if those Avakirs or boghars come back? We can find Silverbell and Brianda can ride her, with a pillow in the saddle or something."

She organized the women who had finished their skimpy meal into search parties. Some were to investigate the kitchens and storerooms for anything that could be carried as provisions. They were to search, too, for anything that could hold water. Others Varian sent looking for the armory; this castle was so similar to Leopard's Keep that it should be in much the same place.

The food they collected was little enough; some dried meat, a few root vegetables, and coarsely ground grain. How Rafel had acquired the food He fed them, nobody knew.

Water containers were scarce, too. The castle itself, like Leopard's Keep, relied on rainwater cisterns and large tanks that served the kitchens and what would have been the laundries. A single well deep within walls would supplement the cisterns in case of siege. But the pipes or buckets that filled them would be of little use on a trek like this.

Mirad returned with news that she had discovered the armory. More than one of the village women said she could use a bow or dagger. There they found weaponry enough to satisfy all of them, a sword for Mirad and better bows than the one Cathlin had found in the guardroom. Here, too, they found a few dried waterskins, insufficient, but again better than nothing.

Cathlin nearly cried when she and her party discovered the stables. Silverbell was there in a dirty stall with

an empty manger and a bucket of scummy water. The
mare was pathetically glad to see her mistress. Cathlin
could take only a few moments to stroke and soothe her,
for a feeling that they must get out *now* or it would be
too late was beginning to nag her.

Varian was feeling the same way. When the parties
reported back on their successes or failures, he took their
reports with the same hard-faced grimness. Sooner than
he had hoped was possible, they were ready to go. He
took a moment to look back at the castle as they topped
the first rise, and Cathlin thought she heard him whisper,
"Someday . . ."

They made better time than he had thought they could.
Though sunset came early these days, his people were
hardy and more than willing to put just a little more
distance between themselves and the place of their captivity. It was nearly full dark before they stopped in the
dubious shelter of a few scraggly trees.

Varian would not risk a fire; the few blankets they
had scrounged were given to Brianda and shared among
the younger girls. Cathlin herself did without one, hud-
dling next to Mirad, waking again and again with cold
and discomfort. She yearned for the feel of Varian's
body to snuggle next to hers, but he was back to the
distant man of the days before their ordeal. He stood
watch half the night, gazing out into the darkness.

The next day was much the same. They trudged on
across the empty waste, occasionally stopping for a brief
rest and a mouthful of water and dried meat.

The only excitement happened about midmorning.
Silverbell stretched out her neck and gave a shrill
whinny, answered by a more distant one. Varian's head
came up at that, and he suddenly put two fingers in his
mouth and whistled. The distant neigh came again, and
soon they could see a dark figure trotting toward them.
It was Rowan.

Varian made as much fuss over his warhorse as Cathlin had made over Silverbell. The horse was covered with dried sweat and a long scratch ran down one haunch. When Varian checked him more carefully, he found dark red spatters on Rowan's legs and hooves. This sign of his stallion's fighting spirit brought the only smile from him that Cathlin was to see all day.

But Rowan's presence made little difference. He would allow nobody to ride him but Varian, and shifted uneasily when his master took one woman or another to ride pillion behind him for a short rest from walking.

Again that night Cathlin slept on the ground in the cold, alone.

17

Last Battle

Year 410 D.S.:
Twenty-fifth day of the month of Redleaves

Corven's horse moved restlessly under him. Hazel was
not a purposely bred warhorse like Varian's Rowan, but
he had his own eagerness for battle. He stamped now in
the frosty morning, eager to be on the move.

He was no more eager than his rider. The last days
and nights had crept by in an agony of slowness for
Corven. The armies, both of them, had grumbled and
complained, but they had moved with astonishing speed.
That is, at any other time Corven would have seen it as
speed, and a great marvel that they could have allied at
all. Perhaps it was true that King Corleon had witch-
blood in his family, for he had met the envoys with the
news that he already knew of the massing armies and
the danger to both kingdoms.

The plains of Sundare were behind them now, as were
most of the impediments of armies. No baggage or supply wagons trailed this army, for their horses and mules
had been drafted to convert infantry temporarily into
cavalry. Every stable in northern Sundare and Leopard's
Gard had been stripped, and any beast that could carry

a warrior faster than his own two feet had been put into service. For them, it would be strike and stand to the last man. If they won, the foemen's supplies would serve them instead. If they lost . . . dear gods, if they lost, they would have no need of supplies.

The long twilight of dawn was just beginning when they moved out of Leopard's Gard, following Corven as he led the way. Scouts, local lads and lasses for the most part, ranged ahead, bringing back reports.

Alnikhias had raised a skeptical eyebrow at the number of female warriors under Corven's command. Corven himself had not bothered to defend their presence. He knew better than the young king did how the girls of the peasantry trained with the bow alongside their brothers here in the North. He knew, too, the quality of warrior that the tough Northern peasant made.

Cathlin awoke stiff and sore. This second night of sleeping on the ground had been easier. At least she hadn't awaked in discomfort *quite* so many times.

When she went to ration out the remaining dried meat, she sniffed it suspiciously, then shrugged and portioned out larger rations so that it was all shared out rather than leaving some in reserve. To Varian's silent look of query, she replied shortly, "It's starting to go bad. Better we eat all of it now than have to throw it away." They filled their bellies and the water containers at the stream and continued on their trek.

It was midmorning when Corven's scouts reported the presence of the enemy. They were not an hour too soon, it seemed, for the Avakirs, too, were on the move. Hastily, Alnikhias met with Corleon. The D'Alriaun king, a middle-aged man with a surprisingly merry eye for so calculating a warrior, nodded at Alnikhias' plans. "An ambushed ambush, eh? I like it, lad. Even more than I liked fighting you. That—well, I'll admit that was a mistake. I'd like to make peace after this is over. Deal?"

"We'll talk about it, Corleon. As you said, after this is over."

Tir-Os, the Avakir High Warchief, had gambled on surprise and a quick thrust into enemy territory before his foes knew he was there. His informant at Dread Keep had communicated with him last two days ago. Every handspan of sun-movement since then had seen his warriors grow more and more impatient to strike. What was their leader waiting for? All of them knew that the yellowhairs were fighting among themselves; now was the time to hit them, while the warriors were away and only women and children and oldsters remained on the settled farmsteads.

Now he cursed to himself as his scouts reported a force riding to meet his own. Where was the warleader, the magic warrior that the Evil One had promised, the one that would make his own countrymen turn and run in terror?

And as the sun had risen in the sky this day, so had grown his belief that he had been betrayed. There was no such warleader. The only help from Him would be these straggles of bogharts, these useless animals with even less discipline than his own warriors. There was no magic, no other help from the sorcerer who had promised him rich plunder with little risk to his own people. *All you have to do is watch them die,* He had said. Liar. Traitor. Snake.

Here, then, was where they would meet the foe. Here would be the fight that the bards would sing of down the long years. Tir-Os took his place at the crest of the hill where all could see him, raised his arms to signal the drummers, turned his face to sacred Father Sky, and began the chant that would make the magic to sustain his warriors through the day.

"I . . . will . . . be . . . *damned*. What are they doing?" Alnikhias muttered. It was clear enough from the scouts' reports. He did not need to see with his own eyes what was happening, did not need to expose himself to danger, but he was here on top of the hill, nonetheless.

Corleon pulled on his own helm and swung up onto his warhorse. "Haven't fought them before, have you? They always fight on foot. Horses are sacred or something. They won't risk them in battle or deliberately target ours."

"I'd heard that, but I couldn't believe it. To give up that advantage . . ." Alnikhias shook his head.

"That shieldwall will be its own advantage, if they hold it. You'll see." The D'Alriaun king spurred his horse and rode off to head his own troops.

Corleon had raised remarkably few objections to Alnikhias' suggested tactics. As the Avakir warchief was raising shieldwall against them, they had deployed their people so that they could strike in rotating waves. First the archers would fire, aiming to break holes in the Avakir lines to give entrance to wedges of foot-soldiers. The mounted warriors would follow to enlarge the holes; as the enemy fell back to regroup, the archers would repeat their fire, and it would all begin again.

At least, that was how it was supposed to work.

The magic was running for him as a wild horse runs free across the plains. Tir-Os could feel it flowing through him with the pulses of the drums and out to his warriors. The weapons of the enemy could not reach them through the magic; their arrows bounced off the shieldwall. Only where the faith of an Avakir warrior faltered did the arrow pierce and kill. And there were few such falters.

Alnikhias scowled down at the valley floor and cursed. Why had he accepted Corven's word that his archers were the best in the kingdom? True, he had seen them in action against Corleon . . . but those were men. How many of the archers out there were women, this time? There had been no time to pull the charging infantry back; they were nearly on the Avakir lines before it became clear that there were no holes to charge through.

What was clear was the decimation of the allied armies under Avakir throwing axes and javelins.

"He's down!" "He's dead!" "The king is dead, Likarion help us!" Rumor flew faster than arrows among the D'Alriaun infantry. Who started it, nobody was ever to know, for the frightened youngster for whom this was only his second battle was killed a few moments later. Perhaps he really had believed his own reports, for Corleon's distinctive red-barded black warhorse had indeed stumbled and gone to his knees in the maelstrom of battle.

The left flank, mostly younger, unseasoned fighters, began to crumble. Corven, from his own position nearer to the center, watched in swift glimpses as he fought, for he had been afraid of just such a happening. *Damn* them, what was their captain doing?

The movement of the battle swept him away from the foe now, and he could spare a longer moment to watch them. The D'Alriaun lord leading them was nowhere to be seen, unless that heap of bright red back on the hillside was his body. And Likarion damn them, they *were* running! He had to stop them, for his men would be the next to go.

There was a shrill war cry from the Avakir ranks, and then they, too, were running in pursuit of the fleeing men. Corven reined in Hazel abruptly. "To me!" he bellowed. "They're breaking—now it's our turn! Evan, Dusan, take our riders and go after those Avakir stragglers!"

His own horse he spurred in a different direction, cutting across the path of the fleeing D'Alriauns. "What th' hell d'ye men think ye're doin'?" he bellowed in his best imitation of Varian's command-voice.

They checked only for a moment, but it was long enough. "The king—he's dead, sir!" one of the youngest fighters cried, his voice near to a wail.

"Then who's *that?*" He wheeled and pointed with his sword. "Will you abandon him to die alone?"

The horse was not Corleon's, but the surcote, shield, and helm certainly were. The gold roses that were the symbol of D'Alriaun caught the light like miniature suns, flaming against their red background.

And at the sight of them the young warriors' faces caught fire, too. "Corleon!" someone screamed as a war cry, and they turned as one and ran back into the fighting, all of them now screaming shrilly enough to burst their throats, "Corleon! *Corleon!*"

"It worked! Just for an instant, but it worked!" Alnikhias cried. He called a courier to him. "Get me that man who is leading the Leopard's Gard troops. We have to know what he did just now."

"Aye, m'lord!" The courier spurred off.

Again and again the allied armies rolled their waves of fighters against the breakwater of the Avakir shieldwall. Now, however, they knew what to expect and broke off just short of the range for the deadly war-axes. The Avakir javelins still took out many a warrior, but for every one that fell in such a manner, Sharrese archers targeted an Avakir as he left himself open for just that instant of throwing.

The sun had moved a good handspan across the sky when Alnikhias realized that Corven had not responded to his summons. Irritably, he sent out another messenger. "We can't take this much longer," he muttered to himself as his attendants pretended not to hear.

Tir-Os redoubled his chants and signaled for a faster tempo from the drums. The Sky had heard him, of that he was certain, for were not his people winning? The yellowhairs had blown at his warriors like the wind, and as long as they stood firm like the rocks, the wind could not win against them. So he had argued for many nights in council, using all the magic of persuasion that the Sky had gifted him, and there, too, he had won! Soon the soft lands of the yellowhairs would be theirs, and they would have many slaves to wait on them, many slaves to give to the Sky. Yesterday he had made sacrifice to reconsecrate the wardrums, and even now the feel of the still-quivering hearts as he tore them out of the slaves' chests remained in his hands. "Soon, Father Sky," he vowed. "Soon you will feed until you are glutted!"

Varian's head snapped up as they paused in their weary plodding to ration out another mouthful of water. "Quiet!" he ordered. He strained his ears, listening, and made an abrupt gesture for silence when Cathlin began to ask him what was wrong.

Mirad nodded, just as alert. "I thought m' mind was playin' tricks, m'lord. But if that's not drums we're hearin', I'm a lizard."

Varian's face was grim. "I hope both of our ears are playing tricks, Mirad. Cathlin, you stay here and take care of everybody. Mirad and I will scout ahead and see what's up there."

Cathlin stifled her demand to go with him. He was right; this time he must go alone, or nearly so. A whole clutter of people would only endanger them all. They were back almost before she and Rhiama the midwife had time to settle everybody safely in the shelter of some scruffy trees.

"Avakir wardrums, and a battle, just over those hills. Maybe three thousand Avakirs, and packs of boghahrts. Against our Sharrese and what sure as hell looks like D'Alriauns. Maybe two thousand."

"D'Alriauns? Fighting with us instead of against us?" Cathlin said in disbelief. Now indeed she could believe in miracles, if their ancient enemies were now their allies. "But what do we do? Try to go around them?"

And once again Varian was caught between millstones: duty to his king and duty to his people. "I can't, Cathlin. I swore fealty to Alnikhias. I can't abandon our people—all of our people—for just this handful."

"You stop that nonsense, m'lord," Rhiama interrupted firmly. "Ye'll not abandon anybody. Leopard's Gard is our home, too. I'll take care of Brianda and the babes and keep them safe here for a day or two until ye can come back. The rest of us will go with ye. It sounds like it's come down to needing every hand that can fight."

"Aye, sorr," said a dark-haired young woman who had named herself as Zalki but who had said little up until now. Her accent was strange, not a mountain accent at all. "M' motherr was Avakirr. I—I c'n tell you about them, maybe things that we could do here behind they lines to frright them. They's rreal superstitious, sorr."

"Yeah, sure," someone whispered sneeringly behind her.

"I m-mean it, m'lor'. *They's* not my people. *They* threw out m' mam when she wouldn't let them kill my da. You let us stay here when nobody else would. This's my home, too, sorr." She was nearly crying, looking up at him with her jaws clamped tight and eyes wide to keep the tears in.

"I believe you, Zalki. Who else is volunteering?"

By ones and twos they raised their hands. Even Brianda raised hers, defiantly jutting out her chin at Rhiama.

"Child, a woman with a newborn can't fight the way we need warriors," the midwife began, only to be interrupted by Zalki.

"She can't fight, no, but she an' t' babe're one of t' best weapons we've got. Look here, Brrianda." She raised her hand coated with pale gray dust and grinned evilly. "How'd you like t' be a ghost?"

Varian began to smile as she explained. "Yes, that just might do it, lass. And—" He hesitated, his belly tying itself into knots at the very consideration of what he was about to do. "Cathlin, you showed me a horseman's word, to make horses obey you. Can you use it on Rowan, so that he'll let Mirad ride him? And is there a word to make them do just the opposite? Something that will make them run in fright, uncontrollable? Especially if something else frightens them?''

Cathlin nodded slowly. ''Not that, exactly, but certain words will make them uneasy . . . Varian, you're not . . . ?''

''What other weapon do I have?''

Alnikhias listened to Corven's report with barely contained eagerness. ''That's it, then. We can bait them out. I'd wondered why they weren't conforming to all the reports we've had about them, about their lack of discipline. Someone is managing to hold them in leash. If we can make them slip that leash—'' He turned to the waiting couriers and began to issue a rapid stream of orders.

Corven didn't like it, but he obeyed. As he rode in the next wave of mounted warriors, the drums of the enemy suddenly seemed to double their sound, drowning the sound of the warhorns that blared signals to their own troops. There were formal prayers to the God of War at such times, but none of them came from Corven's lips. All he could think of was, *Let them stop. Likarion, silence them! If we can't hear the signal, we're all dead! Please, make them stop!*

The rising crescendo of sound seemed to strike terror into the allied armies. One by one, they began to falter. One or two turned back as if to flee—and then their fellows followed.

They had done it! The cowardly yellowhairs were running away! Tir-Os' prayers to the Sky rang with thanksgiving as his men, shrieking war cries, broke shieldwall to let through the packs of ravening bogharts. No need to try to keep those filthy animals in check anymore. Let them run and rend and satisfy their bloodlust.

But—*no,* not that! His men were running, too, after the bogharts, after the fleeing cowards. After all the weeks of training in discipline that he had put them through, they were falling back into the old patterns, the old ways. A cruel smile curved his face. Ah, what matter? Let them satisfy their bloodlust, too. Father Sky would not begrudge the blood of the enemy spilled onto his sister Mother Earth.

Mirad looked at her warband with pride. Female they might be, and few enough trained to the arts of war, but they were warriors at heart. They might have gone white with fear and shock when Lord Varian showed them what he was, but it was not enough shock to send them into witless terror. As they slipped into position, she waited, counting Rowan's heartbeats to keep time. There, there was the ice leopard, poised to charge into the lines of horses, and there was the ashen pale form of Brianda mounted on Silverbell, her baby tucked into a sling bound to her chest.

Four-ninety-eight. Four-ninety-nine. Five hundred. She whistled as shrilly as she could as she swung onto Rowan's back. Brianda kicked Silverbell into a canter and rode toward the top of the hill where the enemy warleader stood. She wailed an odd sequence of unfamiliar words as she rode. Zalki had not translated them, saying only that they were the words of a formal curse when one was banished from an Avakir tribe.

It was her imagination that she heard the *thung* of bowstrings as the arrows streaked across the plains toward two targets: the great wardrums, so big that they required their own wagons to move them, and the lines of Avakir horses, held here in safety by boys too young to take their place on the battlefield but not too young to have their first taste of war.

Those horses began to scream in terror as the first arrows found their marks, for even as they hit, a woman's voice began to cry strange words that she couldn't quite hear and a great dappled silver-white ice leopard, one of their most ancient of enemies, leaped from ambush to spread slashing chaos among them.

And as Mirad charged, screaming Varian's own war

cry and urging on totally imaginary troops to follow her, the Avakir wardrums fell ominously silent.

Corven twisted his head as the drumming ceased, gauging the number of Avakirs following. They were broken from their defensive posture for certain, now. And now, *now* came the cries of the warhorns. As one the mounted warriors wheeled and charged back into the face of their pursuers, cutting them down like wheat before scythes. The archers, too, turned and fired a blistering hail of arrows, shooting in a high trajectory to rain their missiles down into the now undefended Avakir lines.

Cathlin held her breath as she took aim. Her first arrow had punctured the largest wardrum, her second the drummer. She didn't know who had taken out the others. Here was their main target: the white-haired old man who was the heart of the Avakir army.

Tir-Os turned in bewilderment. To have been tricked into breaking shieldwall—that was bad enough. But who was attacking from behind? The screaming of horses fell on his ears as the drums ceased. Who—or *what*—was attacking?

His heart nearly stopped as another sort of wailing began to make itself heard. *No, it cannot be,* his mind began to yammer. *No, not the Wailing Woman, not she who prophesies death for the people.* But it was, it *was* a pale ghostly form, mounted on a wraith-gray spirit horse and holding a screaming infant, crying out the words of Outcasting, damning them all.

And then a tongue of fire grew in his own chest. He had time only to look down at the arrow-fletchings that had blossomed there before he fell.

Likarion, blessed Likarion, thank you! Corven's heart sang over and over as his sword flew. He didn't know why the Avakirs were retreating in a panicked rout, but they were. This was no trick; these warriors were truly running under the spur of terror. Repeatedly, as he caught up to one Avakir or another, the man would throw whatever weapons he had managed to save or snatch up, then pull a dagger from his boot and, with a scream of defiance, cut his own throat.

The camp was a crude affair, only a fire and some hastily scavenged supplies from the abandoned Avakir camp. Alnikhias sat with Corleon as both kings received reports from the troops doing mop-up fighting. They tried to ignore the unpleasant noises that came from not very far away, the sounds of the wounded being worked on by the healers, and the screams of a few Avakir prisoners being questioned.

"I'm sorry, sirs," reported the captain of the mercenary warband that was performing the questioning. "I can't get any more out of them, not even under torture. Just more howling about betrayal and evil spirits and some crying woman. The only man I have who speaks Avakir shuts up like a clam when I try to get any better translation out of him."

"Oh, bloody hell, stop the torture, then. Superstitious animals. I guess if that's what they believe, I'll not argue with the results." Corleon looked to Alnikhias for his agreement and made a gesture of dismissal at the captain.

The man didn't leave. "What should I do with them, sir? Their people won't pay ransom for them. A warrior who surrenders or is captured is regarded as dead in disgrace."

"Triumphal parades," Alnikhias suggested cynically. "And public execution afterward. Give the populace a vicarious thrill so that they know how well their monarchs defend them from the barbarian menace."

Corleon nodded slowly. "Keep them under guard, Captain. Heavy guard, blindfolded, and with their hands kept tied behind their backs until we can put proper shackles on them. They'll pay for what they've done. Blessed *gods*, they'll pay!" He scrubbed his hands down his face, a face that looked older by twenty years than it had just that morning. Among the dead now being prepared for transport home was the body of his son, Prince Thorondal.

"Aye, sir." The mercenary captain had no sooner left than there was another commotion. Stalking through the camp, attended by men who didn't seem to be quite sure whether they were guard or escort, came a dark-haired man and a group of women.

"Varian," Alnikhias said. He made it a statement, not a question. "You come before me now, after having abandoned us on the eve of battle?"

"Aye, my liege." Varian went to one knee before the young king. He unbuckled his sword belt and laid the sheathed sword at his feet. "I am here to await your judgment, my king."

"I think you owe me an explanation first."

Varian's shoulders slumped and his head dropped in surrender. Before he could speak, there was an explosion of female voices as each of the women with him tried to leap to his defense.

"Quiet!" Alnikhias snapped in command-voice, and as a startled silence fell on everyone, he pointed to Cathlin. "You, young woman, who are you, and why are you wearing the rings of a baroness in your ears? I've never seen you before."

Cathlin raised her head proudly. "I am Cathlin of Leopard's Gard, wife to Lord Varian. I accompanied my husband to Dread Keep and helped him kill the Nameless God."

If Alnikhias was astonished at such a claim, he showed little evidence of it. "Indeed, my lady, I would welcome hearing the rest of such a story. Pray continue."

"When my husband returned from the battle with the D'Alriauns, I could see there was something terribly wrong. The next morning . . ." It seemed to take a long time to tell her story. Darkness had fallen while she talked, though it hadn't been that late in the day . . . had it? She felt justified in leaving out a few minor bits, such as how Varian had slapped Amethyst, and equally justified in emphasizing that she and Varian were both under spells of ensorcellment.

When she came to the end, the king nodded and pointed at Mirad. She, too, told her story simply. Her emphasis was on the leadership of her baron as they created havoc behind the Avakir lines.

One by one, the king pointed to the other women. The only time he expressed any emotion was when Brianda, her face still streaked with pale gray dust, described how she had played the wailing, vengeful ghost-woman. That drew a slight smile from him and a nod of final comprehension toward Corleon.

When they were done, he looked at Varian, still kneeling silently at his feet. "Well, Lord Varian. Is this all true?"

"Yes, Your Majesty." Varian steeled himself to confess the parts that Cathlin had left out, the parts that she had never known, but Alnikhias' gesture cut him off.

"You are vindicated before my eyes, at least. I wish all my nobles inspired the loyalty in their people that you do. It seems that you won this battle for us, you and your lady and your shadow Corven. I see nothing to condemn you for. Go get your troops something to eat and some sleep, man." He called an aide to lead the group to where they could sleep and then fetch them some food.

As he watched them go, Alnikhias heard a rough throat-clearing behind him. "There's more to that story than meets the ear, I'm sure you know," Corleon said. "But I take it you're planning to make heroes out of them?"

"Of course. The commons need heroes. If I don't give them some, they'll make them up, perhaps ones much more unsuitable. I'm sure *you* know that."

"My people have scrounged up an Avakir tent for us, lad. We need to talk about that peace between us now."

"Peace? When my father and brother are not yet laid to rest?"

"Or my son. I think we're even there, Alnikhias. And . . . my daughter Ashlana is not yet betrothed."

Alnikhias looked sharply at the older king and nodded slowly. "Aye, Corleon. We do have much to talk about . . . lead the way to this tent of yours."

The Lady

Cathlin watched her husband with increasing worry. Since his vindication by the king, he should have been, if not happy, content to settle back into his life. And there was no reason for him to still avoid her bed. Instead, he became quieter and more somber, if such a thing seemed possible.

The morning after the royal armies dispersed, she watched a flight of white doves sailing over Leopard's Keep and made up her mind. She found Varian with Corven in the armory, going over the inventory of weapons and armor.

"My lord husband, I'm about to do something I've never done before."

He gave her a weary, lopsided smile and asked gently, "What is that, my dear?"

"I'm about to kidnap my own husband."

"Assuming you could do such a thing, where would you drag this husband off to, my lady?"

"A pilgrimage. To the Sanctuary of Byela."

"Good idea," Corven spoke up. "Shall I cosh him on the head and tie him up for you, Lady Cathlin?"

Cathlin studied Varian with compassion. "I don't think that will be necessary, Corven, but thank you. I think our lord will agree that in fairness, it's time for me to give the orders and him to obey."

Varian was silent, no flicker of his heartache showing on his face. This was Cathlin's right. He had tried to give her to the god he was forced to serve; it was only natural that she should want the comfort of her own goddess. And if She was as merciful as She was reputed to be, perhaps She would extend that mercy to him.

The Sanctuary was not a single temple but a complex as extensive as a major castle. Shrines, living quarters for the priestesses, dormitories for students and novices and guests, stables, and other outbuildings were protected by walls and armed guards, but the Grove and Cavern themselves were defended only by their sacredness.

Cathlin and Varian, as nobility, were assigned a tiny room rather than put in the pilgrims' sleeping hall. And as nobility, however minor, Cathlin was accorded a prompt interview with the Mother Priestess Illyana. She had only just enough time for her sacrifice to the Lady. The handful of silver she poured out to the priestess bought her a whole flock of the Lady's sacred doves.

She knew of deities that demanded blood sacrifice; as she felt the beating heart and soft white feathers of the first dove in her hands, her first prayer was thanks that Byela did not. She released it to freedom and watched it take wing for the heavens, wheeling around to the right in a good omen. Again and again as she released the birds, her only other prayer was *help us, Lady, please,* please, *help us.*

Varian stood quietly by, watching her face and listening to her heartfelt prayers, and wishing that he had the right to join her.

Mother Illyana received them in the room where most such interviews took place. She studied their faces as they were shown in, a thoughtful look on her own face. Age had carved many fine wrinkles on that face, and the soothing of many troubles had put a quaver in hand and voice, but she was still a strong woman with a merry twinkle in her eye. "Cathlin, child," she said gently before Cathlin could speak. "This is not the place for your troubles. Come."

Cathlin followed her obediently, and whether he would or not, so did Varian, for she would not let go of his hand. The bustle of the Sanctuary complex fell away as they entered the Grove.

The leaves had fallen from the apple trees, but the sacred oaks still clung to theirs. Their dry, russet leaves rustled faintly in the soft southern breeze, a breeze so warm that it might yet be early fall instead of nearly winter. It was the only noise that broke the hushed silence.

As they approached the entrance to the Cavern, Mother Illyana turned first to Varian. "You must wait out here, Lord Varian. Unless the goddess Herself bids me, I cannot allow a man into Her Shrine."

Varian nodded without speaking. Cathlin squeezed his hand as she tried to release it, only to have him hold it tighter. Hesitantly, he reached his hand to her face; for a moment, Cathlin thought he would step forward and kiss her. Then the open vulnerability on his face vanished into bleak despair.

"Come, child," Mother Illyana said and tugged her away.

Cathlin had been in the Cavern Shrine itself only once before, when she had dedicated herself to the goddess in Her aspect of Mother. She had been too scared then to take any notice of either outer or inner Cavern. The only thing she remembered was the shimmering Veil that separated the two. It had the appearance of mist but was warm and dry to the touch, as if thousands of strands of silk brushed over her face as she followed the Mother Priestess.

Mother Illyana seated herself on the carved throne of the Lady and indicated a stool for Cathlin to sit on. "Now, child, tell me your troubles."

The kindness in her voice was more disarming than

Cathlin would have thought possible. Bravely, she tried to give the plain, simple narrative of the past weeks that she had mentally rehearsed all the way through their journey. When she came to her discovery of Varian's bargain, she could no longer keep her hands clasped in her lap or her voice under control. She raised her eyes to Mother Illyana's face. The pity in the old woman's eyes and the inviting gesture she made were too much; Cathlin lost even the last vestiges of her control.

She threw herself to her knees, her face buried in the old priestess' lap. The words were as unstoppable as her tears as she poured out her story and cried as she had not cried since the night her mother died.

The hands gently stroking her hair might have been those of her mother, indeed. The voice that spoke comforting words was not, nor was it Mother Illyana's. Cathlin sat up with a jerk as the sound of that deep, soft voice penetrated her misery, staring with tear-blurred eyes at the Lady who sat there.

Byela smiled tenderly at Her worshiper, though at Cathlin's look of growing hope, She shook Her head. "I cannot promise, child, that everything will be all right. Your love is deep and strong and true, and the choices you have made were wise, but he must make choices, too. Yes, yes, I understand that your husband did not serve My brother willingly, but the game must be played out. Send him to Me."

Game? What game? Cathlin wondered rebelliously. *Please, Lady, help us; don't chatter of games.* But she rose obediently and left the Cavern.

Varian looked at her with bleak eyes in his still face.

"She wants to see you," Cathlin choked out, struck to the heart, for the look on his face was that of a prisoner awaiting sentence.

Wordlessly, he nodded. There was only one thing left for him to do now, and even though it would rip the heart from him, he would do it.

He strode determinedly through the outer Cavern, seeing nothing, blindly focusing on the shimmering mist that cloaked the entrance to the inner Cavern. It tingled as he stepped through to the shrine to stand warily where no male had ever been permitted before. A tall, regal woman sat on a throne of shining, satiny wood carved in an intricate pattern of grain and vines; she turned eyes on him so dark and deep a blue that they might have been the depths of the ocean he had never seen.

And he knew he stood before the Goddess of Light.

She surveyed him curiously before asking in a soft deep voice, "Is what Cathlin says true? You are a *were*, an ice leopard in your other form?"

For answer, Varian held up his hand, forcing the change so that She could see the thick fur and rough pads, extending the gleaming claws for Her inspection before he relaxed and let it lapse back to a human hand.

"And why is this evil? Do you choose to make it so?"

"*Never!* But—I cannot always control the were-change. When the moon is dark, the Hidden God controls the leopard body . . . and His favorite prey runs screaming on two legs. I know what is happening, I see Him torturing my people before He kills them, and I can do nothing!"

"Cathlin has told Me what happened to her, what you did to her and for her, and how she felt. In fairness, I must hear your side."

"What is there to say, Lady? I admit I entrapped her and meant to give her to Him to buy my own freedom. In the end, I knew I could not, that He had lied to me and would take us and keep us both in torment. I could not let that happen to her, not even if it meant that I would run as an ice leopard all my days." He dropped his eyes, unable to meet the Lady's gaze, studying his mutilated hand as if he had never seen it before. "It was afterward, that I knew—no, that I admitted to myself— that I wanted her for my own, now and always . . . and I wanted her to come to me of her own free will." He faced Her squarely, no longer on the edge of flight, but as if he faced another swordsman, and he asked half in challenge, half in plea, "Is this what they call love?"

"Love? Perhaps. Do you think one such as you can love? She would come to you, yes, for she has enough love in her for both of you. But you know, if she does not, that My brother is not destroyed so easily. You killed only one aspect of Him. In time, there will be another to take his place." She paused, and Her face was full of sorrow. "If He still controls you then, even Cathlin's love may not be enough."

A demon's voice began to laugh somewhere in the back of his skull, whispering, *"Not for you, beast-man, never for you, and you knew it all along."*

Varian bowed his head and closed his eyes. His heart froze as the last spark of hope died in him. Its icy touch spread through his body, numbing even the warrior instincts that urged him to stay alive.

At last he gave a great, shuddering sigh and looked up at Her. He fumbled at the neck of his shirt, pulling out the tiny black velvet bag on its cord around his neck and spilling its contents into his hand. The crystal globe seemed to glow with its own light, the black strand of Cathlin's hair curling into an intricate knot around his own gray claw. If it held his soul, would he finally be free when it was destroyed? Was Cathlin's soul held in it, too?

"I would beg two boons of You, Lady. I made this under His directions, as a geas charm to control Cathlin. I didn't know it would make her think she loved me. Please, I—I don't know how to destroy this so that she will be free of me. Can You?"

The Lady nodded, and he placed the globe gently into Her hand. It seemed to him that the glow increased as She touched it; then the light vanished and there was only a glassy ball in Her palm.

"And the second boon, My son?"

He shook his head in rough denial. "I am not Your son, Blessed Lady, but *His*. He owns me, man and beast, as He has since my birth, and I wear His brand. You know how I sought to escape Him and why I could not.

I would draw my dagger across my own throat, but it would only free the leopard to do more evil.''

She looked at him, he thought, with pity in Her eyes. ''My brother told you this?'' She asked gently.

He nodded mutely, kneeling before Her and bowing his head.

''Then, child, what would you have Me do?''

He spoke so softly She could hardly hear him. ''I am a danger now not only to Cathlin and my people, but to the whole kingdom. Long ago, even before He claimed me, I pledged to my king death before dishonor. I beg you, Lady, kill me—kill *us,* man and beast, so that I can never harm Cathlin or any other.''

He did not see Her eyes as She looked down at him, did not see Her smile change her face as though the sun had broken free from the clouds. She rose to Her feet and cried joyously, ''Let it be then as you will. Look at Me, Varian!''

Startled, with only a brief, bitter thought, *Does She rejoice to slay one of Her enemies so easily?* he obeyed.

The geas charm was glowing, there in Her palm, and so was the goddess Herself. Light trickled between Her fingers even as She cupped Her other hand over the crystal and crushed it between Her palms.

He felt the were-change beginning; then waves of overwhelming white-hot pain rolled over him. Dimly he heard a great cat's scream of rage and fear, but never knew if it was torn from his own throat or another's. Tormenting agony lanced through him, as if he were being ripped apart by his own claws, until he surrendered gladly to a flow of warm, welcoming darkness and knew nothing more.

Cathlin paced fretfully in the outer Grove, trying to do as she was bidden and leave Varian alone with the Lady. She marshaled arguments in her own mind: *''Please, Mother Illyana, he has no knowledge of our goddess and no reason to trust her. I must be with him.''* But even as she did so, she knew what Mother Illyana would say,

with a maddening smile of amusement on her face: *"Is
he a little child, then, that you must hold his hand? Did
you know Her, when first you came to the goddess?
Now, run along and busy yourself with something else!"*

She tried to sit quietly under a tree and found that
stillness was impossible; determinedly she forced herself
to meditation, as she had been taught among these very
trees. She stood and leaned against an apple tree, her
hands and forehead against the rough bark, feeling the
life around her, the sound of birds and insects making a
tapestry of music running in the background of her
thoughts.

The quiet peace was shattered by a triumphant, wordless cry and terrifying screams. The sound jerked her
around and sent her running, bolting for the Cavern in
shock as two thoughts burst frantically into her mind:
*Blessed Lady, no! Please let it not be, don't hurt him,
we came to You for help!* and *It's my fault, it's all my
fault, I knew he belonged to Her enemy and I brought
him here, he's killing Her, Mother, no!*

She raced through the outer cave, knocking aside the
novice who tried to stop her, and through the Veil into
the inner Cavern. It seemed as though she was running
in a nightmare, that her hands and feet moved so slowly,
dragging through the thick, glucy air by the sheer force
of her will. She saw not Mother Illyana but the Lady
standing tall in a column of eye-blinding brilliance, Varian's body lying brokenly at Her feet.

"No, he can't be dead! I won't *let* him be dead!" she
cried as she stumbled to his body. She tried to gather
him into her arms and rocked back and forth, tears
streaming down her face.

The Lady knelt beside her, skilled fingers feeling for
the pulse at his throat.

"Hush, child, hush. He lives. Look, put your fingers
here, and you will feel his heart beating. Do you remember nothing of your lessons in healing?"

It was true. Even under her hand, she felt his racing

heart become slower and steadier. Cathlin raised a tear-wet face to Her.

"But someone—something—screamed, and I felt him dying. I—" She faltered and bit her lip. "I knew I had betrayed one of you to the other, and I didn't want either of you to die."

Byela raised an eyebrow at her and said dryly, " 'Something screamed' indeed, My girl. My brother fights to the last to hold onto His slaves—but he doesn't have this man any longer!

"There was no betrayal, Cathlin," She continued more gently. "He came here wanting to die—"

"Wanting to die? But why? I thought he knew that I love him, that I would willingly have died for him in the Nameless One's keep."

"Because he hates what My enemy has made of him, and because he loves you and wanted to free you from the danger he might bring to you. I fear he does not know much of love, poor boy. He thought only the geas charm held you to him and that his death would release you to love someone else."

Cathlin shook her head firmly. "I don't want someone else. I love *him*."

"Even I cannot help where there is no will. This was My test for him; did he love you enough to let you go, and was he willing to die so that others would live?"

"You asked him to make a Sacrifice like that?"

"No, My child. He *chose* to make it. And between the two of you, you have won his freedom."

Cathlin held him closer and cried harder, this time tears of joy.

Rain. A warm rain, dripping onto his face. Was he drifting in the darkness, or was he being held in a woman's arms? Light, where was the light? Sounds beat at his ears, roaring in his head, buzzes and murmurs that became a woman's voice. "Between the two of you, you have won his freedom."

Freedom? For him? His heart twisted in bleakest despair. Byela had failed him. He was still alive.

Hands clasped his, as gently as a mother's. "Do you know all the Names of My brother, Varian?" Byela asked softly. "In the South they call Him 'Father of Lies.' He lied to you, My child. You and the leopard are one; if one of you dies, so does the other. There is no danger to your people any longer. He has no control over you now, man or leopard."

He made a great effort—and opened his eyes. Cathlin's face swam above him, and she was crying. "C . . . Cathlin . . . no . . . don't cry. . . ."

Her arms tightened on his body. "You almost died, my love! Why shouldn't I cry?"

"Your love? . . . Can't be . . . freed you . . . ask . . . Her."

Byela smiled at them, a smile as warm as a spring day. "You cannot free her where she chooses to love, Varian. You have always been Cathlin's love, and I think you always will be. This is not the first lifetime you have shared, nor will it be the last."

Disbelief warred with sudden hope; he felt some of his weakness ebb and sat up carefully as Cathlin supported him. For the first time, the Lady saw him smile. "One lifetime, my Lady, is enough for me now."

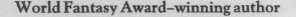